Viking Raid

A Robert Fairchild Novel

By Matthew McCleery

Praise for *The Shipping Man*

From The Shipping Industry...

"Reading this book won't make you a shipping man, but it's a good start." – **John Fredriksen**, *Owner, world's largest oil tanker fleet*

"I feel I have been to Coco Jacobsen's offices in Aker Brygge several times." – **Tor Olav Trøim**, *Director, Seadrill*

"McCleery's *The Shipping Man* is very, very funny...painfully funny, as his characters and stories are often closer to fact than fiction. It is a great insight into our wonderful industry. Go Coco Go!" - **Robert Bugbee**, *President, Scorpio Tankers*

"I don't remember ever reading a book with as much accurate insight into our industry – which, combined with humor and pathos, made it very enjoyable." – **C. Seán Day**, *Chairman, Teekay Corporation*

"*The Shipping Man* brought home the game of shipping in spades. I am still laughing about the picture McCleery has painted, as it matches a lot of my own experiences." – **Seymour Schulich**, *O.C., Co-founder, Franco-Nevada Mining Corporation, author and philanthropist*

"*The Shipping Man* is exciting, well-written and the best guide to our industry I have ever seen." – **George Gourdomichalis**, *Greek Shipowner*

"Why would someone risk millions to own ships? Well, for the sober, textbook answer, you could try Martin Stopford's *Maritime Economics,* but for an explanation involving 'shipowner's punch' and Jägermeister, *The Shipping Man*, a novel by Matthew McCleery, fits the bill nicely." – **Greg Miller**, *Fairplay*

...To Wall Street

"Set at the intersection of finance and the high seas, *The Shipping Man* is essential reading for anyone with shipping stocks in their portfolio, but, for the rest of us, it's simply a great read." – **Forbes**

"It is very hard to marry entertainment with education – especially in the world of finance and shipping, but McCleery succeeds spectacularly in doing so." – **Mohnish Pabrai**, *Managing Partner, Pabrai Investment Funds*

"The book is just phenomenal and had me splitting my sides at various points." – **Guy Spier**, *Aquamarine Capital Management*

"McCleery's ability to succinctly capture so many facets of the Wall Street morass into the characters is the best I have come across. Very skillfully crafted and delivered story." – **Tim Dooling**, *Analytic Firepower*

"A gripping, hilarious novel about a hedge fund manager who buys a decrepit dry bulk carrier at what he thought was 1x EBITDA. It is also a crash course on the shipping business." – **creditbubblestocks.com**

"*The Shipping Man* is really well written, absorbing and fun, and just very well done. I couldn't put it down." – **Richard Hurowitz**, *CEO, Octavian Advisors*

"It's a quick read, it's interesting, and it teaches a lot about ship financing and high yield financing...I promise you that if you read it you'll have begun to put shipping into your circle of competence." – **WhopperInvestments.com**

"Just like Émile Zola's '*L'argent*' can provide you with a unique glimpse into the world of nineteenth century banking, McCleery's book does a great job capturing the state of the shipping and financial markets in the years 2007-2010." – **Clemens Scholl**, *Seeking Alpha*

Viking Raid, Copyright © 2013 by Matthew West McCleery
Published by Marine Money, Inc.
62 Southfield Avenue
Stamford, Connecticut 06902
www.marinemoney.com

ISBN: 978-0-9837163-4-1 (Hardcover edition)
ISBN: 978-0-9837163-2-7 (Paperback edition)
ISBN: 978-0-9837163-7-2 (eBook edition)

Three of the chapters in this book originally appeared in *Marine Money* magazine in 2012. They have changed significantly since their publication.

About the Author

Matthew McCleery is the president of Marine Money International, a ship finance publisher, conference organizer and advisory firm based in Connecticut, Singapore and Athens. He is also managing director of Blue Sea Capital, Inc., where he arranges debt and equity financing for oceangoing ships on behalf of shipowners and investors worldwide. Matt can be contacted at mmccleery@marinemoney.com.

About the Epigraphs

Each chapter of the *Viking Raid* begins with an epigraph, which either provides biographical information about a selected shipowner or features a fact or quotation relating to the shipping industry. Although some of the epigraphs relate to the theme of the chapter they precede, most don't. The source of the epigraphs is Wikipedia unless noted otherwise. Many of the epigraphs come from a fantastic article written by Lewis Berman and published in *Fortune Magazine* in 1974.

About the Cover

The image on the cover of this book is called *Advancing on Blue #1* by Suzy Barnard, 2012, oil on wood panel. The painting was commissioned by Marine Money and depicts a partially laden, two-million-barrel VLCC, similar to the ones owned by Coco Jacobsen, at sea. More of Suzy Barnard's fantastic work can be viewed on her website: www.suzybarnard.com.

With Thanks

I've been fortunate: fortunate that my curiosity led me into the Port of New Haven, Connecticut fifteen years ago and fortunate that I met Joe and Dave, a pair of affable ship agents who invited me aboard a bulk carrier and introduced me to the truly amazing Connecticut Maritime Association (CMA) – and the equally amazing Jim Lawrence.

I was fortunate to be offered a CMA summer internship as understudy to Jim and Alan Ginsberg at Marine Money where I've been fortunate to have spent the past fifteen years working in ship finance – a fascinating business in which the words "client" and "friend" are almost always interchangeable. Someone once told me there are only two ways to get into the shipping business – either you're born into it or you get lucky – and I got lucky.

I've also had a lot of help – with my life, my career, my deals and my books. Without the patience, support and encouragement of dozens of charitable people around the world neither *Viking Raid* nor *The Shipping Man* would exist. So it is with sincerity that I thank my editor, Steve Whelley, for his tireless help with the plot, Julia Hull for devotion, Jan Lindstrom Valerio for good advice, Elaine Lanmon for patience, Annie Gumpel for providing a second wind, Sarah Noonan for keeping an eye on the books after their release and Suzy Barnard for once again contributing what many rightfully consider the greatest feature of my books – the cover.

Thanks also go to my colleagues at Marine Money, especially Jim Lawrence, Lorraine Parsons, George Weltman and Elisa Bybee, who always keep the ship on course. Richard Squires' commitment to bringing Robert Fairchild to Hollywood (as played by Brian Ladin) has gone beyond the call of duty. My brother Mike has continued his lifelong habit of gently stepping in just in time to save me from myself.

I am very grateful to the following friends and family whose good humor, encouragement and insight into the wheeling, dealing, dining and drinking habits in various locales around the world helped bring badly needed veracity to this story: Jeff Parry, John Bradley, Alan Ginsberg, Peder Bogen, Bob Kunkel, Peter Fortier, Lars Juhl, Beth Wilson-Jordan, David Frischkorn, George Weltman, David Capps, Nico Walsh, George Gourdomichalis, Kevin Oates, Witt Barlow, Tor Olav Trøim, Nancy McCleery, Jamie Freeland, Herman Hildan, Paul Goss, Christos Papanicolau, Thomas Söderberg, Seymour Schulich, Tom Roberts, Greg Miller, Michael McCleery, Don Frost, Campbell Houston, Richard Hurowitz, Andy Dacy, Kees Koolhof, Marc Baron, Erik Helberg, Bijan Paksima, Yolanda Kanavarioti, Aristotle Topalidis, Peter Evensen, Morris Morishima, Kim McCleery, Andre Grikitis, Eric Uhlfelder, Gary Wolfe and Robert Bugbee. Any wisdom or wit contained in this book is theirs – all errors, omissions and misjudgments are mine alone.

Finally, I also owe a debt of gratitude to my family for their support of this project. I want to thank my wife Buffy for tolerating the ever-presence of my laptop, my sons Rufus and Murphy for giving me so many great ideas during our daily drive to school and Homer for listening to me read *Viking Raid* aloud without complaint.

Introduction

For as long as there have been people, there has been a fascination with making money on the sea. Even today, especially today, as technology mercilessly strips mystery from most aspects of life and business, the sea remains what it has always been: a physically and financially unpredictable frontier that excites the imagination and creates and destroys fortunes.

Not surprisingly, the type of people capable of thriving in the global shipping business hasn't changed much over the centuries; Greeks still account for the world's largest fleet of merchant ships, the British and Dutch still provide financing and insurance for global seaborne trading and Norwegians still enthusiastically leave the safety of their shores, exactly as their Viking forebears did, in search of greater opportunity.

The Shipping Man and *Viking Raid* focus on the most recent fortune-seekers to join up with the adventurous world of shipping: Wall Street investors. The books follow the adventures of Robert Fairchild, a dethroned New York hedge fund manager whose accidental discovery of the famously private international shipping business changes his life.

The story of Robert Fairchild's indoctrination into shipping was spontaneously conceived as a last-minute, five-page fictionalized article I wrote for ship finance trade journal *Marine Money International.* In the article, I attempted to explain some of the reasons why American investors were having trouble buying discounted shipping debt from European commercial banks during the post-2009 shipping crisis – and the story was meant to end there. But a few weeks after George Weltman published it, I received phone calls and emails from readers around the planet who asked the same question: What will Robert Fairchild do next?

In considering how to answer that question, I realized that a longer story, perhaps even a novel, would be a fun way to follow Robert Fairchild's education in shipping. I also figured that writing a novel would be a great way to capture the spirit of the unique and amazing people running the global shipping industry at the turn of the twenty-first century – a Belle Époque for shipping during which China-led industrialization converged with the hyperactive global capital markets. From 2003 to 2008, anyone with a ship, any ship, got rich. In 2009, the market began to suffer from overcapacity and it still hasn't fully recovered.

So my long-winded answer to the question of what Robert Fairchild would do next took the form of *The Shipping Man* – a homegrown combination of epic-length trade journal article and thriller. My ambition was not literary; it was simply to use an entertaining format to share some of the things I have observed about shipping and ship financing during my career. I enjoyed the process of writing the book so much that I continued the story with *Viking Raid*, which involves largely the same cast of characters when confronted with today's shifting patterns of energy production, consumption and transportation.

I am truly grateful to have had the chance to write *The Shipping Man* and *Viking Raid*. The process has given me a unique opportunity to think seriously about the business of financing ships from the point of view of different participants – and to consider why the business of shipping, despite its considerable challenges, has been so alluring for so long.

I'm sure I haven't gotten everything right in the books, but I sincerely hope reading them is as enjoyable for you as writing them has been for me – and that you come away knowing just a little bit more about the remarkable business of shipping.

"We must free ourselves of the hope that the sea will ever rest. We must learn to sail in high winds."

Aristotle Onassis

For Buffy, Rufus, Homer & Murphy

The Viking Law*

Be Brave and Aggressive
Be Direct
Grab All Opportunities
Use Varying Methods of Attack
Be Versatile and Agile
Attack One Target at a Time
Don't Plan Everything in Detail
Use Top Quality Weapons

Be Prepared
Keep Weapons in Good Shape
Keep in Shape
Find Good Battle Comrades
Agree on Important Points
Choose One Chief

Be a Good Merchant
Find Out What the Market Needs
Don't Promise What You Can't Keep
Don't Demand Overpayment
Arrange Things So That You Can Return

Keep the Camp in Order
Keep Things Tidy and Organized
Arrange Enjoyable Activities Which Strengthen the Group
Make Sure Everybody Does Useful Work
Consult All Members of the Group for Advice

*(*As described on a postcard that Rick Rockhold bought for me
at the Oslo Airport circa 2007)*

Chapter 1

Navigating the Shipowner's Aegean Haven

They are a splendid assemblage indeed, representing most of Greece's special aristocracy: the shipowners and their families. A visitor (to Chios) might well run into a member of the Livanos family, or a Karas, Chandris, Xylas, Lemos, Pateras, Los, Frangos, Tsakos, Fafallos – among others – all of whom by some strange act of the gods hail from Chios. Perhaps the only stars missing are the Onassis family, who come from Asia Minor but are known to have lived on the island. Chios, in fact, is a kind of shipowners' reserve, where ordinary mortals are not barred but have not been encouraged to visit.

The New York Times, 1983

When Coco Jacobsen stepped out of the twenty-seven-foot Riva and onto the island of Chios, the Norwegian tanker tycoon's instincts told him that something monumental was about to happen.

He shuffled quickly through the seaside village of Kardamyla and slipped into the same deserted taverna where he had met the Greek each of the past thirty days. When he walked into the dimly-lit restaurant the two Russians who protected the Greek shipowner looked up from their cigarettes and dominoes and touched their shoulder holsters. Coco flashed a disarming smile as he made his way to the round table in the back corner and the men resumed their game.

"*Kalispera*," the Greek said and smiled as he rose slightly from his seat and sat back down again. As always, the shipowner was alone except for an unopened bottle of local white wine, a basket of sesame bread and a dossier swollen with the deal documents. "Coco, the time has come," he said.

"I sure hope so," the deeply tanned Norwegian said as he peeled off his trademark Ray-Ban aviators and sat down on the wobbly rattan chair, "because I am very hungry today!"

Although Coco was not accustomed to eating so late in the day, as many Greeks did, he never grew tired of the meal they shared: a salad of local tomatoes and fresh feta, fried minnows caught by a village fisherman and a whole red snapper grilled over charcoal and bathed in that life-extending elixir of olive oil, lemon juice and freshly snipped oregano.

"There will be no lunch today," the Greek said gravely.

"No lunch?" The Norwegian was disappointed. "Why not?"

"Because I am going back to Athens in a few minutes," the Greek said, "and it is time for you to leave Chios as well."

Coco shot the cuffs of his blue shirt, crossed his arms defensively and leaned forward. "Ja, but I am not leaving this little island until the deal is done," he said.

More than four weeks had passed since Coco's $150 million yacht, *Kon Tiki*, dropped her anchors into the azure water off the beautiful island of Chios. Ever since his arrival he had been spending every day the same way: rising late, passing the afternoon commanding and controlling his fleet of supertankers and meeting the Greek for lunch at five o'clock. Like sculptors working clay, the men spent hours going over every detail of the deal – often working until long after the fiery sun had dropped behind the barren mountains of Chios.

"I know," the Greek said and paused until the waiter had moved safely out of earshot; almost every local resident of Chios was somehow related to a shipowner and it was absolutely critical that their deal remained secret. "It is time to sign the papers and start wiring the money."

"I'm happy you are feeling so comfortable," Coco said with smile. He was relieved that his plan had apparently passed muster with the Greek. Over the years, Coco had come to believe that there was simply no one more knowledgeable or harder working than a Greek shipowner with money at risk.

"*Comfortable?*" the Greek chuckled as he submerged a small piece of bread into a shallow pool of dark green olive oil. "I don't feel the least bit comfortable, Coco, but if I think too much about this deal I will never do it," he said. "Don't forget, if we get this wrong I could lose everything," the Greek said.

"Ja," Coco replied with a flash in his pale blue eyes, "but this is exactly what makes it so exciting."

As Coco turned his eyes to the diamond-studded sea, the self-made tycoon had an epiphany; the cyclicality of life wasn't so different from the cyclicality of the shipping market in which he trafficked. He had been born poor in the village of Bergen, Norway and he might die poor in a village on a North Aegean island – but he would have had one heck of a ride in the meantime.

"Θεού θέλοντος," the Greek said solemnly – if God is willing. "There's just one thing I must ask you before we go any further," the old man said and placed a giant, callused hand on Coco's. "I need to know whether you will have your share of the money."

The Norwegian wanted to scream with frustration as he calmly returned his potential partner's gaze; Coco had developed this deal himself – the single best money-making opportunity he'd ever seen – but now he was short on cash just when he needed it most. Like most shipowners, he had some "rainy day" funds squirreled away in a variety of offshore banks, $30 million in Liechtenstein and $20 million in Guernsey, but the deal with the Greek required shipping-sized money, *ten times* what he could scrape together at a moment's notice.

"Of course I will have my share of the money," Coco said. A lack of cash had never stopped him before and it wasn't going to stop him now; he had faith that money would always find its way to the really good deals. "I would, however, be grateful if you put your $500 million in first – while my CEO Robert Fairchild gets my money together."

"Okay," the Greek said, "but let me be clear, Coco. If you do not come up with your share of the money in time for the next payment, you will no longer be a part of this deal."

The old man removed a tiny talisman from the front pocket of his short-sleeved button-down shirt and pushed it across the rough wooden table toward Coco.

"What's this thing?" Coco asked as he inspected the pea-sized blue and white eyeball attached to a short gold chain.

"It's called the *evil eye*," the Greek explained and shot a furtive glance around the room, "and my people have been using it since the sixth century BC. I want you to keep it close to you until the deal is done; it will keep us safe when things get rough."

"You really shouldn't worry so much," Coco said and tightened his fist around the charm. The pragmatic Norwegian usually wasn't much for voodoo, but he knew he needed all the help he could get.

"I'm afraid it is you who should worry…" the Greek said slowly as the two Russians rose from their chairs and came to escort their employer to the Mercedes idling outside the taverna, "you and Mr. Fairchild."

Chapter 2

Hilmar Reksten

Few businesses are as nerve-racking as the chartering of behemoth supertankers to carry oil, and until recently few tycoons played the risks with such consummate cool as Norway's Hilmar Reksten. Reksten, a ramrod-straight six-footer and lone-wolf operator, started out as a shipping clerk; in 1929 he bought a freighter cheap, parlayed it into a modest fleet (thanks in part to two rich wives), then seized on slumps to buy up tonnage cut-rate. By 1973 he had amassed a flotilla worth, by some estimates, $600 million. Now, one of the worst depressions ever in the tanker business has left Reksten financially becalmed, if not yet dead in the water.

Time Magazine, 1975

Robert Fairchild's six-foot frame was trembling with terror as he clung to the fluorescent-green safety railing and stared down into the six-story engine room of the supertanker – a vessel longer than the Empire State Building is tall.

Viking Alexandra's 36,000-horsepower engine had slowed to an idle as her turbine-driven pumps regurgitated the last million barrels of sour Saudi crude into a Philadelphia refinery – enough juice to light up Spain for forty-eight hours – but even at rest the bowels of the ship were so hot and loud that it felt as though he'd descended into hell.

Like many ship financiers, Robert didn't have much to do aboard an actual ship. The only reason he was spending the day on the *Viking Alexandra* was because his boss, Coco

Jacobsen, wanted him to experience some of the less glamorous, but altogether vital, aspects of owning and operating vessels…"Just in case I decide to change your job description."

Robert had only been aboard the *Alexandra* for a few hours, but even that small dose was enough to shock the system of a man accustomed to the life of a shipping dealmaker. Instead of dining in Michelin-starred restaurants and ruminating over hundred-million-dollar transactions, he had spent the day sipping cold Sanka in the Captain's day room and reviewing the horrifying hemorrhage of cash that started before the ship had even come in to port.

From the four over-budget tugboats that strained to bring the 1,500-hundred-foot vessel into her berth to the longshoremen's union that demanded overtime because *Alexandra* arrived on a weekend after being re-routed to avoid the wrath of Hurricane Ebbel, Robert quickly gained a better understanding of just how quickly cash evaporated in the shipping business.

He also learned why shipowners like Coco Jacobsen, irrespective of their wealth, fought for every penny as if it was their last: because it might be. Alistair Gooding, Viking Tankers' lender in London, had once told him that copper wire had been invented by two shipowners fighting over a penny and now he understood the joke. The only predictable thing about being a shipowner was its unpredictability.

After spending just ten minutes on his self-guided tour through the stifling heat, acrid air and pounding cylinders of the ship's floating power plant, Robert's pulse was racing and his anxiety was in the red zone; he couldn't wait to get off the ship and start the weekend. While he was visiting the ship, his wife Grace was dropping off their nine-year-old son, Oliver, at her mother's house in Greenwich, Connecticut. Robert had made a dinner reservation at their favorite restaurant, Il Cantinori, that evening and in the morning they would fly to the New England island of Martha's Vineyard.

In addition to spending the weekend celebrating their twelfth anniversary on the island where they were married, they were also planning to attend an open house at their dream home – a nineteenth century Federal-style mansion in a former whaling village called Edgartown. The house had serendipitously come onto the market a few days earlier for the first time in three generations and Robert believed the timing of the listing was a sign from above. Although he had neither the cash nor the income to support the purchase and ongoing maintenance of a $3 million second home, Robert knew he probably wouldn't get another chance at the house; the best opportunities in life, he'd noticed, only came around once.

Desperate to exit the unremitting violence of the engine room, he turned around and climbed up the steep and narrow stairway that stitched together the seven levels of the floating dungeon. Once he reached the next floor, he looked across the canyon of pounding cylinders and spotted a small, brightly lit room populated by a small group of men. With his leather-soled Gucci loafers slipping on the oil-slick diamond-plate floor and his hands gripping the greasy green safety railing, Robert carefully edged around the parapet, pulled open the heavy bulkhead door and stepped inside the engine control room.

When the door latch clicked, Robert exhaled with relief. He savored the room's soundproof walls and inhaled the air-conditioning like it was cold water. After he pulled out the fluorescent-yellow foam plugs from his ears, he cleared his throat but the four Indian officers didn't look up. They were transfixed on the long bank of computer screens that monitored the vital signs of the mighty machinery like bond traders watching the testimony of Fed Chairman Benjamin Bernanke.

A tall man with a long, shiny mustache and a warm smile finally broke away from the intense huddle and moved toward him. All but one tendril of his shoulder-length hair was concealed beneath a fuchsia turban and his lanky body was zipped into blue and red coveralls bearing the infamous, and menacing, logo of Viking Tankers – a Norse longboat resplendent with a serpent's fire breathing head and five sets of oars and shields.

In an attempt to look the part of CEO, Robert secured his hardhat under his arm, straightened his tortoiseshell glasses and mopped the sweat from his forehead with the sleeve of his blue gingham button-down. "Robert Fairchild," he said and extended his hand, "Chief Executive Officer of Viking Tankers."

"Prasanth," the Indian said, playfully echoing Robert's serious tone of voice, "Chief Engineer of *Viking Alexandra.*"

Once the introductions had been made, the two men looked each other over in silence. Unsure what to say next, Robert offered the only compliment he could think of. "This engine room is very clean."

"She's a cougar," the Indian acknowledged proudly as he gazed through the window.

"A cougar?" Robert asked, ready to learn more of the lingo associated with the jargon-filled shipping industry. "Do you mean she's a Cougar-type? Is that the specific model of this ship?"

"No, it means she may not be youngest ship on the sea," the Indian said with a wink, "but she remains highly desirable thanks to a good maintenance regime. There are some charterers who even *prefer* her to the younger models."

"There's no substitute for experience," Robert said, as he chuckled for the first time since boarding the ship. He appreciated the good humor coming from a man who lived his life in a blast furnace below the waterline.

Robert briefly considered making an offhanded remark about Alexandra Meriwether, the forty-year-old investment banker who Coco had named the aging supertanker after during a brief and tumultuous romance, but he quickly thought the better of it; Alex was one of the few topics in which Coco Jacobsen did not find humor.

"Any idea when this cougar will finish her discharge and sail?" Robert asked.

As the money-man at Viking Tankers, Robert was eager to send the $3 million invoice to a trading house in Switzerland for *Alexandra*'s delivery of two million barrels of Saudi crude oil. Unlike dry cargo shipping, in which customers like grain houses and steel mills paid 90% of the ocean transportation cost upon loading, spot market tanker owners didn't get anything until the cargo was discharged. That meant *Viking Alexandra*, a $50 million ship, was living hand-to-mouth, paycheck-to-paycheck – just like her enigmatic owner.

"We are hoping to finish the discharge before tomorrow morning's high tide," Prasanth said proudly, "but I'm not certain when we will sail."

"Time is money when you get paid by the day the way a ship does," Robert said.

"I am familiar with how it works," Prasanth replied.

"What's the reason for the delay?" Robert asked.

"The terminal is having a reception after we finish and they've asked us to stay for photographs," Prasanth said.

"I've never heard of anyone celebrating the discharge of a tanker," Robert laughed.

"That's correct," Prasanth said. "Americans only care about oil tankers when they have a spill."

"So why the party?" Robert asked.

"It is more like a funeral," Prasanth replied.

"Not ours, I hope."

"I'm afraid so," Prasanth said. "After more than one hundred years in operation, *Alexandra* will be the last tanker to ever discharge crude oil into this refinery," the Indian engineer said.

"I hope it wasn't something we did," Robert said.

"Not exactly," Prasanth replied. "The new owners are going to use this facility to export products like propane, butane and ethane that are made from U.S. shale gas; the U.S. is producing more gas than they know what to do with these days."

Robert was stunned. "Does that mean they won't import *any* foreign crude oil to make products like gasoline and jet fuel?"

"That's exactly what it means," the Chief Engineer said. "The U.S. is on the road to energy independence; your country will be an *exporter* of energy once the laws catch up with the reality of the market."

While Robert had been expecting to learn much during his field trip to the ship, he had not been expecting to receive an education on hydrocarbon production and marketing from the Chief Engineer – a graduate of the Indian Institute of Technology (IIT) who had received a considerably more rigorous education than Robert had at Harvard.

"That really does sound like a funeral," Robert said, "at least for crude oil tankers like this one."

After decades of tirelessly trying, a group of maverick energy entrepreneurs in America had figured out how to extract oil and gas from nooks and crannies beneath the U.S. and Canada by combining the established processes of horizontal drilling and fracking, shorthand for hydraulic fracturing, with new technology. As a result of this newfound domestic production, U.S. imports of crude oil had recently hit a twenty-year low and North American production was increasing each year by almost one million barrels *per day* - all of which was apparently starting to have a profound impact on the seaborne transportation of energy.

"It may be a funeral for us, Mr. Fairchild, but it is the beginning of a new life for the people who own the ships that can carry the exported gas around the world," the Indian said.

Too bad we don't have any super-cooling gas tankers, Robert thought, and not just a clutch of middle-aged crude carriers. This was the problem with having a "pure play" shipping company – one that had only a single type of vessel: if the market went against you as the crude oil tanker market appeared to be going against them, you were toast – especially if you didn't have time charters and were as overleveraged as Viking Tankers.

The imminent threat to Robert's livelihood further aggravated his anxiety. He simply had to get off the ship, take a taxi to 30th Street Station in Philadelphia and catch the next Amtrak back to Manhattan. He placed the yellow hardhat back on his pomade-stiffened hair, wrapped his hand around the heavy handle of the bulkhead door and prepared to step back into the hellish engine room. But just as he was opening the door, he felt his BlackBerry begin to vibrate in the pocket of his blue cashmere blazer. Assuming it was Grace calling to tell him Oliver was safely tucked away at grandma's house in Connecticut, he answered the call without bothering to glance at the caller ID.

"Hey baby cakes," Robert said softly so the engineers wouldn't hear him. "I sure hope you're going to wear that tight little black dress to dinner tonight."

"Ja, but only if you find me the $500 million!" Coco Jacobsen shouted over the roar of the Marshall Islands flag flapping violently on the stern of the *Kon Tiki*.

"Oh, um, hi, Coco," Robert stammered as he worked hard to overcome his embarrassment. "What did you just say?"

"You heard me, Fairchild!" the Norwegian insisted as he stared across the teal-green sea speckled with whitecaps. "I need the half billion and I need it now!"

"Half a *billion* dollars!" Robert recoiled. "But, I…"

"Just tell me you with the lawyers right now and everything will be fine," Coco screamed as if force might overcome fact. "Tell me you are getting the paperwork ready. Tell me you are setting up the wiring instructions!" Coco demanded. "I love the smell of an incoming wire transfer in the morning!"

"The *wiring instructions*?" Robert choked incredulously. "Are you crazy?"

Coco had been asking him to find money on Wall Street for months, ever since they bought back the $300 million junk bond, but the more Coco asked, the less Robert listened. But judging from the desperation in his boss's voice, Robert knew the situation had become more serious.

The problem wasn't just the staggering sum Coco was demanding; it was that the Norwegian's fleet was old and leveraged to the hilt which meant Robert couldn't get his hands on any more debt in the newly sober commercial banking market. Moreover, Coco categorically refused to sell shares in Viking Tankers which meant raising equity was out of the question as well; playing Lotto appeared to be Robert's most likely way of raising capital for the shipowner.

"Of course I'm crazy!" Coco shouted above the wind. "If I wasn't crazy I wouldn't be shipowner! So do you have the money or not?"

"Coco, I'm in the engine room of the *Viking Alexandra* right now – where *you* ordered me to go!" Robert reminded his boss.

Coco grunted when he remembered the educational errand on which he'd sent Fairchild. After a long period of silence uncharacteristic of the boisterous shipping magnate Coco finally spoke. "And in the engine room is where you will stay if you don't find me the $500 million!" Coco shouted and hung up.

Chapter 3

The Greek Spirit

The Greek climate, although it had great variety, rarely endured typhoons or very strong gales. The temperature was always pleasant, blue skies, clear atmosphere, and the sun almost a permanent source of light. Such an environment does make for a freer spirit, strengthens the imagination and makes people optimistic, liberal and daring. In other words, it created the necessary conditions for the Greeks to become very good shipping men.

Mr. Spyros M. Polemis
The History of Greek Shipping

The deeply tanned woman floated across the meadow of teak on the stern of the 208-foot Feadship with a shiny silver tray gripped in her hands. She was wearing tight white pants, a blue and white striped sailor shirt and her dirty blonde hair was tousled by the *meltemi* – the warm northerly wind that blew hard across the eastern Aegean during the summer.

"May I offer you a glass of chilled wine, monsieur Jacobsen?" she asked as she approached the sole occupant of the magnificent vessel's outdoor Jacuzzi.

Coco Jacobsen looked up mischievously from behind the gold-rimmed Ray-Bans that were shading his blue eyes from the blazing Greek sun. He had spent the past several hours moving in and out of the 105-degree water as he studied the name and location of every supertanker in the Arabian Gulf with the intensity of a master chess player considering his next move.

"Only if it's Montrachet," the Norwegian announced as he placed the so-called "position list" of vessels on the edge of the hot tub next to a collection of items essential to successfully running one of the world's largest private fleets of supertankers: a red box of Marlboros, a tin of Snus, half-a-dozen mobile phones to communicate with the hundreds of people around the world who financed, operated, crewed and chartered his ships…and now the evil eye charm that the Greek had given him.

"*Bien sûr*," Dominique replied with the accent of her hometown, Cap D'Antibes.

As the yacht's full-time sommelier, she knew full-well that Montrachet was the only variety of wine the six-and-a-half-foot magnate would drink anymore; consuming the dry and costly French wine had become a ritual Coco practiced to worship Alexandra Meriwether – his now estranged lover who had first introduced it to him.

After Dominique had disappeared behind the helicopter that was tied-down to the deck, the shipping magnate swallowed a generous quantity of the ice-cold chardonnay, looked down at the telephones and smiled. He knew it was time to start playing the game he loved most of all: trading ships.

The telephones had been buzzing like a swarm of cicadas for nearly a week but Coco hadn't picked-up a single call. He didn't need to because he knew exactly who was trying to reach him – shipbrokers – and why: to offer crude oil cargoes for his tankers to load in the Arabian Gulf and Africa and haul east to Asia and west to America. Based on the frantic number of incoming calls that day, Coco figured oil companies and traders around the world had begun to notice that something unusual was afoot in the supertanker spot market; demand for ships was rising and so was the number of available ships…yet not a single ship had been chartered, or "fixed" as they say, for days.

Coco took a deep breath examined the updated position list one last time. He liked what he saw. When there were more ships than there were cargoes, charter rates would drop. But when there were more cargoes than ships, even by a small margin, there was almost no limit to how high the market could rise. The cost of shipping commodities by sea was small relative to the value of those commodities, which meant ocean transportation costs could quadruple before it would destroy demand. That's what made the shipping market, which was fragmented with thousands of independent vessel owners, so unusual – and so exciting.

"*God dag!*" Coco boomed to his good friend Peder Hansen who happened to be the lucky caller. The seventy-five-year-old Norwegian tanker broker had been helping Coco buy, sell and charter tankers ever since the oil crisis of 1973 and Coco was happy to give him the business.

"I'm pleased to know you're among the living," the old shipbroker said softly. "People in Oslo were starting to worry."

The über shipbroker was speaking in a hushed voice because he was camped out at BAR, a raucous restaurant near Oslo's famous Aker Brygge so thick with shipowners and ship financiers that a single overheard conversation could destabilize the global tanker market or worse; it could cost him a commission.

"I'm in heaven," Coco said as he admired the magical island of Chios off the port side of his yacht, "but I am feeling more alive than ever."

"You're about to feel even better," Peder whispered with his hand cupped over his telephone, "because I have some very good news."

"Very good for whom?" Coco whispered back playfully.

After more than forty hair-raising years in the tanker business, Coco Jacobsen had come to believe there was no such thing as good news or bad news; there was only the market – that unpredictable amoeba of perception mixed with reality that parceled-out just enough good luck to give struggling shipowners the hope to keep trying.

"American Refining Corporation just called me," Peder said.

"Ah yes," Coco said and smiled as he paced the port side of teak deck wearing only his swimsuit. He had been hoping that Rocky DuBois, the CEO of American Refining Corporation, would be the first beast to wander into his trap.

"He wants to charter *Viking Aphrodite* today," Peder said.

"Ja, but of course they want to fix the ship today," Coco laughed. "Charterers always want to put a ship on subjects on Friday so they can enjoy their weekend knowing they have a free option on a vessel."

"Does that mean you'll take it?" the shipbroker asked hopefully before downing half a bottle of ice-cold Ringnes lager to steady his nerves. "So we can all enjoy the weekend?"

"Peder, I am a shipping man without a family," Coco reminded his friend. "In fact, the closest thing I have to a child is *Fairchild*."

"What is that supposed to mean?" Peder asked.

"It means good charter rates are more important to me than good weekends," Coco said, "and that charter rate simply isn't high enough."

"But I haven't even *told* you the charter rate," Peder replied.

"Okay, fine," Coco sighed. He decided he would go through the usual motions even though he knew exactly how the conversation was going to end. "What's the rate?"

"Forty thousand a day for the ninety-day round trip Fujairah via Houston," Peder whispered with his hand over his mouth so that no one could hear him. "That's $3.6 million for one voyage!"

"No thanks," Coco said, pressed the "off" button and placed the device on the edge of the Jacuzzi.

"Are you delusional?" Peder snapped after immediately re-dialing the shipowner's mobile phone.

The tanker broker's emotional outburst piqued the interest of a pride of ship financiers from Fjord Bank who were gathered around a nearby table. The dozen lenders had been enthusiastically celebrating the closing of a beefy Belgian bulk carrier deal but knew that anything capable of riling-up a veteran tanker man like Peder Hansen was probably market-moving.

"If I wasn't delusional, I'd still be working in a petrol station in Bergen," Coco laughed. "And I am not interested in $40,000 a day," Coco said.

"But Coco, average charter rates were less than $30,000 a day last year," Peder insisted.

"Ja, but this is exactly why I need a lot more than $40,000 a day," Coco explained. "I need to make up for last year's bad market; I'm still in the hole to my banker."

"You're *always* in the hole with your bankers," Peder laughed. "In fact, most people think you must have photographs of Alistair Gooding or else he would have foreclosed on your fleet ten years ago."

"Having the right information has always been the key to making money in this business," Coco said.

"If you don't like the rate," Peder said, "let's just make them a counter offer."

"A counter offer?" Coco gasped. "Don't you know how I feel about the CEO of American Refining Corporation?"

The tanker broker knew it was a kamikaze mission to broker a deal between the two greatest foes in the oil shipping market, men whose rivalry was as legendary as it was mysterious, but a successful shipbroker was nothing if not tenacious.

"Everyone in the world knows how you feel about the CEO of American Refining Corporation," Peder sighed and slowly massaged his temples. He was enjoying the sight of a huge Color Line ferry move slowly across the beautiful Oslo Fjord a lot more than his conversation with Coco.

"That man is *Kraken*!" Coco shouted, likening the American oil executive to the giant, legendary sea monsters known for scuttling sailing ships off the coast of Norway.

"Well, I think ARC's offer is generous," Peder pouted.

"Ja," Coco laughed, "but you should always beware of oil companies bearing gifts."

"But we are moving the market in the right direction," Peder urged. "This rate is higher than your last fixture of *Viking Penelope*."

"Then it sounds like you should have waited a little longer before chartering *Penelope*," Coco said.

"Yes, Coco, and if your aunt had *balls* she'd be your uncle!" Peder blurted out.

"I don't have an aunt or an uncle," Coco said solemnly. "I am all alone in this world and I am getting older."

"Well your ships aren't alone in the Arabian Gulf, Coco," Peder said, "and they too are getting older. If you don't take this cargo I will be forced to offer it to another shipowner with a more modern and fuel-efficient vessel."

"I appreciate your loyalty," Coco said.

"A man has to eat," the well-fed shipbroker said and instinctively rubbed his stomach.

Peder suddenly remembered his hunger and spread a glob of freshly churned butter on a slice of Russian pumpernickel. Then he laid a blanket of smoked salmon over a slice of cucumber with the care of a mother tucking a young child into bed.

"So do you want the cargo or not?" Peder asked as he tucked a white cloth napkin into the collar of his shirt. Then he lifted his fork and knife and began cutting his delicate sandwich.

"*Nei,*" Coco said casually and then stuffed a giant wad of Snus between his upper lip and gums.

"No?"

"No," Coco asked once his tobacco was securely in place. He wrapped his hands around the shiny mahogany rail and stared at the magnificent little island of Oinousses. "And would you like me to tell you why not?"

"Do I have a choice?" Peder asked as he reclined in his rattan chair and settled in for another one of Coco's rousing rants. The celebrity shipbroker lifted his arm to order another bottle of Ringnes; getting a counter offer out of Coco was going to take a while.

"It is because I'm tired of charterers like Rocky DuBois beating up on me like I'm his baby brother," Coco said.

"Yes, but your big brother is offering you very good money right now, Coco," Peder pleaded.

"Ja, but this is only because he knows he has a problem," Coco said. "Most of the time he won't pay me enough to keep my fleet properly maintained, never mind give me a respectable return on my capital."

"Return on capital!" the shipbroker groaned. "Coco, you started life as poor as a potato and you are now the wealthiest person in the history of Norway."

"Ja, but Norway was a very poor country until the 1960s when we found the oil," Coco said. "Besides, you know I don't care about money."

"Yes," Peder muttered, "except when you lose it."

"I care about what's fair," Coco continued.

"Give me a break, Coco," Peder said as he sat up in his chair and took the offensive. "Oil companies pay the market rate and there's nothing fairer than that. The real problem is that ever since opportunistic tanker owners like Hilmar Reksten and Aristotle Onassis started building vessels on speculation instead of against long-term time charters from oil companies, this market has been nothing but a high stakes game of tug-o-war."

"That's right," Coco smiled. "And now it is time for me to drag Mr. DuBois through the mud."

"But that's just the point Coco; forcing Rocky to pay $40,000 per day *is* dragging him through the mud," Peder said. "The Americans are importing less and less crude oil because of all the fracking and the crude tanker market is sure to suffer."

"I am not smart enough to predict the shipping market," Coco said, "but I assure you that there will always be someone in this world who wants to burn the cheapest form of energy – and that will always be crude oil and coal."

"Oh yeah," Peder challenged after confirming the stat on his iPad, "then why are there are so many empty VLCCs in the Arabian Gulf?"

"You're the shipbroker," Coco mused, "you tell me."

"I can't," Peder said. "There's not a shipbroker in the world who understands why the charter market is so firm considering how many idle VLCCs there are. Not one ship has been fixed for a week and an agent at Kharg Island told me the tanker crews are so bored they've even started fishing off the ships. These vessels are like taxi cabs queuing up outside the airport and one of them is about to pull over and pick up the ARC cargo."

"Not for a $40,000 daily fare they aren't," Coco said as he used his tongue to push the huge wad of Snus higher into his gums to make room for more – the "turbo pincher" as Magnus Magnusen, Coco's semi-exclusive investment banker at Haakon's Gate Capital, liked to call it.

"How can you possibly think that?" the shipbroker demanded.

Peder knew the clock was ticking. If he didn't get the ARC cargo "on subjects" with Coco in the next few minutes another tanker broker in Monte Carlo, Singapore, London, Paris or New York would fix the business with another ship and Peder would have ruined a perfectly good lunch for nothing.

"Because I just took control of the market," Coco said, "and I'm about to have a tanker party."

"Oh, now I understand," Peder said after a period of silence.

"You do?" Coco asked.

"You've gotten into the Ouzo again, haven't you?" Peder asked. "Don't you remember what happened at the Posidonia party at the Island Club last year?"

"I am serious," Coco said softly and lifted his nearly empty glass of Montrachet to inspect it in the sunlight.

"But you can't have taken control of the market," Peder said. "That's impossible."

"Anything is possible," said the seventh grade dropout. "I'm proof of that."

"But I'm looking at the position list and I can see every open supertanker from the Gulf of Aden to Mumbai," Peder said.

"Don't believe everything you read on the worldwide web machine," Coco said.

The tycoon's interest in modern communications was limited to text messaging; he liked those purely because the truncated style and lack of grammar reminded him of the telexes he was paid to sweep off the floor of Hilmar Reksten's office in Bergen fifty years earlier.

"But Coco, the names of your tankers start with the word *Viking* followed by the name of a character from Homer's *Odyssey*," the shipbroker explained. "Everyone knows your naming pattern, even though no one knows why a Norwegian would possibly name his ships after a Greek epic poem."

"Isn't it nice to know there are still a few mysteries left in this world," Coco said. "Goodbye, Peder."

"No! Wait!" the shipbroker shouted as he read the ship name on the screen of his device. "How about the *Junonia* – I suppose that ship is yours?"

"Yup," Coco said by way of a sharp gasp of breath that was unique to Norwegians. "She is actually *Viking Telemachus*."

"And *Fighting Conch*?" Peder asked dubiously as he recited the name of another vessel on his screen. "Is she yours, too, in this little Ouzo-soaked fantasy world you're living in?"

"Bravo!" Coco said, playfully parroting the favorite expression of his Hellenic partner. "She is *Viking Argos*."

"*Murex?*"

"*Viking Odysseus*," Coco volleyed back.

"That's strange," the shipbroker said as he skimmed the list again. "Unless I'm mistaken, all the ships presently positioned in the Arabian Gulf are named after seashells."

"You are finally starting to pay attention," Coco said.

"But I don't recall ever seeing a fleet of supertankers named after seashells other than the ones owned by Shell Oil," Peder said. "And these ships definitely aren't theirs."

"Ja, but that was Oddleif's idea," Coco chuckled as he spun the evil eye charm on his index finger. Oddleif was Coco's only shore side employee besides Robert Fairchild.

"Excuse me?"

"It was my idea to play with the position list," Coco said. "But using the seashell names was Odd's. He and his wife just bought a very nice house in Miami and his little boys have been finding very pretty seashells on the beach which is what gave us the idea," Coco said. "You really need to get creative to come up with a unique naming pattern for the ships these days."

Peder jumped to his feet with a vigor he hadn't experienced since Spain beat the Netherlands in the World Cup. "You can't be serious!"

"We didn't really change the names," Coco said, "because that would have required getting new inspections and approvals from all of the charterers. We just changed the names on the position list. A computer hacker in Connecticut named Jimmy K helped us do it."

"But what about the other forty ships in the vicinity?" Peder asked eagerly. "The ones I know for a fact belong to George, Nicos, Andreas and Peter?" Shipping was the only business in the world in which billion dollar companies were still ubiquitously referred to by the *first* name of their owner.

"Ja, but those guys agreed to charter most of them to me for thirty days when we were out playing golf together on the Algarve a few weeks ago," Coco said. "And the ships I don't control will just come along for the ride; everyone is invited to Coco's tanker party."

"But if what you're saying is true, Coco," Peder said slowly, "then you are the first shipowner to have ever cornered the VLCC market."

"Ja, but this is a little dramatic."

"Dramatic?" Peder said, stunned. "Coco, *you* control the lifeline between the money addicted Middle East and the power addicted people in America and China! You are living the dream!"

The seventy-five-year-old shipbroker pumped his fist and spun around on the heel of his suede loafer like a breakdancing boy. Not only did he appreciate the artistry of Coco's handiwork, he was also thrilled that the 1.25% commission he levied against the transportation costs was about to increase in lock-step with the short-squeeze in charter rates.

"Dreams don't last forever," Coco said as he thought briefly about his failed relationship with Alexandra Meriwether – the prize he wanted most of all and only one he hadn't had been able to keep.

"And neither do tanker parties," Peder said, "but they sure are fun while they last! And I guarantee this will be a surprise party for Mr. DuBois."

"You know surprise parties are my favorite," Coco sang. "I've been waiting almost ten years to get even with that no-good wrangler and now I've finally got my chance."

"So what should I tell him?" Peder asked.

"Please inform Mr. DuBois that I require $100,000 per day for the *Viking Aphrodite* and that he has one hour to reply *firm*," Coco laughed.

"One hour?" Peder said. "I don't know if I can even reach him in one hour. It is Friday, you know."

"People can always be reached if they want to be," Coco said. "Oh, and tell him the price will go up when he comes back from his rodeo on Monday. That will get his attention."

"But Coco," Peder said, "I believe Rocky DuBois has at least ten cargos to load in the next two weeks," Peder said. "Are you actually proposing to charge him $100,000 per ship, per day?"

"Oh no," Coco said sweetly. "I would *never* do such a thing to a fine gentleman like Mr. DuBois."

"Thank God," Peder exhaled. During his decades of shipbroking he had learned that while a strong market was good for almost everyone, an overheated market usually ended up hurting more people than it helped.

"I am only proposing to charge him $100,000 per day for the *first* ship," Coco howled. "The next one will be higher."

"*Higher?*" Peder swallowed hard.

"Strap on your lifeline, Mr. Hansen, because we are taking the VLCC market up to $250,000 per day!" Coco announced. The tanker party wouldn't yield enough cash to satisfy the $500 million he owed the Greek, but it was a good and symbolically powerful start.

"Aye, aye, Captain!" Peder said.

"There's just one more thing," Coco said. "Be sure to tell old Rocky that I'm currently in Aegean Sea on the $150 million yacht he bought for me the last time I had a tanker party in 2006," Coco laughed.

"Will do," Peder smiled. "What will Mr. DuBois buy you this time: a couple more Van Goghs?"

"No," Coco said with a smile as he admired the evil eye pincer gripped between his fingers. "This time Mr. DuBois will buy me eternal salvation."

Chapter 4

John Fredriksen

John Fredriksen (1944-) is widely considered to be the greatest shipping tycoon of all time. Born in Oslo, the welder's son dropped out of high school to work in a shipbroking company before starting his own business at age twenty-seven. With a gift for assessing risk, a belief in empowering people, a drive to build value for shareholders and a strong work ethic, Fredriksen has amassed a fortune of around $15 billion, making him Norway's richest citizen. Fredriksen and business partner Tor Olav Trøim have been a creative force in shipping and ship finance - dramatically transforming the way maritime companies utilize the capital markets.

Marine Money

"Mr. DuBois, you have a telephone call on line one, sir," Brittany Davenport said, her soothing New Orleans patois drifting like smoke from the triangular speakerphone on the corner of his massive black desk.

Although the CEO of American Refining Corporation had clearly heard his twenty-five-year-old personal assistant summon him, Rocky DuBois didn't acknowledge her right away; he preferred to prolong the pleasure of terrorizing Coco Jacobsen and the silver-tongued tanker broker who fronted him.

To kill time, Rocky sucked a breath into his twice-broken nose, pushed his inhumanly rough hands into the pockets of his gray flannel trousers and began to move slowly across his corner office; he was as far from his natural environment as a lion in a cage.

It was a beautiful autumn Friday and while many high-ranking oilmen were looking forward to hitting the links at River Oaks, Rocky was looking forward to a enjoying a different sport: trading ships. Although some oil companies considered the vessel charter market to be nothing but a necessary evil, a two-bit Turkish bazaar in which their transportation department had to procure vessels from time to time, a self-made wildcatter like Rocky DuBois felt at home there; he took the same hardscrabble pleasure in trading vessels as he did in exploring for stranded pockets of oil and gas – especially when those vessels belonged to Coco Jacobsen – the man who had ruined his Thanksgiving dinner and embarrassed him in front of his family ten years earlier.

Rocky slowly paced his acre of office. When he finally arrived at the wall of floor-to-ceiling windows that insulated him from Houston's stifling heat and humidity, he paused to study the view – not of the endless industrial prairie his company was finally helping to electrify with domestically produced power, but of himself. Rocky felt like he was staring at a complete stranger.

He studied his perfectly coiffed chestnut-brown hair, the red power tie and clerically-crisp white spread-collar as if they belonged to someone else. He scowled at the perfect fit of his J. Press suit and the mirror shine of his Jermyn Street wingtips. Rocky would have been more comfortable in the dirty blue jeans and steel-toed boots he'd be wearing for decades, but his investor relations team asked him to wear his CNBC costume because he'd been on *Mad Money* earlier that day explaining the potential of hydraulic fracturing and watching his stock price gush to yet another all-time high.

"Are y'all taking a nap in there?" Brittany finally asked her non-responsive boss. "I can always take a message if you're feeling sleepy," she added.

"No, I'm not taking a nap," The eighty-year-old man said as he moved toward the speakerphone. "I just wasn't ready to talk."

"Well are you ready to talk now?" she asked.

"That all depends who I am talking to," he said. "Not if it's that Matt Damon calling again to interview me for that anti-fracking movie of his," Rocky said, shamelessly showing off for his attractive aide-de-camp.

"It's not Matt Damon," she said.

"And not if it's one of those boobs inside the beltway accusing me of poisoning the aquifers," he said. "There's nothing worse than being an oilman during a Democratic administration; I give them the miracle of energy independence and cleaner burning fuel and they give me nothing but grief."

"I don't think it's…"

"Did you know that Congress hauled me in over that *Deepwater Horizon* fiasco, even though ARC doesn't even *drill* offshore!" he continued his rant. "I tell you, Britt, if this stress keeps up much longer I'm going to head up to Big Sky once and for all," he grumbled.

"Oh, no," the young woman gasped into the telephone. "There's no need for a vigorous man like you to talk about death," she said. "Not just yet."

"I'm not talking about death!" the old man replied into his telephone. "I'm talking about cashing in my chips, giving a bunch of money to charity and moving out to my new ranch in Montana."

Deep down, Rocky knew it was time to get out while he still could. He had spent his life preaching about the possibilities of fracking, making and losing half-a-dozen fortunes along the way, and now America finally believed him. But Rocky knew that the fracking party would invariably come to an end, at least for a little while, and he didn't want to be holding five-million shares of ARC when it did. After all, with all this hype about alternative energy and global warming, the next time a cyclical bull market came around for a fossil fuels man like him he might be dead. Rocky knew that a business owner rarely got two chances to sell out; he had bought the rumor, now it was time to sell the news.

"The caller's name is Peder Hansen, sir," Brittany said.

"I'll take him," Rocky sighed as he snatched the telephone from its cradle and pressed the blinking button. "So I assume we're *on subjects*," he said into the black handset; he deliberately used the shipping parlance to remind the Norwegian tanker broker that he was a bareknuckle businessman and not some pampered American executive there to be hustled in the spot market like a tourist in a taxicab.

"I'm afraid not," the Norwegian said softly as he began his twenty-minute walk home through the Oslo twilight. When Peder noticed that people had begun to arrive at BAR for dinner, he'd decided that his lunch should probably be over.

"Come again?" Rocky asked with his mouth agape as he untied his uncomfortable shoes and pulled on his faded yellow "Cat Diesel" baseball hat.

"Coco countered," Peder said as he walked into the magnificent Frogner Park and added softly, "sort of."

The lovely one-hundred-acre park located in the dead center of Oslo was home to the sprawling bronze and granite sculptures created by his countryman Gustav Vigeland. While Frogner Park was the most popular tourist destination in Norway, even natives like Peder couldn't get enough of the place. He had learned to ride a bike with his parents in the park when he was a little boy, met his future wife on the lawn during a Frisbee game in university and now took his grandson for a walk along the pathways every Sunday; the place was a part of his soul.

"What do you mean he *sort of* countered?" Rocky was still stunned. He had been expecting to put the *Viking Aphrodite* on subjects over the weekend with "no money down" and then fail the deal or lower the charter rate if he was able to find a cheaper ship on Monday.

"I mean that…"

"That Norwegian has $10,000 of operating costs per day and $20,000 of financial costs per day and I am offering him $40,000 per day; he should be thanking me not countering me."

"Coco has a different view," Peder said.

"*How* different?" Rocky grumbled. He picked up a pair of binoculars from his bookshelf so he could read the name on a fully laden freighter making way up the Houston Ship Channel – M/V *Tanna Schulich*.

"About $60,000 a day different," Peder replied. He sat down on a park bench and prepared for the crabby old man's rage.

"Are you saying he wants $100,000 per day?" The Texan laughed. Rocky had expected a counter offer from Coco on the order of $10,000 per day higher, which they would finally agree to split down the middle after dancing a tango of eight counter offers made in increments of $1,000 each. "Is this some sort of joke?"

"I'm afraid not," Peder said as he resumed his walk past the sculpture-adorned fountain located on the Monolith Plateau of the park.

"Then let's just forget that crazy, long-haired Viking and find us another ship," Rocky said. "Actually, this is just as well. I never want to give too much of my business to any one shipowner," Rocky said. "You know I like them better when they're all hat and no cattle."

"There are no other available ships," Peder said.

"Well now I know you're kidding around," Rocky chuckled. "There are always desperate ships loitering around the Arabian Gulf like stray dogs in search of a meal."

"Not this time," Peder said.

"Why not?"

"Because Coco has managed to get control of more than half the fleet of supertankers within ten days steaming of the loading ports," Peder said.

"So let's charter one from the other half," Rocky said. "I'm not picky about boats."

"I'm afraid the market doesn't work that way," Peder said. "Coco has told all the shipowners what he's done and now no one will fix below $100,000 per day. Coco said he's hosting a big tanker party and he's invited all the shipowners to come along as his guests."

"Did you say *tanker party*?"

"Yes," Peder said. "That's what he's calling it."

"What am I supposed to do now?" Rocky asked, suddenly feeling vulnerable. "I can't put thirty million barrels of oil on an airplane – and I'm pretty sure I can't send it by email!"

"If you recall, sir, I advised you to put a ship on subjects *last* Friday but you were out elk hunting," Peder reminded him. For better or worse, rarely did anyone remember a broker's market call.

"Well I'll be dipped in diesel," Rocky chortled.

The Texan's complex tone reflected both his anger and his admiration for what Coco Jacobsen had apparently pulled off. The aged oilman had seen dozens of shipowners try to corner the VLCC market over the years but every one of them had been led to slaughter. In many ways, the Norwegian was just like him: a self-made and able adversary.

"Did you tell him I have *ten* cargoes to move this month?" Rocky finally asked.

"I did," Peder said.

"And did he offer me a volume discount if I give him all the business?" Rocky asked hopefully.

"Actually," Peder said, "Coco said the cost for your next shipment is going to be higher than this one and the one after that will be higher still. Coco said he is going to squeeze the market up to $250,000 per day."

"I do believe Mr. Jacobsen has got me by the short and curlies this time." Rocky was distraught about being caught short on ships, but invigorated by the prospect of entering another battle against Coco Jacobsen. "Did he say anything else?"

"He did," Peder said.

"What?"

"Coco said that if you hadn't taken away his ability to legally enter the United States of America ten years ago, he would fly to Houston in his G-5 right now and urinate in your ten-gallon Stetson," Peder covered his mobile telephone with his hand so Rocky wouldn't hear his uncontrolled laughter but it was Rocky who started laughing.

"I really put him in the penalty box with that North Korea stunt," the oilman chuckled proudly as he recalled one of his career highlights.

"You have no idea," Peder said, thinking briefly of Coco's inability to travel to America to try and patch things up with Alexandra.

"That's a gift that keeps on giving," Rocky said. "But you know I can't pay a hundred grand a day for a boat even if I wanted to."

"It's still only a few cents a barrel," Peder said.

"That's not the point," Rocky said.

"Then what is the point?"

"The point is that an army of green eyeshade accountants downstairs make me mark my vessel charter book to market, and I sold thirty million barrels of crude on a delivered basis two months ago when charter rates were less than $30,000 per day," Rocky explained. "That means if I let Coco extort me for $100,000 per day I will lose about…"

Rocky paused as he pecked the figures into the big-button calculator positioned on his desk and then gasped. "I will lose $45 million of earnings!"

"That's less than a quarter of the value of the cargo," Peder said.

"Yes, but since ARC's shares are valued at ten times earnings, Mr. Jacobsen's short-squeeze is going to take a $450 million bite out of my company's market capitalization! And since I own 20% of the stock of ARC I am going to lose $10 million! That Viking barbarian is trying to steal $10 million of the money I've been planning to give to charity!" he shouted causing a lightning-bolt-shaped vein to bulge from the side of his forehead.

"If it makes you feel better," Peder offered, "Coco took you for almost $300 million in 2007. That's when he bought the yacht he's on in the Aegean right now."

At that moment, Rocky DuBois had a moment of clarity; it was the time to hang up his spurs once and for all and put ARC up for sale. He had watched too many of his buddies round-trip their fortunes and there's just nothing sadder than watching an old man blow his wad when he was mentally and physically incapable of earning it back.

As the shipbroker waited for the oilman's reply, Rocky collapsed into his black leather chair, put his clenched fist to his cleft chin and considered how he could solve his first problem; he needed at least ten ships as soon as possible. Having spent his long career in the oil and gas business there was hardly a fact pattern he hadn't experienced. He'd lived through Acts of war and Acts of God, coups d'états, dictators, despots, earthquakes, volcanos, typhoons, canal closures, hostage crises and oil shocks. Most recently, he'd watched the world get caught short on ships when a perfect storm of global credit expansion converged with China's industrial boom of 2003-2008.

Recalling that mixed-up four-year period, during which supertanker rates rose from $15,000 to $150,000 per day and ship values soared from $65 million to $165 million, Rocky realized there was only one solution to his problem; he had to agree to long-term time charters with Viking Tankers at a lower rate instead of taking short-term ones at a higher rate.

Rocky knew Coco would never agree to such a plan, which was why the Texan figured he had to entice Coco's lenders and his executive officers into doing it. Rocky had noticed a natural tension between shipping lenders and shipping borrowers; lenders had an incentive to de-risk their loans in the long-term even if that meant borrowers had to surrender a strong market in the short-term.

"So do you want to fix *Aphrodite* or not," Peder prodded as he slipped into the darkness beneath a red and green canopy of maple trees. "I can assure you that there are plenty of desperate traders who will."

Rocky began slowly hunting and pecking at the keyboard of his computer. After no more than two minutes of keyword searching on Google the technologically challenged Texan had downloaded the four-hundred-page prospectus for the $300 million Viking Tankers junk bond offering. Smack dab in the middle of the cover page was the name and telephone number of Coco Jacobsen's Chief Executive Officer – Robert Harrison Fairchild.

"Naw," Rocky said.

"Naw?" Peder repeated.

"Where I come from, steer wrestling is a solo sport," Rocky said with a smile.

Chapter 5

The Future of Swashbucklers

If, indeed, landlubbers in pinstriped suits do become major factors in marine transport, there may also be some changes in the management style of the industry. Private equity investors tend to be buttoned-down, methodical, numerically focused executives who use deliberative and analytical process and tend to use outside consultants and this approach is almost the antithesis of the intuitive entrepreneur, who may bet his whole business on a judgment call...making swashbuckling, larger-than-life characters typical of the industry less common going forward.

Wilbur Ross, Billionaire Investor & Shipowner, Marine Money Week 2013

Alexandra Meriwether leaned over the railing of the gallery suspended above the New York Stock Exchange – a neo-classical conduit for capital formation with more flashing lights than Times Square. With the golden pendant around her neck glinting in the afternoon sunlight, she had all the grace of a figurehead on the bow of an eighteenth century sailing ship.

"It's show time!" a host from the New York Stock Exchange boomed to Jimmy Lee Brown, the CEO of recently listed Clear Sky Airlines. "Are you ready?" he asked as he slapped a stubby wooden gavel into his guest's hand.

Although the celebratory closing of the NYSE or NASDAQ usually didn't happen until many months after the completion of an Initial Public Offering (IPO), a last-minute cancellation by sub-prime residential mortgage lender *Dough Nut*, which had been indicted by Elliot Spitzer the previous evening, had created the opening in the calendar.

"That's why we're here," Jimmy Lee replied smoothly. He looked down at the host and then over at his trusted investment banker. "Are you ready, Alexandra?"

Alex raised a pair of clenched fists into the air and emitted a howl so primitive that it attracted the focus of a CNBC camera floating nearby. "Yahoo!" she wailed.

"Wow," one of the lawyers in the back row said with excitement, "that young lady is wild."

"And she can't be tamed," Jimmy Lee replied over his shoulder.

Alexandra had always been energetic but vitality was especially impressive considering that just twenty-four hours earlier she had touched down at JFK after the three-week global roadshow for Clear Sky – the world's first fuel-efficient airline. In order to generate enough investor demand for the environmentally-advanced-but-unproven business concept, Alex and Jimmy Lee Brown had circled the world visiting two hundred and fifteen investment funds in eighteen countries. They had slept in thirteen different beds, spent eight nights on airplanes and ate in one hundred and twenty-four different restaurants. Most people would have been tired but Alexandra Meriwether was stoked.

Upon her return from the airport, she spent just twenty minutes freshening-up in her Chelsea loft before working the graveyard shift on her firm's Equity Capital Markets desk. With the help of her colleague, a Scottish expatriate named Rufus Streit, her jet lag and a staggering quantity of café latte from nearby Bodega del Vino, the indefatigable duo had dialed for dollars around the planet until they'd "built a book" of investors willing to buy shares in the whopping $750 million IPO – before construction had even started on the first airplane. Wall Street loved a story.

Now, as Alex proudly stood beneath the 10 x 19-foot American flag flapping in the breeze of a patriotically-placed HVAC vent, she did her best to soak in every detail of the highly symbolic NYSE closing – because it was likely to be her last. After nearly twenty years of helping businesses form capital in order to develop products, employ people and create shareholder value, she knew it was time to step out of the game.

While her status as a single person had been a competitive advantage during her successful career, allowing her to work through the night and jump on airplanes at a moment's notice when other bankers were worried about missing anniversaries and kids' baseball games, her solo status was about to change. During her brief but intense romance with Coco Jacobsen, the Norwegian shipping magnate she'd helped tap the junk bond market, she'd accidentally become pregnant – on the very same night in St. Bart's when their relationship came to a dramatic end.

Alex knew that the unplanned conception was a blessing that would force her to make an overdue change in her life. And while she didn't know exactly what the future would hold for her, she did know what her next move would be; she was going to retire from investment banking, move out to the Thimble Island off the coast of Connecticut where her father lived, toss her BlackBerry into the ocean and focus on raising her kid.

When the time came to rejoin the workforce she was going to use her talents and experience in a slightly different way, she had decided. Maybe it was because she'd spent so much time in the presence of an inspiring environmental entrepreneur like Jimmy Lee, or maybe it was because of a primal desire to try and make the world a little better for her unborn child, but as she sat in the lobby of the Hotel Georges V in Paris a few days earlier, she decided her next job would be a little different.

As luck would have it, it was a perfect year for her to retire from the transportation investment banking department at Allied Bank of England because she was about to have an epic year-end payday. She had been the sole underwriter of a $300 million junk bond for Viking Tankers and earned another fee for buying back 80% of those same bonds at a discount five months later. She had advised on the merger of two short-line railroads, been the sole arranger of Road King's bond deal and been lead bookrunner on the $750 million IPO for Clear Sky. All told, she was looking at a year-end bonus of nearly $8 million. The only problem was that she had to hang-on until bonuses were paid-out three months later; she hoped she could make it that long.

"You're the captain of this closing," Jimmy Lee said with his smooth southern drawl as he pressed the market-closing mallet into Alex's hand.

"Don't be ridiculous," Alex laughed as she handed the mallet back to him. "It's your deal; bang the little hammer and have some fun."

"No, it's *our* deal and it never would've gotten done without you," Jimmy Lee replied as he crossed his arms and refused to accept the tiny hammer.

"I hope you won't think less of me, Jimmy, but you have a right to know that this isn't my first time," Alex said. "In fact, I have opened and closed this exchange on more occasions than I can remember."

"I don't care who does it," the NYSE executive laughed nervously to the occupants of the gallery – a group of senior executives, lawyers and bankers that had clapped their hands long enough and now were hungry to taste fresh email. "But would someone *please* get ready to press the button."

"Tell you what," Jimmy Lee said. "I'll press the button, you bang the gavel. Deal?"

"Deal," Alex smiled.

But just as the airline entrepreneur prepared to push the round red button that would unleash the violent clanging of the metallic bell that preceded the hammer-slamming market close, Alex felt her BlackBerry emit a seductive tickle from the pocket her tailor had sewn into her dress for the sole purpose of holding the device. She closed her eyes and hoped the vibration would stop – but it didn't.

When the device buzzed for the third time, Alex experienced the helpless feeling of addiction: that haunting sensation of being physically unable to resist the impulse to do something you absolutely, positively knew to be self-destructive. So she tucked the historic hammer under her bare right arm and unsheathed the diabolical little device with her left hand. Like a novice poker player examining an unfavorable hand, she dramatically winced when she noticed the last name in the world she wanted to see – *Pearl*. It was her boss, Piper Pearl, the head of Allied Bank of England's investment banking business.

Had her life-altering bonus not required the formal approval of Piper Pearl, in his capacity as Chairman of the compensation committee, she truly believed she would have ignored the call, slipped the evil machine back into her dress and quarterbacked the closing of the NYSE with Jimmy Lee Brown. But only in books and movies was life that simple. The reality was that if she really wanted to have the luxury of retiring from banking to raise Coco's child she would be Piper's slave until the $8 million wire transfer hit her account three months later; she would chew the man's food if he asked her to.

"Heya Piper," Alex cooed as she began to squeeze out of the crowded gallery, "to what do I owe the pleasure?"

Alex may have sounded relaxed, but she wasn't. Every interaction she'd had with Piper Pearl over the last ten years had put her stomach in a knot. As she waited for her boss to reply she twisted the singular dreadlock concealed beneath her torrent of cascading blonde hair. Like a well-concealed tattoo or an old Porsche 911 tucked away in a dusty barn, Alex just hadn't been able to part with the symbol of her youth – in her case the post-Dartmouth summer she'd spent on the island of Corsica with a French reggae singer called "Pork Chop."

"Miss Meriwether, the market closes in like twenty seconds!" the host gasped in stunned disbelief after she casually pushed him aside while handing back the hammer. "And *you* are the one closing it."

"I bet the boys can handle it," Alex said over her squash-strengthened shoulder as she exited the gallery and wandered into the empty hallway to resume her conversation with her overlord.

"You have ten minutes to get yourself to Four Seasons Hotel on 57th Street," Piper ordered from the other end of the telephone.

"I didn't think we had that kind of relationship," she said.

"I'm in the bar," Piper replied.

"That's a shocker; what's up?" Alex asked.

"What's up is that my freshman roommate from University of Texas called me last night and gave me authority to sell his oil and gas business," Piper said. "He even gave me the name and phone number of the guy who wants to buy it," he laughed. "I swear this deal is too easy."

"Those are famous last words," Alex warmed.

"This time is different," he replied.

"So what company are we peddling today?" Alex asked as she strolled slowly down a dark and abandoned hallway like an athlete leaving a stadium, the rushing roar of the stock exchange now barely audible in the background.

"It is a little business called American Refining Corporation," Piper said with the pride of a cat presenting its owner with a dead mouse. "Perhaps you've heard of it?"

"Heard of it?" she said. "Are you kidding? ARC basically *invented* fracking and they also have substantial oil reserves in the Middle East," she said. "That's a real company."

"Don't sound so surprised," he laughed. "I *am* the chairman of the investment banking division at this bank."

"That's a juicy mandate, but who can eat a company that big?" Alex asked.

"Another little organization you may have heard of," Piper said. "It is called the People's Republic of China."

Alex stopped in her tracks. She was stunned by the mere mention of selling a major American energy company to the Government of China. "You can't be serious."

"And why not?" he challenged.

"Because the United States Congress will never go for a deal like that," Alex said. "They wouldn't let CNOOC buy Unocal and they wouldn't let the Dubai Ports buy the Port of New York. Lest you forget, Piper, there are plenty of people in this country who believe our domestic energy production should be used *domestically*. I have seen this movie and I know how it ends."

"This ending is going to be a little different," Piper said.

"What makes you so sure?" she asked.

"*Because I've got friends in low places*," the investment banker sang the words to the tune of the Garth Brooks song as he considered the long list of his former and future colleagues who occupied virtually *all* the highest economic and monetary positions in D.C. "Besides, it's my *civic duty* to do this deal!" Piper proclaimed.

"Yeah," Alex laughed, "How do you figure that?"

"Because this transaction is the ultimate win-win; we create jobs, generate tax revenue, help restore the balance of trade and share clean energy with the planet's biggest polluter. How can you possibly argue about that?" Piper asked. "Now get yourself over here right now so we can do this thing with the man they call Mr. Xing."

"But I'm closing the New York Stock Exchange," Alex reminded him.

"I know," he said. "I was watching CNBC and saw that eerie moan of yours. That's what made me think to call you. By the way, you look great in that red dress and I love that necklace you're wearing."

Alex reached down and touched the golden Picasso charm that Coco Jacobsen had spontaneously purchased for her at a Bonham's auction in Paris one week before the regrettable night in St. Bart's. The necklace, called *Le Faune Grande*, was a sun-shaped splotch of gold with a smile that would forever remind her of her estranged Norwegian lover.

"It belonged to my grandmother," Alex lied.

"She must have worked-out a lot," Piper marveled.

"I'm referring to the necklace," Alex said. "My grandmother gave me the necklace, Piper, not the dress."

"Oh," he grumbled, "the only thing my grandmother gave me was a bald spot and high blood pressure."

"You are so deprived," she said.

"Alex, my black Sprinter is idling in front of the statue of George Washington on the corner of Broad and Wall," Piper said of the Mercedes van he had customized into a mobile office and trading desk that shuttled him around the island of

Manhattan. "So if you ever want to collect that little year-end bonus I might possibly owe you, I suggest you get into it."

"That's cruel, Piper," she said.

"To the contrary," he replied. "A boss' job is to motivate their employees and what could be more motivating to an investment banker than money?"

"You got me," she said. "See you in ten."

Chapter 6

Tung Chao Yung

Born in 1911, C. Y. Tung was a self-made Chinese shipping magnate, founder of the Orient Overseas Line and father of Tung Chee Hwa the first Chief Executive of the Special Administrative Region of China. After the end of World War II, Mr. Tung financed $2.87 million to purchase 10 Liberty ships, 3 Victory ships, 8 CIMAVI ships, 10 N3 ships, 3 tankers, 16 Great Lakes Ships and 4 auxiliary naval ships from the U.S. government. At the peak of his career, he owned a shipping fleet with over 150 ships. He was one of the world's top seven freight moguls; he was often called the Onassis of the Orient.

Bobby Xing was breathing hard when he finally reached the top of the stairs leading up to the bustling Bar 57/57 in the Four Seasons Hotel.

He didn't know if it was the five glasses of Suntory he'd consumed while singing karaoke with some friends from MIT the previous night or if he was just wiped-out from working one-hundred-hour weeks since his nation joined the World Trade Organization twelve years earlier, but whatever the cause Bobby Xing felt like he could fall asleep standing up.

Mr. Xing knew sleep would have to wait until he boarded the 14-hour Air China flight back to Beijing later that evening. As the human being tasked with converting a portion of his country's massive U.S. dollar reserves into the energy needed to power the most profound industrial experiment in history, Mr. Xing did not have the luxury of turning down meetings just because he was tired. If China's growth was to continue at its current pace, which it had to, the growing need for energy wouldn't pause – and neither would he.

After mopping the sweat from his forehead with his shirtsleeve, the weary traveler began to scan the dimly lit room in search of his host. He had received the cold call from the man named Piper Pearl late the previous night to request a meeting to discuss what the American modestly described as "The Greatest Synergy Ever."

After a few seconds of searching, Mr. Xing spotted a slowly swaying arm in the far corner of the bar. He felt his pulse quicken. Squinting behind the rectangular rims of his eyeglasses, he recognized the aristocratic face that he'd only seen on television and in newspapers. It was Piper Pearl – and he had not come alone.

Mr. Xing swerved around an obstacle course of tables and chairs filled with rowdy corporate revelers as he moved toward the corner table. Just as he arrived, his host sprouted a wide smile and tilted forward as if on a hinge. Piper held back his bright orange Hermes necktie to his chest with one arm and slowly swept the other around the room as though the Four Seasons Hotel was his own private grounds.

"Welcome," the banker announced to the man with the world's largest checkbook. "And thank you for meeting us on such short notice."

"The pleasure is mine," Mr. Xing replied as he withdrew a business card from a silver case and used both hands to solemnly present it to Piper Pearl. Piper responded by casually passing Mr. Xing one of his cards and said, "This is my colleague, Alexandra Meriwether."

"It's nice to meet you," Alex said as she lowered her head and presented Mr. Xing with her business card using the same respectful protocol that he had used.

A few second later, a perky waitress wearing a black skirt glided toward the table. She punctuated her arrival by shifting her thick blonde French braid and her narrow hips in opposite directions. "Hiya, Pipes!" she said.

"Good afternoon, Samantha," Piper said proudly before turning to his guest. "What can Samantha bring you, Mr. Xing?"

Although she had no idea what Piper Pearl did for a living, Samantha Algood couldn't help but enjoy the thrill of being the man's co-conspirator. Had the Juilliard-trained hostess been a student of global leveraged finance rather than classical cello she might have confused Piper as a minor character in the book *Liar's Poker* – and would definitely have had more insight into the capital-seeking people whose inhibitions she had lowered over the years.

Parked at Piper's round corner table had been Icelandic investors, Brazilian oil executives, Argentine soybean farmers, social media moguls, dot com geeks, buyers *and* sellers of sub-prime mortgages, Australian iron ore promoters, South African gold miners, Montenegro waterfront developers, Angolan plantation owners…and now the youthful but exhausted looking man with the backpack.

"Ladies first," Mr. Xing said and smiled politely at Alex.

"It's good to know there really *is* one gentleman left in the world," Alex said and shot a glance at Piper. Mr. Xing blushed.

"What would you like?" Samantha asked.

"A glass of Montrachet, please," Alex said with a smile.

Alex's accidental pregnancy with the Norwegian prevented her from drinking her favorite white wine, but that was beside the point. The critical thing now was that Piper Pearl didn't discover that her BlackBerry wasn't the only thing she was carrying 24/7. Her boss had a bad habit of hoarding every scrap of information until he found a way to use it to his advantage; she needed to collect her $8 million bonus before he figured out she might resign.

"Your turn, sweetie," Samantha said after her eyes flashed at Mr. Xing.

"May I have a ginger ale, please," Mr. Xing said politely, hoping it would soothe his troubled stomach.

"I must apologize, Mr. Pearl," Mr. Xing said after Piper Pearl had ordered his third martini. "The last flight to Beijing leaves in two-and-a-half hours and I must be on it. I am meeting with our president upon my arrival tomorrow evening to update him on our country's most recent energy acquisitions."

Mr. Xing had spent the last forty-five days on a billion-dollar shopping spree all over Africa and the Americas during which he had acquired massive oil reserves in Angola, bought a mountain made of coal in Canada and loaned Venezuela $50 billion in exchange for one supertanker full of staggeringly sour crude oil every week for the next twenty years. His country had committed to spending about $1 trillion on natural resources in Africa alone in the coming years which meant Mr. Xing still had plenty of work ahead of him.

He had bought everything on the shopping list his colleagues in Beijing had given him – everything except the one commodity his country wanted and needed most of all – clean burning liquid natural gas and the products made from it.

"Then let's just get down to business," Piper smiled with excitement as he unhitched his cufflinks, a pair of bulls cast in gold, and methodically folded back his starched sleeves.

Like most serial dealmakers, Piper Pearl preferred the excitement of doing transactions to just about anything else in his life: more than playing golf at St. Andrew's or sail fishing off Bimini, more than buying trophy real estate in the Hamptons or collecting early twentieth century Impressionist paintings at Sotheby's and even more than the earthly delight of the many beautiful women he had known during his endless bachelorhood. The business of doing deals, it turned out, was the perfect therapy for Piper's Attention Deficit Disorder.

"Thank you," Mr. Xing said as he inspected a singular smoked almond before laying it on his tongue like a Communion Wafer.

"Mr. Xing, I suspect it will come as no surprise to you that the natural resource complex is under a severe capacity strain these days," Piper said clinically before lowering his lips to the wide rimmed martini glass and slurping Ketel One like it was a Slush Puppy.

"We are painfully aware of this," Mr. Xing acknowledged.

Mr. Xing knew all too well that the price of every industrial commodity had skyrocketed in the last ten years mostly due to the hyper-development of his populous country. From food to energy to iron ore, China's raging consumption had caused the collective and disturbing realization that maybe the planet's supply of cheap natural resources, and the environment's capacity to absorb pollution, *weren't* sustainable after all.

It wasn't simply a question of money and industrial growth, it was also food; global production of carbohydrates and protein was now barely adequate to meet current demand and that was only thanks to enhanced yields from genetically modified crops. Throw in extreme weather events caused by climate change and a diminishing supply of fresh water and it was clear that the world was approaching an entirely new phase in its development. Mr. Xing's noble job was to make sure that his country had access to the energy needed to power a rapidly improving standard of living.

"I'm here to relieve your pain," Piper said dramatically.

Before continuing his riff, the investment banker raked a pair of green olives off a plastic toothpick with his gleaming incisors. Then he winked at Alexandra and gave her his *aren't-I-the-best-little-boy-in-the-world* look. Alex rolled her eyes and formed a dubious smile – the complex expression of a mother who was secretly amused by her impish son.

"What do you have in mind?" Mr. Xing asked as he checked his watch.

It wasn't in Mr. Xing's cultural profile to be so direct. He had been trained to always act indifferent but respectful for as long as humanly possible. However, he had spent so much time with American oilmen lately that he'd been infected with their blunt protocol and high efficiency.

"American Refining Corporation," Piper said the words slowly.

Mr. Xing was silent, and stunned. He had been watching fracking pioneer American Refining Corporation for years – and even more closely since ARC had become America's largest producer of domestic shale gas in addition to its foreign oil holdings. He'd taken a meeting with Rocky DuBois, ARC's maverick CEO, when he was in Houston the previous week. Mr. Xing admired the organization and envied its 550,000 acres of oil- and gas-rich American farmlands, but he hadn't made an offer for fear of the political backlash.

"Are you actually proposing that China buy ARC?" Mr. Xing asked as he carefully experimented with a beer nut.

"That's why we're here," Piper smiled and then poured a handful of mixed nuts into his mouth. "This is the most exciting transaction I have ever been involved with; it's real win-win."

"Are you suggesting that my country import American oil and gas products from America?" Mr. Xing asked.

"Fill up the boats and haul it away," Piper said.

Easier said than done, Mr. Xing thought with frustration. His country had spent hundreds of billions of dollars in its quest to dominate the global shipbuilding industry and had succeeded spectacularly when it came to building low cost bulk carriers. But in the realm of designing and building technologically complex vessels like the ones that carried LNG, Korea and Japan still controlled the market...for now.

"Correct me if I am wrong," Mr. Xing said, "but aren't there certain laws that prohibit the export of U.S. energy?" He knew the official answer, of course, but was always curious to hear how Americans viewed their country's policy on energy.

"Actually," Alex interjected, "the U.S. only prohibits the export of crude oil and it looks like even that might change soon as long as the exporters pay a tax. There is no law against exporting products made from gas such as ethane, butane and propane and you can even export LNG; all you need is a permit and they are being issued all the time."

"Interesting," he said. While Alex's over-simplification of American LNG export-laws was technically correct, in reality the government had issued few permits for the export of gas.

Mr. Xing knew that the acquisition of a company like ARC, with its massive reserves of gas, was exactly what his country had been searching for. Ever since the U.S. Embassy in Beijing had begun tracking the city's air quality, people from China and around the world had been demanding that the country enforce tighter emissions standards and use higher-quality fuels. Everyone recognized that it was impossible to increase the standard of living without improving the quality of life.

In response to those concerns, China had made a commitment to spend billions of dollars converting some of their six-hundred and fifty power plants from coal and oil to clean burning natural gas. Mr. Xing's job was to find the gas – and figure out how to get it to China.

On a personal level there was no one who was more committed to improving the air quality in China than Mr. Xing whose own son had developed severe asthma. That was why he'd made it his personal as well as professional mission in life to do whatever was necessary to import as much clean burning gas as he could find around the world.

Mr. Xing had heard all he needed to hear – and he had a plane to catch. "I am afraid I must leave now to reach the airport," he said as he stood up and prepared to exit the bar. "I thank you for presenting me with this opportunity. I will discuss it with my colleagues upon my return; if there is interest I will contact you immediately," he said, hoping they had not seen the appetite in his eyes.

"That sure was weird," Piper said after Mr. Xing had disappeared down the stairs toward 57th Street. "Was it something I said?" Piper asked, disappointed that his deal got so little traction.

"No way," she smiled. "You were awesome."

Although she did see the nobility in sharing natural resources like food and energy, Alexandra Meriwether was relieved that the politically-charged deal between the People's Republic of China and American Refining Corporation was dead on arrival – but she couldn't have been more wrong.

Chapter 7

Playing Hunches

Each fleet is customarily treated as an extension of one man's personality – never "National Bulk Carriers" or "Olympic Maritime" but "Ludwig" or "Onassis." And it is generally accepted that the head man is entitled to play his hunches.

Fortune Magazine, 1974

"Ladies and gentlemen," the impeccably dressed real estate agent said with flourish as she floated up the first few steps of the wide central staircase. "Prepare yourselves to hear something absolutely wonderful about the special home you have just entered."

After stopping halfway up the wide and gracious stairs, the petite woman turned around and lifted her palms into the air like a preacher preparing to deliver a sermon to the parish of twenty potential purchasers. "There is magic in this home," she said dramatically.

"This place had better not be haunted," Grace whispered into Robert's ear, "because I will *not* share a bathroom with a ghost. Two boys are quite enough."

"According to the local historian here in Edgartown," the agent continued with a dramatic whisper, "the Daniel Fisher House was built by a prominent shipowner and ship captain in 1840. Some people even believe it was the inspiration for the Admiral Benbow Inn featured in the novel *Treasure Island.*"

Robert's eyes bulged and his body tingled with excitement as he absorbed the words. "Did you just hear that, Grace?" he whispered to his wife after jabbing her with his elbow.

"What? Did you hear something?" she replied and looked around nervously. "Was it the ghost?"

"No, first our dream house comes on the market the day before we were planning to come out here for our anniversary and now we learn it was built by a shipowner and might have even been the inspiration for Oliver's favorite book! Oh, Grace, it's a sign."

"It's a sign alright," she said. "It's a sign that you are crazy."

The agent continued. "Fearing he might not return from one of his long voyages at sea, Captain Fisher built this house for his only child...a boy named Oliver. Only later was it turned into an inn for sailors and then restored by members of the Fisher family."

Robert emitted a gasp so loud that his wife slapped her open hand over his mouth. They had walked past the stately white house a hundred times since they started visiting the island, but not in their wildest dreams did they imagine living there – never mind having such a close *connection* with the place. Robert suddenly felt possessed with the same kind of self-determination that had been getting him into trouble for as long as he could remember; he had to have it.

"It's more than a sign," he said. "It's *two* signs and do you know what that means?"

"What?"

"It means there's another sign coming," Robert said. "These things always happen in threes."

"We don't have the $3 million required to buy the house," Grace reminded him. "Maybe that's the last sign. You lost your hedge fund and now you work for a sweet but financially unstable Norwegian playboy who lives on a yacht and needs a haircut."

"We'll find a way," Robert said, just as the telephone in his pocket rang. "We always find a way."

Needless to say, Robert Fairchild was in a receptive frame of mind when he answered the incoming call from Houston, Texas. "Hello," Robert whispered with his hand cupped over the telephone.

"Good afternoon," the gentleman caller said with a gracious southern drawl. "May I have the pleasure of speaking with Mr. Robert Fairchild?"

"This is Robert Fairchild," Robert said as he slowly drifted away from the herd of house hunters. "May I help you?"

"I hope so," the voice said. "My name is Thompson DuBois and I am with a little company here in Texas called…"

"American Refining Corporation," Robert finished the man's sentence. Robert was stunned. He knew exactly who Mr. DuBois was. The man's story was legendary; he was a geologist turned wildcatter who never gave up on fracking even after the big oil companies had. Heck, Robert had seen him on CNBC that very morning when he and Grace were waiting in the JetBlue lounge at LaGuardia. "I know it well."

"I'm honored to hear that," he said modestly. "May I have a few moments of your time, Mr. Fairchild?"

"Absolutely, Mr. DuBois," Robert said.

"Please call me Rocky," he laughed slowly.

"Rocky?" Robert asked.

"That's the name my daddy gave me when he noticed I couldn't stop cracking open rocks in the backyard of our house in West Texas to see what was inside of them," he chuckled.

"That's a great story," Robert said.

"It's been a long, strange trip," Rocky said. "Mr. Fairchild, I'm calling you today because I'd like to take some of your boats on long-term time charter to move some my Middle Eastern oil to America."

"Excuse me?" Robert said.

"You *are* the CEO of Viking Tankers, are you not?" Rocky asked.

"Yes," Robert said slowly.

"And as CEO you *do* have authority to enter into charters on behalf of your company, do you not?" the Texan asked.

"Of course I do," Robert bluffed.

The truth was that he had never been approached to charter a ship. In fact, Coco and Oddleif had never even included him in a *conversation* about chartering a ship. The only thing the swashbuckling Norwegians did was perpetually pester him to find "the free money" on Wall Street – as if he was searching for loose change under the seat of a car.

"Then I'll be straight with you, son," he said. "I need some boats to move my crude oil and I would prefer to work with someone in my own time zone," Rocky said. "I need someone who speaks my language, if you know what I mean."

"I understand," Robert said as he slipped out the front door of the house and stood on the colonial cobblestone sidewalk.

"Mr. Fairchild, I'd like to start by having my ocean transportation subsidiary charter-in ten of your VLCCs for five years," Rocky said. "How does that sound?"

Robert swallowed hard and said, "Come again."

"And I believe this is could be just the beginning of the kind of mutually beneficial business that our organizations can do together, Mr. Fairchild. You see, what I am looking for here is a long-term relationship," Rocky said. "I want maritime monogamy."

"Maritime monogamy?" Robert repeated the words slowly, wondering whether they had ever resided next to each other in a sentence before.

As if hypnotized by the pair of tiny barge ferries shuttling back and forth between Martha's Vineyard and the neighboring island of Chappaquiddick, Robert listened with fascination as an elder statesman of the U.S. fracking community eloquently espoused the importance of cooperation between shipowners and oil companies.

"Well, how much are you comfortable paying for the ships," Robert finally asked. He didn't particularly want to leave the fantasy world he was enjoying, but he knew that shipping deals always started with talk…but ended with dollars.

"How about $50,000 a day," he proposed. "Each."

"I believe the spot market is quite a bit stronger than that," Robert said.

"It won't be this strong for five years, which is exactly how long my subsidiary is willing to commit to your boats," Rocky said.

"I will have to talk to the owner of Viking Tankers, Coco Jacobsen."

"What's there to talk about?" Rocky asked. "I just offered to pay you $900 million over five years. It sounds to me like you don't have much juice at the company. Are you sure you're really the CEO?"

"I'm sure."

"But I thought you said that gives you the authority to enter into a five-year charter agreement," Rocky said.

"Technically, I do, but…"

"Good deals don't hang around for long," Rocky said. "I am offering these charters firm for reply right now. You have just sixty seconds to make up your mind and after that I will call another shipowner."

"Sixty seconds? You can't be serious," Robert asked, but the Texan didn't reply. He just asked someone named Brittany to bring him a skim latte.

Robert turned around and stared lovingly at the stately sea captain's house. Looking at the elegant edifice and its finely carved architectural details, he thought about how much his family would enjoy living in it. He also rationalized that the charters to ARC might help him raise the $500 million that Coco had been demanding on a daily basis for the past three months. Lord knows he had tried everything else.

In an effort to placate the Norwegian's desperate and mysterious need for half a billion dollars, Robert had scoured the capital markets like a pig in search of Périgord truffles. He had hunted in the austere Hamburg KG houses, rooted around in the Norwegian bond market and been sniffed over in the khaki-colored offices of thirty-four private equity funds perched high above midtown Manhattan.

He had sat with a white-shoe investment bank on Park Avenue and a boiler room in Bayonne where he had discussed everything from IPOs to SPACS, convertible bonds to preferred shares to private placements. He had met with "unregulated" banks, family offices, sovereign wealth funds, credit wrappers, offshore insurance companies, onshore insurance companies, residual value guarantors, a Sharia-sheik in Dubai and a "crowd funding" geek in San Francisco.

His quixotic quest for capital had even led him to look into creating a late night infomercial named "Owner Ship" on which he would dress-up in a rented captain's uniform with epaulets and hawk *faux* antique share certificates in Viking Tankers to insomniac investors with a longing for the sea.

But the intimate examination of fifty shades of ship finance had yielded a singular reply: "Sure, Mr. Fairchild, we'd be happy to give you money just as long as Viking Tankers has profitable, long-term charters on his ships with a financially solid counterparty."

The lack of time charters had always been the deal breaker when it came to raising equity and now he had the solution right in front of him. The world famous CEO of an investment grade American oil company was apparently willing to take the ten vessels at a good rate for a long-term. It was a miracle, Robert decided, and it was undoubtedly the third and final sign that he and Grace were meant to buy the Captain Fisher house.

Robert knew Coco would hate the idea of chartering-out the ships, but he figured he could deal with his objections later. In the final moments, the thing that gave Robert the courage to accept Rocky DuBois' offer were the words of advice that Coco shared with him a year earlier.

"Listen carefully to me, Robert, and remember my words," Coco had said. *"Teach them to your little boy some day when he is ready; there will always be many good reasons not to do things in life but people who achieve great things are the ones who believe in themselves and find reasons to do things, even when sometimes they do things that are not so smart."*

Robert knew it was now or never. Like most people involved in the shipping business, he might get only one good cyclical opportunity in his career to place a big bet – and deep down he believed this was probably it. It was time to play his hunches like real shipowners did. It was time to use his gut instincts. Due diligence and decision-by-committee be damned!

"Congratulations, Mr. Rocky DuBois," Robert said. "You've got yourself a fleet."

Chapter 8

Daniel Keith (D.K.) Ludwig

D.K. Ludwig (1897-1992) was a self-made U.S. shipping magnate who had the distinction of being ranked #1 on the first Forbes 400 Richest Americans list published in 1982. Ludwig's first venture into shipping was at the age of 9, when he salvaged a 26-foot boat. He left school at the end of eighth grade to work in various shipping related jobs, directly learning such trades as machinist, marine engineer, and ship handler. In Port Arthur, he sold supplies to sailing ships and steamers. At 19, Ludwig established himself in the shipping business when he began transporting molasses around the Great Lakes. In the 1930s, he developed a novel approach to financing further expansion, by borrowing the construction cost of tankers and using pre-agreed charters as collateral. In 1971, the low-profile Ludwig used a significant portion of his fortune to establish the Ludwig Institute for Cancer Research.

Robert Fairchild slurped creamy clam chowder from a thick ceramic mug at the Black Dog Tavern and reflected on the reckless acts he had just committed.

As he sat in front of a crackling fire at the Martha's Vineyard landmark restaurant, his ripped khaki pants and red flannel shirt camouflaging him to look like every other middle-aged preppy working through a hangover, he began to reconstruct the series of events that preceded his billion-dollar rogue trade.

Robert's "risk-on" binge didn't stop with the ten time charters to ARC. He also convinced Grace to let him make an offer on the Captain Fisher house overlooking Edgartown harbor, which was immediately accepted by the three siblings in Boston who'd just inherited the house from their parents. Later that evening, as they enjoyed their anniversary dinner at the Outermost Inn just below the Aquinnah lighthouse, Robert had proposed to Grace that they relocate to the island of Martha's Vineyard in pursuit of the Holy Grail for young families: a backyard, a garage filled with bicycles, a minivan, sidewalks, a dock, and maybe even the black Labrador retriever that Oliver wanted so badly.

As a shipping man with clients and colleagues around the world, Robert said, it didn't really matter where they lived as long as he had a telephone, a valid passport, an internet connection and access to an airport. They both agreed that Oliver would be thrilled by the prospect of living in an old sea captain's house that had once belonged to a boy named Oliver and may even have been the inspiration for the Admiral Benbow Inn featured so prominently in his favorite novel – *Treasure Island.*

Now the buzz of impulsive decision-making had worn off and the hangover of having to confess his crimes to Coco was setting in. Robert felt his chowder-laden stomach flutter as he searched his BlackBerry for the numbers of the Norwegian's half-dozen mobile telephones. It was with fear in his soul that he dialed one of the numbers and took a deep breath. It was time to come clean.

"I sure hope you are calling to tell me you've found the $500 million!" Coco sang upon answering the phone.

"Not exactly, Coco," Robert said and swallowed the sizeable lump in his throat.

"Ah, then you must be calling to advise me *Viking Alexandra* has left Philadelphia ahead of schedule," Coco interrupted. "That is also good news because the tanker party is about to start in the Arabian Gulf and that ship had better not be late! When the market is this strong, every minute matters."

It wasn't as good as hauling in $500 million on Wall Street overnight, but every ship Coco managed to get into position while the market was hot would be worth close to $10 million in voyage revenue.

"I thought you said every minute mattered when the market was weak," Robert replied.

"That is also true!" Coco cried. "But make no mistake, Fairchild, if freight rates have slipped by the time that ship gets back to the AG then the difference is coming from *your* paycheck!"

In his tireless pursuit to teach his inexperienced underling the agony and ecstasy of being a tramp shipowner, Coco Jacobsen had indexed Robert's monthly salary to the average daily rate that charterers paid for each of his two-million-barrel supertankers. When the spot market was strong Robert made a boatload of money, but most of the time he didn't – most of the time he, like the ships, was living dangerously close to cash break-even.

"How could I forget?" Robert muttered.

"What did you just mumble, Fairchild?"

As he waited for Robert's reply, Coco ran his hand across the white canvas shell that protected his helicopter on the deck of the *Kon Tiki*. He had briefly considered popping down to Mykonos to meet another Greek shipowner friend who might be willing to make up for Coco's cash shortfall, but he'd quickly decided against it; having one partner was tough but having two would be sheer torture; there were simply too many tough and unsubstantiated decisions to be made in the shipping business every day.

"Actually, *Viking Alexandra* was caught-up in the port for some, um, issues," Robert said, careful not to share the bad news about the refinery no longer accepting crude oil tankers.

"But the good news is that she will be sailing tonight and is still on budget according to the voyage calculation."

"Ja, but we make money in this business by doing *better* than the voyage calculation," Coco said. "And besides, if everything is fine why are you calling me?"

"Can't I just call to say 'hello,'" Robert said.

"No one calls a shipowner just to say hello," Coco said. "People call shipowners when they want money or when there is a problem; so which is it, Fairchild – problem or money?"

"Neither," Robert said, even though knew it really *both*.

"You're lying," Coco said.

"We need to talk," Robert said.

"Then talk."

"No," Robert said spontaneously as he shook his head back and forth and stared into the orange flames dancing in the stone hearth.

"Excuse me?"

"This is a conversation we need to have face-to-face," Robert said. He had called Coco to confess his sins but he realized there was simply no way he could be persuasive enough over the transatlantic telephone line to overcome his boss's inevitable objections.

"Ah," Coco sang with amusement. "Let me guess; my little American Boy Scout has decided to raise the $500 million from Tony Soprano and now you are afraid to talk on an unsecure mobile phone line, is that it?"

"I am definitely afraid," Robert conceded.

"Fear is good," Coco said. "Fear means you are alive. Fear means you are pushing yourself by taking some chances. I am proud of you."

"We'll see about that after we speak," Robert said. "When can we meet?"

"Ja, but I am still on *Kon Tiki* near Chios," Coco said. "Although my work here appears to be finished."

Robert had no idea why, or with whom, his cagey boss had been spending so much time on the fabled Aegean island of Chios but his curiosity was agonizing.

"No problem," Robert said as he glanced down at his watch. "I'll be there the day after tomorrow."

"I am working on a transaction that doesn't concern you," Coco said.

"But I'm the CEO of Viking Tankers," Robert countered.

Coco chuckled and said, "That's funny."

"What's funny?"

"Come on, Robert," Coco said. "CEO is just the title we gave you when you did the roadshow for the junk bond deal so that the Americans would take you seriously. Alexandra made me give you that title, but we all know that it doesn't actually mean anything."

Robert closed his eyes and shook his head; this was going to be bad -really bad.

"Would you like to meet in the Oslo office instead?" Robert asked.

"I can't," Coco wailed. "If I spend one more day in Norway during this calendar year it will cost me $50 million in unpaid taxes."

"But I thought Wade Waters came up with a legal strategy that allows you to spend more time in Oslo," Robert said.

"He did, but he's not quite ready to test it out," Coco said.

"How about New York?" Robert asked.

"Nope," Coco said. "I'm still on the naughty boy list with the FBI; I can't clear U.S. customs until the matter is resolved."

"That's right," Robert said. He had always followed the theory of "Don't Ask, Don't Tell" when it came to Coco's travel restrictions.

"Don't you see what's happening here, Robert?" Coco pleaded. "Between laws and taxes I am running out of places to go. Once all the countries connect their computers, I might never be able to get off this yacht ever! I will be like an astronaut stranded in outer space! I will be like Major Tom!"

"There are worse places to be confined than the *Kon Tiki*," Robert said.

"Confinement is confinement," Coco replied.

"Tell you what, let's just meet in London," Robert suggested calmly; it was a common refrain in the international shipping industry.

"Yes, London is still safe," Coco said as his dark mood suddenly turned bright. "I will meet you in London tomorrow evening to hear this fabulous news you are going to tell me."

I never said the news was fabulous, Robert thought, but instead he said, "Fantastic!"

Although Coco would not normally have jumped onto his Gulfstream just to hear whatever balderdash Fairchild felt the need to ventilate, his work on Chios appeared to be finished. The Norwegian was desperate for something that would cheer him up. Even though he was on the brink of completing the biggest deal of his lifetime and that his fleet of supertankers was about to corner the supertanker market, he didn't feel particularly happy. Although Coco had come to possess more assets during his rags-to-riches lifetime than many sovereign nations, the two things Coco wanted most of all were still outside his grasp – Alexandra Meriwether and a family.

"But I am warning you, Fairchild," Coco said, "this had better be something really good, or else…"

Chapter 9

Malcom McLean

With only a high school education, Malcom McLean (1913-2001) pumped gas at a service station and saved enough money by 1934 to buy a second-hand truck for $120. From that beginning, with his single pickup truck, he built it into the second-largest trucking company in the U.S., with 1770 trucks and 32 terminals. McLean Trucking became the first trucking company in the nation to be listed on the New York Stock Exchange. In 1956, McLean developed the metal shipping container, which replaced the traditional break bulk method of handling dry goods and revolutionized the transport of goods and cargo worldwide. McLean secured a bank loan for $500 million and in 1956 bought two World War II T-2 tankers, which he converted to carry containers on and under deck. McLean's company, Sea-Land Services, Inc., was sold to A.P. Moller of Denmark in 2006.

Twenty minutes after the G-5 touched down at Biggin Hill airport, a triple-black Maybach with the license plate "VIKING" was cruising slowly up a snow-covered Dover Street in Mayfair. Before the luxurious land yacht had come to a complete stop beneath the fluttering Union Jack suspended from the illuminated façade of Browns Hotel, Coco Jacobsen sprang from the back seat.

The Norwegian bounded up the hotel's stone steps, burst through the double doors and strode purposefully down the long, black-and-white tiled hallway. He didn't stop until he'd arrived in the taproom where he had agreed to rendezvous with Robert Fairchild. The towering tanker tycoon still had no idea why his Ivy League lackey had summoned him from sunny Greece to freezing London but as a naturally optimistic shipowner, he assumed something great must be about to happen.

As he shook the unseasonable snow from his raven hair, Coco appeared not to notice that the multicultural occupants of The Donovan Bar were studying him like he was an exotic animal. Representing the handful of nationalities that had colonized Mayfair real estate, the ultra-wealthy French, Arabs, Chinese, Indians and Russians were puzzled by Coco's chestnut skin, intrigued by his rock-star length hair and curious that his powerful six-foot-six-inch frame was swaddled in that boyish Norwegian business uniform of Levis, a blue button-down shirt and a blazer blooming with a lime green pocket square – a gift from Anwar Sadat to commemorate their first deal together. But what really captured their attention, more than their inability to determine which ethnic group he belonged to, was the man's energy; it was a force that filled the bar as completely as the smell of wood smoke and the sound of Cole Porter.

Once they had adjusted to the dimness, Coco's pale blue eyes moved across the room like a searchlight. They moved over the antique brass sconces, the walls packed tight with black-and-white Terence Donovan photographs, the magnificent stained-glass window behind the bar and the curvilinear chairs on which lounged a species of stateless souls seen in most of the five-star restaurants and hotels of London, New York, Paris and Hong Kong.

The oil tanker czar had nearly exhausted his search of the taproom when he spotted Robert Fairchild reclining in the "Naughty Corner" – a banquette nook on the far side of the room named in honor of Mr. Donovan's nude photographs which decorated its walls. Coco was momentarily puzzled to see Fairchild sitting next to his single largest lender, Alistair Gooding from Allied Bank of England. And while the shipping tycoon would normally have been furious to find his CEO fraternizing with his financier *sans* chaperone, Coco didn't care; he was just too excited to hear Fairchild's fabulous news.

The moment Robert and Alistair noticed that the towering Norwegian was staring at them the two grown men jumped to their feet and began waving him over. They were as nervous as schoolboys eager to please a favorite teacher.

"Thanks so much for coming up from Greece," Robert said enthusiastically after Coco had crossed the room in a few long strides and stopped abruptly in front of them. "How was your trip?"

Without uttering a word, Coco shot his cuffs and crossed his powerful arms across his chest – a maneuver that revealed one of his sixty-five pairs of sterling silver ship propeller cufflinks. Coco had taken possession of cufflinks (along with one hundred and seventy-five ascots, several hundred engraved silver pens and twenty-two supertankers) after his hostile takeover of a courtly two-hundred-year-old Norwegian tanker company called Knut Shipping. "Ja, I paid $300 million for Knut's man jewelry and I got the VLCCs for free," Coco said when he leaked the story to *TradeWinds*.

"And a good evening to you, Coco," Alistair Gooding oozed in a slow and syrupy British accent. With his head tipped back and his eyes locked on the towering tanker king the banker resembled a baby bird waiting to be fed – an image that was not altogether inaccurate. "How are you these days?"

"How am I?" Coco laughed. "Haven't you been reading the Financial Times, Allie? I've already squeezed tanker rates up to $125,000 per day and most of my ships are still on the starting line. The only guy who's printing more money than me these days is Benjamin Bernanke."

"Yes," Alistair laughed, "and my bank very much appreciates your efforts."

"Excuse me?" Coco said slowly.

"Well, as you know, Coco, you have a substantial breach in the minimum value clause of your loan agreement," Alistair said. "And since you do not have a personal guarantee on the loan, Allied Bank of England has decided to retain all freight income in Viking Tankers' operating account until further notice; this is permitted according to the terms of the loan agreement."

"You *what!*" Coco said with his mouth agape.

"Relax, Coco, it's still your money," the banker said. "We are just going to hold it for you until loan is back in compliance."

"How much will that require?" the shipowner asked.

"Based on recent vessel appraisals," Alistair replied, "we estimate that $200 million should do the trick."

"Ugh!" Coco cried. "But I need that money."

If what Alistair was saying was true, Coco wouldn't get a single penny out of his tanker party – and neither would the Greek. He had pulled off the greatest coup in the history of the oil tanker market and he *still* didn't have a dime to show for it. This was the problem with having an over-leveraged and over-aged fleet; you couldn't even make money in great market because the bank took it all. Coco might as well of had the name "Allied Bank of England" on his business card because that's exactly who he was working for.

"We appreciate the fact that you need some money to run the ships," Alistair said. "That's why we are more than happy to pay the ships' operating expenses directly. We must be careful; it appears that the crude oil tanker market is heading into some very heavy weather."

"Heavy weather!" Coco cried. "Why do you think that?"

"Because the U.S. is importing less and less light, sweet crude oil now as a result of fracking; everybody knows that what's happening in the tanker market today is nothing but a blip."

"Blips are how you get rich in this game," Coco said. "Besides, Allie, this is shipping; just when everyone thinks something is going to happen, the opposite usually does."

"Thanks, Coco," Alistair laughed. "The rigor of your analysis will give great comfort to my colleagues on the credit committee."

"May I ask you something, Allie?"

"Sure."

"How did you get so darned pessimistic?" Coco asked.

"Simple," Alistair replied, "by financing optimists like you."

"Okay, Fairchild," Coco said with expectant eyes after turning toward a truly terrified looking Robert Fairchild, "why am I here? I am counting on you more than you can imagine."

Robert Fairchild had been expecting to enjoy at least a few minutes of conversation, canapés and cocktails in the cozy corner booth before delving into the brutal commercial matter at hand, but Coco was clearly ready to get down to business.

"Coco, do you remember when we were on the brink of bankruptcy last year and you said you wanted to make some changes to our strategy?"

"Wait, wait…don't tell me!" the Norwegian blurted out as he began rubbing his hands together so fast and forcefully that they might catch fire. "I think I know why we're here!"

"You do?" Robert asked and shot a glance at Alistair, wondering if the banker had spilled the beans about the ten time charters to ARC.

"You finally found the $500 million on Wall Street that I need!" Coco shouted.

"*Excuse* me?" Robert gasped.

"You know how much I adored those bonds," Coco said and closed his eyes.

The mercurial Norwegian spoke wistfully of the junk bonds as though recalling a spectacular bottle of wine or a particularly adventuresome lover – which, in fact, he was. It was during the process of selling that $300 million tranche of unsecured junk bonds to U.S. institutional investors that Coco happened upon the dazzling and energetic investment banker Alexandra Meriwether – and the pleasure of chilled Montrachet.

Although Coco had been attracted to Alexandra the moment he first saw her pitching him via videoconference he had fallen hopelessly in love with her when she somehow managed to use the bondholders' escrowed funds to help Coco buy back his bonds at a substantial discount just weeks before the Suez Canal closed and the tanker market spiked. From that moment on, Coco had wanted Alex to be his star – a guiding light to steer by throughout the whipsaw ride that was his life. Instead, she'd been nothing but a comet that flashed brightly but briefly and disappeared as quickly as she came; Coco hadn't felt quite right ever since.

"I…I… but…I…um," Robert stammered.

"As you know, the free American money is so helpful to my business model," Coco whispered after leaning across the table, as if his words were a trade secret. The Norwegian was now so close that Robert was enveloped in a mysterious mélange of mastic chewing gum, Marlboros, cedar shavings and Snus. "Did you know that renting capital is the single largest daily expense of running a supertanker? That is why the free money is so important."

"But the junk bonds came with a coupon of 20%," Robert pleaded. "That was hardly free money, Coco."

"I have no problem with expensive capital as long as I can buy it back at a discount," Coco explained.

"I'm sorry to be the one to break the news to you, Coco, but there is no such thing as free money in this world," Robert said and he felt as though he was sharing the bad news about the Easter Bunny. "And that's *not* why I asked you to come to London."

Robert closed his eyes and waited for the type of unrestrained temper tantrum for which the Norwegian was internationally famous. He waited and waited, but the rage never came. When Robert slowly opened his eyes a minute later he was startled to find Coco's smiling mug hauntingly close to his own. The Norwegian's psychotic smile reminded him of Jack Nicholson in *The Shining.*

"So you're not upset?" Robert asked as he slowly backed away from Coco.

"Of course not," Coco beamed as he leaned toward Robert.

"And you're not disappointed?" Robert asked and leaned back a little further.

"Why would I be disappointed? In fact, I feel happy again because now I *definitely* know why we are here!" The giant unfolded his tall frame and rose from the stool. "And this is the one thing, the only thing, that's even better than the free money!"

"Really?" Robert looked at Alistair.

"Oh yes! The only other good excuse for you to drag me to London, and for my lender to effectively steal $200 million from me, is because you are having a surprise birthday party in my honor," Coco announced and looked around the room.

"What?" Robert gasped. "Did you say *surprise party*?"

"Yes! And that must be why all the fancy people are staring at me," Coco said. "Allie knows I love them more than anything! My parents used to have a surprise party for me every year in

Norway! Is Alexandra here to celebrate my big day?" Coco asked manically as he scanned the room with a flash of excitement in his blue eyes. "If Alexandra comes to my birthday party I'll be the happiest boy in the whole world!"

Robert cleared his throat and prepared to offer the sobering news.

"Coco, we already had your birthday party three months ago, aboard the *Christian Radich*," Robert said, referring to the beautiful full-rigged training vessel built in 1937 whose homeport is downtown Oslo. The vessel was a stirring reminder of Norway's seafaring history and a popular party venue for nostalgic shipping professionals.

"We did?"

"Yes, don't you remember jumping off the bow of the ship into the Oslo fjord with the woman's volleyball team from the University of Nebraska?" Alistair asked.

A smile suddenly stretched across Coco's face. "They were *awesome*!" the Norwegian declared as the warmth of the memory rushed over him. "This reminds me, Fairchild; don't *you* have a big birthday coming up soon?"

"It's not for a few months," Robert sighed, "and I certainly don't have time to worry about it now. In fact, that's the least of my problems at this point."

While Coco Jacobsen couldn't seem to get enough of celebrating his birthday, Robert Fairchild always dreaded the attention and self-analysis that came along with his...especially now that he was inching ever-closer to the dangerously self-destructive decade of the 40s.

Coco laughed and turned to his banker. "Hey Allie, you ever notice how Americans don't think they have time for anything?"

"They've always been a bit confused about what's important," the banker said. "They've gone from drinking three martinis *for* lunch to feeling guilty about enjoying a single glass of wine *with* lunch."

"So maybe we should cook up a little surprise party for Fairchild's fortieth," Coco said. "What do you think?"

"No one does surprise parties better than you," Alistair conceded with a chummy wink and a knocking of the Norwegian's considerable knuckles. "The one you had for our Venezuelan friend on the island of Corsica was best in class!"

"Thanks, Allie, but I think I can do even better, especially if we think up a good theme," Coco said.

"You'll come up with something," the banker said. "You always do."

"But now I am confused, Fairchild," Coco said as he resumed his line of questioning. "If you still haven't found me the free $500 million, and I am not here for my birthday party, then why on earth did you drag me all the way to this freezing cold city?" Coco demanded with patience nearly exhausted. "What is this great news?"

"You're about to find out," Robert said.

Chapter 10

America's Richest Shipowner

George B. Kaiser, whose $10 billion net worth ranks him #40 on the Forbes 400, is currently America's wealthiest shipowner. In addition to his principal ownership of the Kaiser-Francis Oil Company and The Bank of Oklahoma, and his varied activities in the oil and gas business, Mr. Kaiser owns Excelerate LNG which is active in the transportation of Liquid Natural Gas. He is based in (landlocked) Tulsa, Oklahoma.

"The chief executive officer of a blue chip oil and gas company in Houston, Texas called me two days ago and offered to charter some ships from Viking Tankers," Robert said.

"How did he get to you?" Coco grumbled suspiciously as his eyes narrowed on Fairchild.

"I'm not exactly sure," Robert said. "He probably just found me on the internet." He was trying to remain confident as he prepared to lay out his confession-disguised-as-a-business-proposition, but Coco's reaction to his opening sentence made for a discouraging start.

"I hate the internet," Coco snarled. "That machine has been worse for the shipping business than Somali pirates and new Chinese shipyards…combined!"

Robert stoically pushed forward with his pitch like a soldier heading into a battle that he was sure to lose. "The CEO of this American oil and gas producer offered to time charter ten of our VLCCs for *five years!*" Robert announced, failing to mention that he had legally committed Viking Tankers into performing the fifty years of high-seas haulage.

Although Robert knew the Norwegian was euphoric about the state of the short-term spot market, Robert was praying the financial security of having fifty years' worth of time charters would hold some analgesic appeal for a man who'd recently returned from a financial near-death experience.

"So?" Coco said.

"So isn't that great?" Robert asked.

Robert lifted his hand and offered a high-five – but Coco failed to even acknowledge the rudimentary attempt at human bonding. The Norwegian just closed his eyes, shook his leonine head back and forth and yawned.

"Great for *whom*?" Coco asked.

Although Coco's signature question always sounded like a simple one, Robert and Alistair struggled to come up with an equally simple answer. The two money-men knew the time charter deal was great for Alistair and Allied Bank of England, because it would increase the odds that Viking Tankers would repay its loan. They knew it was great for Robert, whose employment and income would instantly become so secure that he might even be able to get a mortgage on the Vineyard house. They also knew it was great for ARC, because the oil company would get a fleet of ships at a discount to the current spot market. But the question of whether or not the deal was great for Coco was a much more complex one. The answer depended entirely on what actually *motivated* Coco Jacobsen – and neither Alistair nor Robert had a clue about that.

"It's great because we can lock in excellent returns that are guaranteed," Robert finally said.

"Why would a major oil company guarantee great returns to a little shipowner like me?" Coco asked.

"Because shipping is not their core business," Robert said.

"Nei," Coco shook his head back and forth as he worked hard to restrain his impatience with the naïve Robert Fairchild.

"Oh, I know why they want to do it!" the American called out. "Because they don't have time to mess around in the charter market every time they need a ship. They want monogamy."

"Any other brilliant theories?" Coco asked.

"Yes, they want the time charters because the financial returns generated by actually owning ships simply can't successfully compete for capital with their shale gas exploration and production projects," Robert said but his statement sounded more like a question.

"Are you finished now?" Coco asked.

"It sure sounds like it," Alistair said under his breath.

"Fairchild, the only reason Rocky DuBois and people like him would offer to take my ships on *long-term* charter is because they can't afford to take my ships on *short-term* charter," Coco explained. "And fixing a short-term problem with a long-term problem is generally not a good idea."

"Do you know Rocky DuBois?" Robert exclaimed when he heard Coco first mention the oilman's nickname before he had even mentioned it. "What a small world!"

"I know Rocky DuBois," Coco snarled, "and I *hate* Rocky DuBois. He is an evil squid."

"He seems like a very good guy to me," Robert said.

"You think Rocky DuBois is a *good guy*?" Coco choked as the memory of his altercation with the Texan surfaced like bile in his mouth.

"He sounded nice," Robert said.

"Takers always sound nice when they're taking, Fairchild," Coco said. "Listen to me gentlemen and listen carefully: long-term chartering-out our ships to that man in this market would be the dumbest thing in the world we could do."

"What happened between you and Mr. DuBois anyway?" Alistair asked.

"Ten years ago I agreed to put the *Viking Telemachus* on a long-term time charter to Rocky DuBois. Three weeks later that Kraken cowboy ordered my captain to halt two miles off Lagos and declared *force majeure*."

"What was the Act of God that gave him a legal excuse for getting out of the charter?" Robert asked.

"He claimed there was an 'armed revolution,'" Coco chortled.

"Well was there?" Robert asked.

"The ship got hit with one lousy bullet," Coco scoffed.

"But Coco," Robert said calmly, "did you ever consider that having an oil tanker hit by a bullet might actually be Rocky's idea of *force majeure*?"

"A man who's afraid of rough water shouldn't go to sea," Coco blasted. "Besides, that was just Rocky's excuse to put the ship off-hire because he could replace my ship with a cheaper one. I wouldn't be surprised if he *paid* to have the shot fired. Would you care to know what your new BFF said to me when I complained about his back-trade?"

"Not really," Robert said.

"He said, 'Go cry to the arbitrator in London three years from now, Coco Puff.'"

"Did he really call you 'Coco Puff'?" Alistair asked.

"Ja, but we were all a bit heavier in the 80s," Coco said.

"So what did you do next?" Robert asked.

"It's like I've always tried to teach you, Fairchild; there are some problems that you can't solve by searching on Google or sending an email," Coco said. "I flew down to Lagos, hired a helicopter to take me out to *Telemachus*, brought the ship into port and handed out greenbacks until the terminal workers agreed to load Rocky's lousy cargo."

"All's well that ends well," Robert said.

"That's not the end," Coco said without taking his piercing blue eyes off Fairchild. "Once *Telemachus* was on her way across the Atlantic I flew to Houston to find Rocky and collect the money he owed me."

"Oh boy," Robert said as he took note of another important feature of the shipping industry; everyone had a history with everyone, whether they admitted it or not.

"I tracked down Mr. DuBois in a private dining room in a place called the Petroleum Club located on the top floor of the Exxon Mobil building," Coco said. "I burst into the dining room just as old Rocky was asking God Almighty to bless the Thanksgiving dinner he was about to share with his beautiful family."

"So he agreed to pay you," Robert said hopefully, "in the spirit of sharing for which the Thanksgiving holiday was first created?"

"Actually," Coco said, "he picked up an electric turkey carving knife from the table, lifted it over his head and began moving toward me."

"Did the man actually try to kill you over a time charter?" Alistair gasped.

"It wouldn't be the first time a man has been killed over a time charter that's gone bad," Coco said as he kept his eyes on

Robert for an unnaturally long time. "And it may not be the last."

"Oh dear," Alistair said.

"Just as the Kraken was about to carve me up like a big bird, Rocky's six-year-old granddaughters started going wild," Coco said.

"What do you mean 'going wild'?" Robert asked.

"It started with your basic kicking and screaming and then each of the girls grabbed onto one of his legs like a Koala bear on a Eucalyptus tree," Coco said. "Rocky dragged those two little screaming kids halfway across the dining room until one of them bit into his knee. That's when he finally stopped."

"Children have an excellent sense of justice," Alistair interjected.

"What happened next?" Robert asked.

"Rocky agreed to cough up the $64,000 of unpaid charter hire," Coco said with satisfaction. "I won."

Alistair Gooding's mouth dropped open before he spoke. He was stunned. "Are you saying that your legendary, multi-decade feud with Rocky DuBois started over $64,000?"

"That was a lot of money back then," Coco said.

"A lot of money? Coco, I've seen you spend more on a sushi. My God man, you paid $5 million for the bauble you bought Alexandra at Bonham's."

"Ja, but this thing with Rocky isn't just about the money," Coco said. "It's about justice."

"And at least there was a happy ending," Robert said. "And I bet your relationship is all the stronger for having gotten through that difficult time. They say that…"

"That's still not the end," Coco interrupted.

"Of course not," Robert sighed.

"Just as I was saying thanks to that little girl for biting old grandpa's knee, Rocky called the police and told them I'd assaulted him," Coco said. "Ten minutes later a dozen heavily-armed Houston police stormed the building and dragged me out wearing handcuffs."

"So that's where *TradeWinds* got the photograph," Alistair said. "Coco, you must remember to send them a nicer picture for their file."

"Once the cops had me in the clink, Rocky's lawyers tacked-on half a dozen more charges to the complaint including trading with North Korea and Iran," Coco said. "One of my bunker suppliers in Houston was kind enough to pay my bail but now I'm wanted by the FBI because I was too busy to go back for the trial."

"So that's why you can't enter the United States," Robert concluded.

"But that was a long time ago," Alistair said. "I'm sure you'd get along with Rocky DuBois now."

"Once a back trader, always a back trader," Coco said. "I don't know exactly how we will do it, but the moment my tanker party ends Rocky will figure out a way to default or re-trade the time charters at a lower level – precisely when I have no leverage to defend myself."

"I think you're being paranoid," Robert scoffed. "American Refining Corporation is an investment-grade corporation. They don't just go around renegotiating on every contract that doesn't go their way."

"Ugh," Coco moaned as he began rubbing his temples. "Can we open up this bottle of aquavit and stop talking about this; it just reminds me how much I still have to teach you, Fairchild. So what on earth is this exciting news you wanted to tell me?"

Robert stared at Coco with bulging eyes and said, "That *was* the exciting news."

"What was?" Coco asked. "Did I miss something?"

"The exciting news is that American Refining Corporation has agreed to pay ten of our ships $50,000 per day for five years."

Robert watched the color drain from his boss's brown face. "Are you actually telling me that you dragged me all the way to London just to tell me that Kraken DuBois will pay me $50,000 for ships that are about to earn $250,000?"

"For *five* years," Robert added weakly. "And it will be good for our long-term relationship."

"There's no such thing as long-term relationships in this business," Coco said. "Shipowners are hunters, not farmers."

"Yes, but…"

"I control most of the open ships near the Arabian Gulf and there are close to eighty cargos that need to be loaded in the next ten days. Robert, I am about to kick off the biggest tanker party in *history* and you want me to go to bed early?"

"Well…"

"*This* is your great news?" Coco shrieked in Robert's face.

"Yes," Robert confessed as he watched the sparkle fade from Coco's eyes like the scales of a dying fish.

"Let me give you some advice, Robert; it's never a good idea to enter into a long-term charter in a market that is either very good or very bad," Coco said. "Because someone will always get hurt – and that someone is *always* the shipowner," Coco said.

When Robert failed to respond to the logic, Coco turned to his lender for moral support. "Allie, please tell me he's kidding," Coco begged. "Fairchild is a rookie who needs an education, I get that and I am trying to be patient with him, but you are a veteran shipping banker. You should know better. Tell me there is some good news, and that you guys are just torturing your old pal Coco before sharing it with me."

"Long term employment for some of the vessels isn't such a bad idea," Alistair said. "I hate to point out the rather fragile state of your finances, Coco, but we did cut things a tad close last time."

"You think *that* was close, Allie?" Coco asked with a dismissive swat of his hand.

"Coco, you were one bunker arrest from disaster," Alistair reminded his behemoth borrower that if an unpaid fuel supplier had put the equivalent of a "mechanics lien" on one of his ships for non-payment it might have started a cascade of worldwide vessel arrests as creditors scrambled to get their hands on collateral.

"Allie, *every* shipowner who plays hard is one bunker arrest away from disaster," Coco explained. "It's called cash flow management."

"But keeping all your ships in the spot market is no different than driving a car on a twisty road at night with the headlights switched off," Alistair said. "You have no idea what's coming at you."

"And this is why it makes me feel alive," Coco said. "Guys, if my ships were on time charter I would have no reason to get out of bed, which would be okay if Alexandra was still in the sheets," Coco smiled. "Are you absolutely *sure* she's not here?"

"I did it," Robert blurted out, the three words escaping from his mouth like gas that could no longer be contained. After the spontaneous eruption he and Coco looked at each other with equal parts of surprise and confusion.

"Excuse me?" Coco said slowly as he glared at his deputy. "Did what?"

"I agreed to put ten of our ships on time charter to Rocky for five years and a rate of $50,000 per day," Robert said. "I already lifted the subjects and went firm."

"But this is impossible," Coco laughed.

"No, it's not."

"But you aren't authorized to buy office supplies without my consent," Coco said, "never mind charter-out a substantial number of my vessels to the squid."

"Actually I am," Robert replied. "According to the by-laws contained in our corporate governance documents and Limits of Authority manual, the Chief Executive Officer of Viking Tankers has the full authority to enter into legally enforceable contracts of this quantum."

Coco's eyes bulged as he turned to Alistair who nodded solemnly. What Robert declined to mention was that such a large commitment of tonnage *did* require the consent of Allied Bank of England – and that Alistair had personally signed off on the request earlier that day when Robert came in from Heathrow.

"But how could you do this without even telling me?" Coco asked.

"I did it because you told me to," Robert said.

"What do you mean I told you to?" Coco shouted.

"Coco, don't you remember telling me that there will always be many good reasons not to do things in life, but people who achieve great things are the ones who believe in themselves and find reasons to do things even when sometimes they do things that are not so smart."

"Well," Coco sighed, "you certainly embraced the part about doing things that are not so smart. Now it looks like we've *both* been played by Rocky DuBois," Coco said.

"I guess we have that in common," Robert said thoughtfully, hoping he could use his folly as a way to bond with his Norwegian boss.

"Hey Robert," the Norwegian said calmly as he sipped the aquavit.

"Yes, Coco?"

"Do you remember when we were sitting on the terrace of that nice restaurant on the cliff in the South of France drinking wine with Grace?" Coco asked.

"Oh yes, we were in the village of Eze-sur-mer, high above Cap Ferrat," Robert smiled just as Coco's telephone began to ring. "That was a lovely afternoon."

"And do you remember when I gave you a hug and told you that you had finally become a Shipping Man?" Coco asked as he examined the screen of the tiny phone.

"That was one of the best days of my life," Robert said.

"Well I take it back!" Coco snapped as he rose to his feet.

"You *what?*" Robert gasped.

"I take it back," Coco repeated.

"What? But why?" Robert begged.

"Fairchild, you have put me in a very bad position here…*very* bad. And what troubles me most is that you've been playing at the shipping game for more than a year and you still don't seem to understand that this business is volatile and *cyclical*," Coco said, pronouncing the word as though it was a mental state.

"I know, Coco, and that's why I am using the charters to eliminate the volatility," Robert said.

"Eliminate the volatility?" Coco shouted. "Fairchild, the volatility is the only way to make any money in shipping! Without the volatility, this would be like the railroad business and I would be competing against guys like Jimmy Buffett."

"Warren Buffett," Alistair interjected.

"Exactly!" Coco shouted and slammed his fist down on the table. "I am *not* going to war with that old guy. He is too smart for me."

"But every business in the world uses hedging strategies," Robert defended himself.

"Shipping is *not like* every other business in the world," Coco snapped back. "Fairchild, I swear if you weren't so old I would send you to Cass Business School here in London so Professor Costas Grammenos could give you a proper education in ship financing," Coco grumbled.

"But…"

"But nothing!" Coco snarled just before answering the incoming call on its fourth and final ring. "I know I said I would be your mentor just like Hilmar Reksten was a mentor to me, but this is just too much work. I give up."

"You give up?" Robert asked with panic. "What's that supposed to mean?"

"It means that you're fired, Fairchild!" Coco said.

Chapter 11

Aristotle Onassis

Aristotle Onassis arrived in Argentina in 1923, reportedly with $60 in his pocket. He worked as a telephone operator by night and imported Turkish tobacco by day, a venture that earned him his first million. Noting freighter prices had dropped in the Depression, Onassis used his savings to launch the scrappy beginnings of a global shipping empire. In 1932, he bought six freighters for $20,000 each, their scrap value. By 1940, recognizing increasing demand for oil, Onassis started building supertankers. At the time of his death in 1975, Onassis had amassed more than 50 ships and had a personal net worth of $500 million, $1.97 billion in current dollars.

Forbes

The industrial orange lights of rain-soaked Gimpo International Airport glowed through a blanket of fog as the gleaming white Falcon 7X shot down the 11,800-foot runway. Propelled by a trio of Honeywell turbo fans producing 19,000 pounds of thrust, the aluminum aircraft tipped upward and shot skyward as if flung from slingshot.

Within seconds the fifty-two-foot cylinder of riveted flesh had slipped into green-black clouds, tearing through the foul weather like a shark through a school of fish. Once the aircraft had battled its way to the prairie of cornflower blue sky at 30,000 feet above the Sea of Japan, the pilots throttled back to a cruising speed of 560 miles per hour and picked up a heading bound for Athens.

"Sir, you may use the telephone now," the pilot, a former captain of the Greek Air Force, announced to the sole occupant of the narrow cabin. The shipowner picked up the small white telephone affixed to the bulkhead wall next to his seat and dialed a mobile telephone number he had committed to memory.

"*Kalispera*, Coco," the Greek said when he answered on the fourth ring.

"*Ti kanis, kapeteine*," Coco replied.

"Coco," the Greek said as he rolled a string of worry beads between his nine-and-a-half fingers, "I wanted you to be the first to know that I have just finished the final negotiations."

"And…" Coco asked.

"And everything is in order," he said. "I must admit that have never seen anything quite like this in all my years," he added. "As soon as we finish this call I will instruct my bankers in Zurich to wire the $500 million."

"But this is good news," Coco said, "so why do you sound so serious?"

"I learned today that we have just three months before the next $500 million installment is due, and I am referring to *your* installment," the Greek added. "Are you *still* confident that Robert Fairchild will have the money ready?"

"I'm more confident than ever," Coco sighed as he watched his CEO throw back a shot of aquavit and then lay his head down on the table. "Robert is putting the money together as we speak."

***

No more than twenty feet away from the bar at which Coco was talking on the telephone, the increasingly intoxicated Alistair Gooding and Robert Fairchild were in Naughty Corner commiserating and debating whether or not Robert should leave the room and end his shipping career with a whimper. Despite their hours of rehearsing the good cop/bad cop routine in advance of Coco's dramatic arrival that evening, the two men knew they had blown their pitch badly. The only thing left for them to do, they concluded, was beg Coco for mercy after he finished his telephone call.

"I give him a lot of guff but the truth is that Coco is the best client I've ever had," Alistair said thoughtfully as he stared at his client whose head was now resting on the bar.

"Why do you say that?" Robert asked.

"Because there are two kinds of borrowers in the world: the kind who pay you back even when they can't and the kind who don't pay you back even when they can," Alistair said. "Coco is the first kind – *and* he's willing to pay fees."

"And I totally spoiled him with those junk bonds," Robert sighed. "That was when he figured out that money that misprices risk is the same thing as free money."

"Yes, but what Coco fails to appreciate is that he's damaged his reputation on Wall Street," Alistair said. "The man borrowed $300 million of ten-year money and didn't make a single semi-annual interest payment."

Like many European lenders, Alistair Gooding felt there was something morally hazardous about creditors writing off principal before the company's equity was wiped out – either that or he was just jealous of Coco's cat-like ability to land on his feet again and again.

"I respectfully disagree," Robert said. "The only investors that we bought-out at a discount were the ones who wanted to sell and most of them had also bought the bonds at discount. There's nothing wrong with that in the U.S. Capital Markets," Robert said. "The only thing we did was provide those investors with liquidity."

"Oh please," Alistair said, "you guys used the money the bondholders put in escrow to buy them out at discount and you didn't pay a single *coupon*!"

The moment Alistair Gooding said the word "coupon," Robert Fairchild experienced a badly needed flash of inspiration. Although he was sitting in the Naughty Corner at the swanky Brown's Hotel he felt as though he'd been magically transported back to the investment bank high above Park Avenue where he had listened to an orange-haired banker describe the benefits of a structure called the Master Limited Partnership – known on Wall Street as an MLP.

Because an MLP had the tax benefits of a limited partnership and the liquidity of publicly traded stock, the banker explained, investors would determine its fair valuation based on the dividend it produced – not solely the value of the company's assets the way traditional shipping investors did. There was only one catch: the MLP had to have contracts with financially solid counterparties in order to pay a reliable dividend – which was exactly what Robert had thanks to the ten rogue time charters he had fixed to ARC.

Robert shot a glance at the bar and watched Coco close his telephone.

"Coco, I can do it!" Robert shouted across the room.

"Do what? Destroy my company even more?" The Norwegian asked as he lumbered back to the Naughty Corner. "You know something, Fairchild, during the course of my career I have survived half-a-dozen shipping crises, countless pirate attacks, jail time, typhoons, earthquakes, a nuclear meltdown and even a missile strike in the Red Sea but you, Robert Fairchild, a skinny little kid from New York City are going to be the thing that takes me down. Risk lurks in the most unlikely places in the shipping business," Coco said philosophically.

"Actually," Robert said, "I am going to be the one who gets you out of whatever mess you're in that requires $500 million.

I can get you the $500 million in America!"

"You can?" Coco's face went from sullen to smiling. He knew that whatever Fairchild had just schemed-up was probably completely naïve and unrealistic but the truth was that since Alistair was stealing his tanker party money, the American was Coco's only remaining chance – a fact he found highly distressing.

"But how are we going to get the free money this time, Fairchild? Will we do another junk bond?"

"We're not going to do a bond, Coco, but we are going back to Wall Street," Robert said.

As Coco Jacobsen and Alistair Gooding looked on with wonder, Robert Fairchild went to work sketching out the MLP transaction on two alcohol-soaked cocktail napkins. It was the second time in his shipping career that he had performed his analysis in such a manner.

He began by drawing half-a-dozen rectangles and filling them with unusual looking names like "NewCo," "VesselCo," and "OpCo" to illustrate the various special purposes companies that would be involved in the structure. Next, he began linking the boxes together with solid lines, dotted lines, diagonal lines and all kinds of arrows and curlicues. Moving with the speed and sleight of hand of a three-card Monte dealer, Fairchild finished his masterpiece by scribbling the economics of the charters he had concluded with Rocky. In the end, his work resembled the series of Miro etchings that hung in the guest rooms aboard the *Kon Tiki*.

"What is that yucky thing?" Coco asked with disgust as he looked at the pair of soggy serviettes.

"It's a financial structure called a Master Limited Partnership and it's the key to getting the $500 million you need," Robert said.

"Really?" Coco asked.

Free Money…Economics – Per Ship

\+ $50,000 charter hire

($10,000) operating expenses

($20,000) principal and interest

=$20,000 free cash x 355 days/year= EBITDA $7,000,000

Times 10 Ships = $70 million

Raise $500 million of new equity through MLP

Dividend Yield on New Equity: 14%!!!

"Yes, just as long as you agree to honor the five-year time charters with American Refining Corporation on ten of your ships I am highly confident we can capture a meaningful valuation arbitrage by marketing the Initial Public Offering of Viking Tankers as a synthetic MLP with a high-dividend yield."

Coco grumbled, but Robert pressed on.

"This will either make an attractive pair trade or a meaningful arbitrage opportunity. And don't worry, we will put the ten ships into a new company," he said and put his finger on the box that said NewCo. "And keep the rest of the Viking Tankers fleet out of the deal…just in case."

Robert deliberately put up the thick smoke screen of Wall Street mumbo jumbo to disable Coco's arguments. "It will even have some tax enhancements we can leverage."

"But I don't *want* to do an IPO of Viking Tankers," Coco said.

"Why not?" Robert asked.

"I don't even know where to start," Coco said. "I hate having shareholders, I hate having time charters, I can't stand doing business with Rocky DuBois…and don't even *mention* the word tax! There must be another way."

Robert had always caved-in to Coco's unrealistic expectations about the cost and terms of capital, but not this time. Like a seven-year-old in a new classroom, the American knew it was time to test his boundaries and hold his ground, even if that meant suffering some consequences. After all, how much worse could the situation possibly get?

"Coco, do you remember when you just said that free money is helpful to your business model?" Robert asked.

"If it weren't for the cost of capital, shipping would be a decent business," Coco confirmed, temporarily tranquilized by the mention of free money.

"And do you remember when you said that the free money lowers the daily breakeven on the tankers?" Robert asked.

"Don't start what you can't finish Fairchild," Coco said with swelling enthusiasm, "because I'm getting very excited right now!"

"And you *should* be excited, Coco, because doing the MLP IPO in America is the solution to all your problems!" Robert said. "You've been begging me to find $500 million of free money and now I've found it!"

"Ja, but…"

"Don't 'Ja, but' me Jacobsen!" Robert snapped at his boss with a degree of self-assured independence that silenced the giant Norwegian and startled the British banker.

"I'm so sorry," Coco cowered. Maybe the Greek was right after all; maybe Coco did need to give Robert some room to run so he would gain confidence; it seemed to be working already.

"Don't you get it, tanker man? If I can sell 50% of Viking Tankers at 200% of net asset value through the MLP then it's like you haven't sold anything at all!" Robert proclaimed.

Coco turned to face his banker as he aggressively scratched his considerable cranium. "Allie, does that make any sense?"

"Of course it makes sense," Robert chimed in without having thought through the logic of the deal. "What's more, you can buy back the shares whenever they get cheap and unlike the junk bonds you never have to pay the IPO money back! Not even for fifty-nine cents."

"Never?" Coco asked.

"Ever!" Robert confirmed. "What money is freer than that?"

"That sounds pretty free," Coco Jacobsen agreed as he drummed his long fingers on the varnished table and considered which scenario he despised more – putting his ships on long-term time charter to Rocky DuBois or missing an opportunity to haul in a huge slug of free money in America that he could invest alongside the Greek.

As Coco was hesitating, Robert Fairchild knew it was time to use his secret weapon.

"And here's the best part, Coco…doing the IPO is going to be just like launching a *Viking raid* on Rocky DuBois – a real Viking raid in which you will be triumphant!"

Coco instantly cocked his head askew like a curious canine. "Did you say a '*Viking raid*'?"

Had the towering tanker tycoon known more about his own genealogy he would have known why his eyes brightened the moment Robert spoke the magical words – Viking raid. Coco would also have known why he possessed substantially more pigmentation than your average Norwegian. It was because Coco Jacobsen was a direct descendant of the risk-seeking and highly emotional Viking leader Jarl Olav, AKA Olav the Unpredictable, who had met his wife Zaraya while plundering North Africa five hundred years earlier.

"Ja!" Robert proclaimed. "If we have the ships on charter to Rocky DuBois we will be able to raise *two times* the value of those ships on Wall Street!" Robert Fairchild boomed. He was delighted that the Viking raid metaphor had produced the desired effect. "This will be like Rocky DuBois handing you $500 million from his own pocket! What better way to get even with him for trying to steal $64,000 from you as a result of the minor gunplay in West Africa ten years ago?"

"Now *that's* a good return on my equity," Coco smiled.

"It sure is," Robert said.

"You know something, Fairchild, maybe you're right," Coco said and nodded. "Maybe a Viking raid on Rocky DuBois will do me good. Maybe that's just the sort of activity that will make me feel happy again," Coco said.

"Let's do it!" Robert cried.

"Yes," Coco said. "Let's do it; why not? And my only condition is that we go on this Viking raid together," Coco said.

"One for all, and all for one," Alistair exploded with an upward thrust of arm as though he was celebrating his winning horse at the Royal Ascot.

"My boys, we will be together in blood and glory," Coco said.

"Did you say *blood*?" Robert asked.

"Be not afraid," Coco said like a charismatic cult leader as he laid his hand on top of Robert's. "If this Viking raid succeeds then we all succeed, but if it should fail and not price at 200% of NAV like you have just promised me, then we will all go to Valhalla together," Coco said as he eagerly tore off the green foil from the neck of the second bottle of aquavit. "We will *all* have skin in the game this time and not just Coco."

"Valhalla?" Robert asked and shot a look at Alistair. "Coco isn't even allowed to enter the country; why would we go to Westchester County, New York?"

"No, Robert, Valhalla is where Viking warriors go after they die in battle," Coco explained solemnly and then rose to his feet. "Valhalla is where Odin will reward us for our bravery in this valiant battle against the evil, bloodsucking monster sea monster known as Rocky DuBois."

After he finished speaking, the towering Norwegian walked to the dead center of the crowded room and climbed onto one of the few unoccupied chairs. His overflowing glass of liquor was still in his hand.

"Is he okay?" Robert asked Alistair as the multi-cultural occupants of the taproom stared up at the massive, dark-skinned man perched atop the wobbly chair. "He's acting sort of crazy."

"This is perfectly normal. Coco always sings a Swedish drinking song called Helan Går before he goes into battle," the banker said before popping a handful of peanuts into his mouth. "He's says it's the only thing he likes about Sweden. You should have seen him the night before he and Oddleif launched their raid against Knut Shipping. They camped out in Knut's lobby like Occupy Wall Street and sang that song all night."

"What does it mean?" Robert asked.

"It means something like 'he who doesn't take the whole, doesn't get the half one either,'" Alistair said, "which pretty much sums up Coco's approach to life."

After Coco had sung the song, he closed his eyes and chanted the following words: *"Vel keðu vér um konung ungan sigrhljóða fjöld" syngjum heilar enn inn nemi er heyrir á geirfljóða hljóð ok gumum segi!"*

When Coco finally opened his eyes and stepped down from the chair, the thoroughly confused but wildly enthusiastic 1% of the 1% gave him a standing ovation so thunderous that it seemed to rock the Donovan Bar. The big man took a dramatic bow before returning to the Naughty Corner.

"What did those sounds mean, Coco?" Robert asked unsteadily.

"It's Viking and it means *let us ride our horses hard on bare backs with swords unsheathed away from here!*" Coco said. "The Viking raid on Rocky DuBois has officially begun!"

Three Months Later

Chapter 12

Cornelius Vanderbilt

Known as the "Commodore," Cornelius Vanderbilt was an American industrialist and philanthropist who built his wealth in shipping and railroads. Vanderbilt was born in Staten Island, New York and began working on his father's ferry in New York Harbor as a boy, quitting school at the age of eleven. At the age of sixteen, Vanderbilt decided to start his own ferry service. According to one version of events, he borrowed $100 from his mother to purchase a periauger (a shallow draft, two-masted sailing vessel). He began his business by ferrying freight and passengers between Staten Island and Manhattan. Vanderbilt bought his brother-in-law John De Forest's schooner Charlotte, and traded in food and merchandise, in partnership with his father and others.

What on earth was I thinking? Robert Fairchild derided himself as the Hawker 900 bumped across a narrow taxiway and inched toward the main runway at Teterboro Airport, a private airfield ten miles west of Manhattan.

Exactly ninety days had passed since his life-altering encounter with Coco Jacobsen at Brown's Hotel in London. During that exhausting three-month period he had spent most of his waking hours in Wade Waters' conference room high above New York Harbor assembling the phonebook-thick prospectus for the Initial Public Offering of Viking Tankers.

During the process of drafting the offering document for the MLP-in-drag, Robert had lived on sandwiches and cookies wheeled in on a cart, debated grammatical principles with first-year associates and massaged the financial model to make the offering appear more like a floating pipeline and less like a clutch of crude oil tankers.

The biggest setback to the process came when the U.S. Securities and Exchange Commission (S.E.C.), the government agency charged with approving any offering of securities before it was brought to market, casually advised that they considered each ship to be its own individual operating "company." As a result of this seemingly subtle distinction, the S.E.C required Viking Tankers to produce three years of audited accounts for each and every one of Coco's vessels – a process that required more forensic analysis than the season finale of *CSI*.

By the time the so-called "red herring" offering document was deemed effective by the regulators in D.C., Robert Fairchild had spent nearly $1 million on accounting expenses, legal fees and a variety of sundry services. He had nothing to show for the investment but the dark circles under his eyes and the stack of paper sitting on the tiny table in front of him – a document that would probably be read by fewer people than his senior thesis.

But all that was history. Now he was fifteen minutes away from launching a ten-day roadshow for the $500 million Initial Public Offering of Viking Tankers. Like a sailor in days of yore, Robert had packed his bag, kissed his wife and son goodbye and told them he wouldn't come home until he was victorious in his epic battle to raise the cash and preserve his job.

The equity-raising road trip was scheduled to officially kick off in a few hours at the trendy Delano Hotel in South Beach, Miami. The urban resort was the unlikely location where he was scheduled to meet with none other than Luther Livingston, the same money manager for LOF, the Lutheran Opportunism Fund, who had fired Robert from his own hedge fund a year and a half earlier for the misdeed of buying the old freighter from Spyrolaki in his personal account and not with the fund's money. Luther's interest in Robert's deal was proof that investors couldn't afford to hold a grudge.

As the stubby little jet engine wheezed outside his window, Robert felt uncomfortable knowing he had more at stake than his job and his reputation; he had put his own family on the line. After an inexplicably open-minded Coco finished his phone call, the Norwegian agreed to go along with the IPO as long as Robert and Allie have "skin in the game." It was not until they had finished the second bottle of Aalborg that the financiers learned just how much of their flesh Coco had in mind.

By the time the three inebriated men stumbled back into the blizzard on Dover Street several hours later both Robert Fairchild and Alistair Gooding had sold their souls. Alistair had agreed to stretch-out the pay-back period, known as the "amortization profile" in banker-speak, of Viking Tankers' loan from twelve years to twenty years. This unorthodox amendment to the loan agreement allowed Viking Tankers to generate even more free cash flow – which would be used to give Coco "a little walking around money in my jeans."

While Allied Bank of England's commitment to the success of the IPO was substantial, Robert Fairchild's was substantially more personal; Coco agreed to rescind Fairchild's firing from Viking Tankers, but only on the condition that Robert to put at risk the 10% of the company he had given Oliver Fairchild in lieu of his father's cash bonus the previous year.

Coco had insisted that Robert wager the boy's shares in Viking Tankers, double or nothing, that the MLP IPO would price at no less than 200% NAV as Robert promised. Simply put, if Robert wasn't able to deliver on his late-night promise he would likely be unemployed and homeless after his wife summarily divorced him for reckless risking their child's only financial safety net.

To memorialize the various agreements, Coco had made Alistair and Robert sign their names on the back of the same wet napkins on which Robert had initially scribbled the structure and economics. The Norwegian had even dragged a barrister from a London law firm out of bed to serve as witness – and affix a legal seal to the soggy serviette.

The following morning, as Robert Fairchild lay in bed trying to sober up by scanning valuation tables that appeared on the website of *Marine Money*, he came to the horrifying realization that he'd made a grave mistake. According to the information provided by the ship finance publication of record, not only had a shipping IPO never been priced at 200% of NAV, but many had priced *below* the value of their ships. The idea that Robert had suggested, selling a shipping deal as a Master Limited Partnership, had never even been attempted never mind achieved.

The only time deals were valued at more than the liquidation value of the ships was if they happened to operating in a red-hot sector or had new ships with time charters double or even *triple* the duration of the ones Robert had agreed with ARC. Unfortunately, neither the lawyers nor Alistair Gooding or Coco had been well-versed enough in the U.S. Capital Markets to save him from himself. Robert had once again done the unthinkable; his unbridled enthusiasm had led him to recklessly gamble his son's financial well-being on an outcome over which he had no control.

The only thing Robert Fairchild had going for him was that it was a decent time to try to sell the deal. After being watertight for years, the relentless flooding of money by the U.S. Federal Reserve had brought the yield on Treasury bills *below* zero, which served to shamelessly coax-out enough yield-starved capital to revive the dead IPO market.

As he stared through the plane's tiny oval window, Robert recognized the Viking raid metaphor he had used to convince Coco to do the IPO was about the only thing he'd said that was accurate. Just as the longboats left the fjords of Norway after the Vikings outstripped the agricultural potential of their native land, the armada of thirty-five rent-a-jets humming all around him at the private airport ten miles west of Manhattan was preparing to embark on a similar quest – a quest for other people's money.

Robert loosened his pink Vineyard Vines necktie, removed the jacket of his gray flannel suit and wiped the sweat from his brow with the sleeve of his blue button-down shirt. Lulled by the vibration of the tiny jet engines outside, he gazed pensively at the leafy New Jersey suburbs. In an attempt to ease his troubled mind, he tried to shift his focus to that lowest of all common human denominators – the unseasonably warm autumn weather – but even that gave him pause.

Although he was happy that Oliver would have an unusually warm autumn afternoon for his weekly soccer game on Roosevelt Island, Robert knew the current weather pattern meant trouble for him; trying to sell shares of a crude oil tanker company during the warmest week in the largest hydrocarbon-consuming country in the world wouldn't make his job any easier. Nor would the fact the U.S. suddenly realized it is sitting on top of more oil than the Kingdom of Saudi Arabia.

Robert took a sip of Diet Coke and returned his eyes to the drift of paper spread out on the table in front of him. There was the 286-page Viking Tankers' prospectus and the forty-five-slide PowerPoint roadshow presentation that had been aggressively marked-up with red pen after his video conference "rehearsal" with the equity sales force at Haakon Gate Capital, the sole bookrunner on the deal.

Off to the side of the stack of paper sat the roadshow meeting schedule which was almost entirely blank. When Robert had asked Magnus Magnusen, the managing director at Haakon Gate Capital, why there wasn't a single meeting scheduled after his two appointments in Miami, the Norwegian said, "Equity roadshows are just like ships, Fairchild; the best ones don't know where they will go next. Just proceed to the deviation point and remain flexible for arbitrage opportunities," Magnus added.

"What deviation point?" Robert complained. "You guys haven't even told me what city I am supposed to sleep in tonight!"

"Don't worry, be happy," the banker said and the line went dead.

Chapter 13

The Greek Grandfather of U.S. Shale Gas

While large U.S. oil firms began migrating operations to other continents in the 1980s and 90s, fracking pioneer George Mitchell (1919-2013) was convinced that the gas reserves located beneath the U.S. could be developed economically. He was right; in 2000 shale accounted for just 1% of U.S. gas production and now accounts for a 30% share that is growing. Mr. Mitchell's story personifies the American Dream. His father, a goat herder named Savvas Paraskevopoulos, immigrated to the United States through Ellis Island in 1919 and changed his name to Mike Mitchell because it was easier for Americans to spell and pronounce. Before his death, Mr. Mitchell joined Bill Gates and Warren Buffet in "The Giving Pledge," agreeing to use the majority of his $2 billion fortune for philanthropic causes. "Throughout my life I've seen firsthand how even a little financial assistance could mean a chance for struggling students, dedicated scientists, and families to reach their goals," he said of the gift.

Compiled from information contained in
The Economist and The Giving Pledge

Mr. Xing's posture was perfect as he sat at his handcrafted, British-made desk sipping decaffeinated green tea and staring out across the pink glow of a dawn that would never really break.

For the past ten years he had occupied the same office on the thirty-third floor of Green Earth Tower, once the tallest building in Shanghai but now dwarfed by dozens of taller ones, yet the view had never stopped changing. He could see his city's development when he was working late into the night thanks to an ever-growing galaxy of twinkling lights, but in the daytime the changes were almost unbelievable.

From his lofty perch, Mr. Xing could see a hundred massive buildings growing as fast as bamboo shoots, a thousand cranes reaching toward the sky like creatures from a science fiction movie, a fifty-mile snake of traffic slithering toward Pudong and a swarm of aircraft filling the sky like locust. Then there was the *sound* of progress reverberating through the soundproof glass around him – an unrelenting thud of metal pounding on metal.

Even after the construction boom that preceded the Beijing Olympic Games in 2008, the scale of industrialization in the People's Republic of China was staggering. His country had spent close to $750 trillion on transportation-related projects alone in the past few years – building 50,000 new miles of roads to accommodate the 100,000 cars that were added to the road *every day* as more than twenty million people relocated from rural communities to urban ones.

It was the largest human migration to occur during a time of peace, ten times bigger than immigration to the U.S. around the turn of the century, and it was underpinned by a singular theory: people who lived in cities would be more likely to stimulate economic activity than people who lived on farms.

While the economies of the world were mostly thankful for the ripple effects created by China's hyper-stimulated double-digit GDP growth, Mr. Xing had been deeply challenged by it. He had been challenged by how to satisfy his country's ever-increasing need to find power that was cheap enough and *clean enough* to be sustainable now that China had surpassed the U.S. as the world's largest importer of energy – burning more than ten million barrels of oil each and every day.

Now he finally had the answer: American Refining Corporation.

Mr. Xing turned his eyes away from the sooty world outside his windows and focused on the sleek black Japanese telephone sitting on his desk. It had taken unbelievable self-control to have resisted calling Piper Pearl for the past three months and he could wait no longer.

Mr. Xing and his team had agreed that there was simply no greater bang for the buck than taking a run at buying ARC. In addition to their oil holdings in the Middle East, ARC's massive reserves of Marcellus and Utica shale gas would give them the clean fuel they needed to run their power plants. The politically aggressive overture would also send a priceless powerful public relations message to the world; China was so committed to protecting the environment by transitioning to cleaner energy that it was making a play for a brand name American energy company. The road would be bumpy, but in the end he knew the strategy couldn't lose.

It was time to make the call.

***

Piper Pearl stumbled out of the private elevator that opened onto his $95 million penthouse apartment. As the investment banker gazed at the necklace of lights strung around Central Park, an eight-hundred-acre preserve he considered to be his own backyard, he felt as though he'd attained a state of grace.

It was nine o'clock on a Sunday night and he had just come home from a three-hour huddle at the back table of the Carlyle Hotel with the Chairman of the United States Treasury – who happened to be Piper's former mentor at Allied Bank of England. Over the course of one-hundred-eighty minutes, the two men consumed forty ounces of Lobster Thermidor, submerged thirty-eight stone crab claws in butter and emptied two bottles of Grand Cru white Burgundy; it was the sort of meal that might have immediately preceded the French Revolution.

The banker's trance was broken by the melody of his mobile phone coming from deep within his brown corduroy trousers. He paused when he examined the screen of the device and saw the word "Xing" illuminated in green; he couldn't immediately recall anyone with that name.

Although just three months had passed since his meeting with Mr. Xing and Alexandra at his usual table at the Four Seasons Hotel, Piper had pitched more than *two-hundred* transaction ideas in the meantime. Even as he grew older and rose to higher and higher positions within the bank, he never failed to practice one of the first lessons he'd learned in his career: if you threw enough deals at the wall something was bound to stick.

"This is Piper Pearl speaking," the banker said with the slightest of slurs. The alliteration of his name not ideally suited to his quotidian consumption of wine. "Who is this?"

Piper spilled a collection of loose change, three packs of matches, an assortment of keys and a swollen money clip onto the elegant table standing on the black-and-white marble tiled foyer floor.

"Good evening, Mr. Pearl," Mr. Xing said softly. "I am Mr. Xing," the man said and then, after a pause, added, "from Shanghai."

"Oh, hey pal!" Piper cried out as he remembered who the man was. "What a nice surprise!"

Although Piper had been initially excited when his freshman roommate University of Texas, Rocky DuBois, asked him to sell his company, the banker had quickly lost interest when ARC's inflated stock price turned off every potential buyer.

"Thank you," Mr. Xing said.

"I thought you had forgotten about me," Piper said.

"I will never forget you, Mr. Pearl," Mr. Xing said. "I realize it has taken some time but I have now had the opportunity to discuss your proposal for American Refining Corporation with our new leaders in Beijing," Mr. Xing said as he stared dismally into his computer screen at the upward price trend of every form of energy.

"And…" Piper asked as he stepped out of his trousers and into the freshly pressed pajama pants that his housekeeper laundered, folded and placed under his pillow every day.

"And I'd like to talk to you more about the deal," Mr. Xing said.

"I should tell you up front that I've received a substantial offer for the company from another party," Piper fibbed as he lay down on his bed. "And those folks are already halfway through their due diligence process."

"Is that so?" Mr. Xing asked doubtfully as he studied his manicured cuticles, admiring the bright white of the orderly half-moons.

"You bet," Piper said. "The buyers have about fifty lawyers camped out in ARC's office in Houston *right now* going through the data room," Piper said as he felt himself drifting off toward sleep.

"We will do it," Mr. Xing said. "We will buy American Refining Corporation. Please inform Mr. DuBois of our intentions immediately."

Piper was tired, but he was never too tired to play.

"That's great, Mr. Xing, but I just don't think you'll have time to play catch-up on this one," Piper said. "I'll be sure to keep you in mind if and when another deal like this ever comes around I heard the Canadians might sell off some gas-producing assets within the next five or ten years. Of course, I can't even imagine where energy prices will be by then," he chortled.

"What if I told you that we will pay all cash?" Mr. Xing asked. "What would you say then?"

Piper's eyes opened wide and he suddenly felt alert. "I would tell you that cash is king," Piper smiled. "And that might make all the difference in a transaction with so much potential execution risk."

Gazing into the beautiful darkness of Central Park from his perch on the corner of 59th and Fifth Avenue, Piper Pearl did what every natural-born broker does the moment a deal may have been conceived – he calculated his own M&A fee – 1% of $15 billion – or $150 million. Not a bad payday for having a few cocktails at the Four Seasons Hotel in the company of Alexandra Meriwether.

"This leaves us with just one other matter," Xing said slowly.

"Which is?" Piper asked. He had begun his soothing nightly ritual of counting airplanes as they made their final approach down into Newark Airport.

"As you may know, Mr. Pearl, clean burning natural gas is important to us," Mr. Xing said.

"The twentieth century was the century of oil," Piper said, parroting something he had read in the newspaper recently, "but the twenty-first century will be the century of gas. This is especially true for you," he added.

"And what is that supposed to mean?" Mr. Xing asked.

"It means that you guys really get a bum rap when it comes to pollution," Piper said.

"Proceed," Mr. Xing said cautiously as he pushed the tip of a freshly sharpened German pencil into his finger.

"Here's how I see it; the entire world wants you to be their factory and manufacture all the junk they don't want to make themselves – stuff that all just ends up in a landfill or in the ocean anyway, right? Everyone expects you to make all this stuff cheaper than anyone else can make it because you pay your people less money and you're a little looser on the rules."

"This is the economic doctrine of Comparative Advantage," Mr. Xing said.

"Exactly, but then all these developed countries hassle you for having a pollution problem," Piper said. "That just doesn't seem right to me since without China there wouldn't even *be* a Wal-Mart. And without China people might actually realize their standard of living has been *dropping* for the last twenty years."

"I appreciate your sensitivity on the complex matter of global development, Mr. Pearl," Mr. Xing said. "There are many trade-offs and sacrifices that must be made if my people are to enjoy the same kind of opportunities that your people have been enjoying for the last one hundred years. I can assure you, however, that we are taking this situation very seriously. In fact, our next five-year plan specifically tasks us with switching many of our power plants from coal and oil to clean-burning natural gas."

"Then ARC is perfect company for you to buy," Piper said. "Rocky's boys have discovered a quarter-million acres of shale gas up in Utica and Marcellus. Far as I can tell, the entire United States of America is sitting on top of that stuff. It's a good thing nobody smokes around here anymore!" Piper chuckled and immediately thought about stepping onto his terrace to have one last cigarette.

"Importing American gas is exactly what we intend to do," Mr. Xing said as he looked out at the sooty gray-green morning, wondering whether his son would be able to attend school when the air quality was so poor.

Mr. Xing knew from the time of day that the sun had risen above the horizon but the ashen sky was still devoid of sunlight. He missed the vibrant colors of Europe and America and was looking forward to going to Davos, Switzerland the following week to make a presentation that would telegraph the "mega changes" that China was making to its energy policy.

"Sounds like we're on the same page," Piper said. "What's the issue?"

"The issue, Mr. Pearl, is that in order to transport the American gas and its related products to China we will need to gain control of a fleet of highly specialized gas tankers," Mr. Xing explained. "This is our condition."

"What's your condition?" Piper asked. His mind was still foggy from the evening's excessive consumption.

"The ships, Mr. Pearl," he said with a hint of irritation. "We will need gas carrying vessels to come along with the deal and there happen to be a fleet of fifteen such vessels under construction at Regal Shipbuilding in Korea that would suit our requirements perfectly."

"So go buy them," Piper said. "I sell companies, not boats."

"We have tried to buy the vessels and we have failed," Mr. Xing explained.

"What's so hard about buying some boats?" Piper asked.

"Shipping is not our core business and we are not experienced in such matters," Mr. Xing said. "That is why we need the assistance of Mr. DuBois."

"What do you mean his *assistance*?" Piper asked. "Rocky DuBois is an oilman not a boat broker."

"The point is, Mr. Pearl, that these fifteen LNG vessels must come along with our purchase of ARC or we are not interested in buying the company. We are happy to pay for the vessels in addition to the full $15 billion asking price that we will pay for American Refining Corporation. All we ask in return is that ARC find out who owns those LNG carriers and then structure a deal for us to gain control of them," Mr. Xing said.

"Whatever," Piper said having grown bored with the conversation.

"Does that mean we have a deal?" Mr. Xing asked and crossed his fingers as he awaited the reply from the sleepy banker. "Will you help us gain control of the vessels?"

"Yeah," Piper said, figuring he could hold Alexandra's bonus hostage until she found the boats. "Let's do this thing, Xing."

Chapter 14

Shipowners as Children

You capital providers need to remember we shipowners are all children and we will always be. So you need to understand that if you keep giving us sweets we will eat them. Do not blame us when we get sick and you have to clean up the mess because it will be your fault…once again!

Robert Bugbee,
President, Scorpio Tankers, Inc.

"It's time to Rock and Roll!" Robert Fairchild announced to no one in particular after he sprang from a taxicab on Miami's Collins Avenue and bounded up the stone steps toward the lobby of the Delano Hotel.

As the figurehead CEO of Viking Tankers dramatically parted the twenty-five-foot wall of billowing white linen that served as the front door of the trendy hotel, he felt like an actor stepping on stage to give the performance of a lifetime – which is exactly what he was about to do. The problem was that when his eyes slowly adjusted to the dim light in the cool and cavernous lobby he realized the theater depressingly deserted.

Even after he had stepped further into the empty hotel and peered into a warren of crevices and corridors he couldn't seem to locate any human life. That was when Robert Fairchild considered the unlikely possibility that the hard working and hard playing Norwegian investment banker Magnus Magnusen had made a scheduling snafu. After all, why on earth would Luther Livingston, a teetotaling bachelor from the Lutheran church in Salt Lake City, possibly want to meet Robert in a fashionable South Beach hotel to discuss the high-octane IPO of Viking Tankers?

With the heels of his freshly polished wingtips clicking like a metronome on the gray concrete floor, Robert moved toward the ethereal glow and briny breeze filtering into the seaward side of the lobby. He glided past an abandoned sushi bar and a dozen purple couches, a mahogany pool table and an immense wood-paneled wall twinkling with a séance worth of votive candles.

When he arrived at the oceanfront side of the hotel and walked onto the elevated terrace, he witnessed a scene that reminded him of Bosch's *The Garden of Earthly Delights*. At the bottom of the steep set of stairs in front of him was a long, thin swimming pool lined with lounge chairs positioned beneath two rows of towering royal palm trees, their bushy green fronds rushing in the steady onshore breeze. At the far end of the pool was a large group of scantily-clad men and women who were swarming around an oceanfront Tiki bar like moths on a light bulb.

The visceral scene immediately took Robert back to his life-altering visit to the Astir Palace Hotel in Greece a little more than a year ago where he had met the smooth-talking shipping scion named Spyrolaki – and his man-eating companion, Aphrodite. It was there that Robert consumed the mind-altering "Shipowner's Punch" and agreed to buy the 1977-built *Delos Express* in a deal that forever altered the arc of his life.

But what reminded him most of his Hellenic adventure was the warm wind blowing in from the Bahamas. Like centuries of men before him it had been the mysterious Greek wind that had given Robert the confidence to take a chance and buy the old cargo ship – a type of confidence that was more emotional than financial and one he had never experienced while huddled behind his computer screens in Manhattan.

Although he knew that Magnus had probably made an innocent scheduling mistake, Robert hoped he hadn't. He hoped that Luther Livingston really was in the fashionable South Beach hotel because he knew first-hand that the meteorological conditions were ideal for selling a shipping deal.

Robert's pulse quickened when he noticed the smudgy silhouette of half-a-dozen cargo ships suspended in the place where the smoky blue sky met the shimmering teal-green Atlantic Ocean. He hadn't been in the industry for long but his brief ownership of the *Lady Grace* and his visit to the *Viking Alexandra* had taught him much about the ghostly apparitions floating on the horizon.

While most Americans would have indiscriminately thought of the vessels as "tankers" Robert knew from the cranes extending from their decks that they were actually bulk carriers or possibly small container ships. He also knew these ships were capable of loading and discharging cargo in the primitive ports of the Caribbean that didn't have cranes on shore.

Although the anonymous and transient specks on the horizon would appear insignificant to most people, Robert knew each was in fact a multi-million dollar, multi-national corporation; they might have been built in Korea, China or Japan, owned by Greeks, Norwegians or Danes, financed by a bank in Germany, England or Holland, crewed by Indians, Filipinos or Ukrainians, and flying the flag of either the Marshall Islands, Panama or Liberia from their stern.

And while the geometric shapes appeared uninhabited from a distance, Robert knew there were at least twenty hardworking officers and crew representing a variety of nationalities and religions co-existing onboard. At that very moment, the ones on duty were working on the bridge, chipping paint on the deck or working in the burning hot boiler room. The off duty seafarers were watching movies, playing instruments or sleeping. If the shipowner had provided for an internet connection most were undoubtedly exchanging email with friends and family on the other side of the world.

Most significantly of all, Robert knew that every one of the ships on the horizon were "in ballast" because of how high they were sitting in the water. The high freeboard meant the ships were empty and every day a ship is empty is a day the shipowner loses money that can never, ever, be recovered; cargo space was the ultimate perishable commodity.

Deflated by the anticlimactic start of his first-ever roadshow, Robert withdrew the BlackBerry from his pocket and called Magnus to check in. But just as the telephone began to emit the heavy tone of a European telephone number, Robert's eyes were drawn to a figure emerging slowly from one of the white canvas cabanas next to the swimming pool. He switched off his phone and watched the silhouette lash the sash of a robe and raise his left arm directly above his head, as if striking a sun worshipping yoga pose.

When Robert Fairchild squinted and placed his hand over his forehead to block the glare of the afternoon sun, he instantly recognized that among models and movie stars, has-beens and would-bes, rappers and their hangers-on, stood his former boss – Luther Livingston.

Despite the tropical conditions, Robert instinctively tightened his necktie and began to walk slowly down the steps toward the pool for his dramatic entrance. Having spent the last fifteen years on the "buy-side" as an investor at Eureka! Capital he had grown accustomed to wearing a more subtle uniform of zip-neck cashmere sweaters, Patagonia vests and gray flannel trousers. But for the next ten days, he would be on the "sell side," which meant asking for money, begging for it – an activity that called for altogether different attire. The unspoken sartorial understanding on Wall Street was a simple one: the people who had cash didn't wear ties and the people who needed it did.

As he drew closer, Robert realized that the man standing in front of the white cloth cabana was altogether changed. Luther's trademark navy blue suit had been replaced by the white terrycloth robe. His wingtips had yielded to white Japanese slippers and his perpetually porcelain skin had been baked to a fiery red. The two men stood several feet apart, silently examining one another with mutual amusement; Luther was amused that Robert looked like he now had a real job and Robert was amused that Luther looked like Jack LaLanne on steroids.

"I don't think I've ever seen you wearing a necktie," Luther said as he opened his arms and exposed his cherry-red trunks.

"I know I've never seen you wearing a red Speedo," Robert chuckled as he surmised that Luther had lost his marbles as a result of too much clean Lutheran living.

"Where are all the baby bankers?" his host asked with renewed energy as he peered over Robert's shoulder at the stairs leading up to the white Art Deco hotel. "Are they bringing your luggage upstairs or looking around for a Kinko's to make copies of the pitch book?"

"Nope," Robert said. "I'm flying solo."

"You're doing a $500 million IPO roadshow and you don't have any young kids running around carrying spiral bound books and critiquing your performance?" Luther asked.

"It's just me," Robert said and couldn't help but laugh at his own ridiculous predicament. "Coco Jacobsen is sensitive to expenses so he is making me do the first ever self-service IPO in exchange for paying the investment bank a smaller underwriting commission."

"Smart guy," Luther said. "Does he have you flying commercial?"

"Not yet," Robert smiled, "but if you don't order some shares in the next twenty minutes I bet I'll be going home in the back of a JetBlue plane."

"We can't have that," Luther said.

"So how have you been, Luther?" Robert asked. His soothing tone was intended to invite a discussion of the potentially compromised mental state of the investors who had first put him in business at Eureka! Capital.

"Never better, kid," Luther said as he pulled open his robe to showcase his ripped abdomen. "Punch me, baby!"

"Excuse me?" Robert asked as he looked at the man. He couldn't help but wonder whether this entire encounter was part of a new reality TV program that tracked the movement of out-of-work hedge fund managers like wild animals tagged with GPS beacons. He scanned the carnal scene at the Tiki Bar but couldn't find a single Kardashian sister.

"There's just nothing like a young wife, a few milliliters of human growth hormone and a little synthetic testosterone with your organic granola every morning," he said.

"Sounds like the Breakfast of Champions," Robert said. "Listen Luther, I appreciate your taking the time to learn about the Viking Tankers deal," Robert said gently. "I know how precious vacation time is and it means a lot to me that you are."

"I'm not on vacation," Luther snorted.

"Oh," Robert said, "are you down here for a conference?"

"Hell no, baby, there's no vacation and there's no conference – that's my new office!" Luther said and pointed toward the cabana enshrouded by white linen curtains. "I live here now. My wife and I live in the penthouse suite of the Delano Hotel – and it's free, dude, totally free."

"Your wife?" Robert said to Luther, a man who had spent his life married to his portfolio of distressed investments.

"Things happen fast in the tropics," Luther said.

"I bet," Robert said. "Congratulations."

"Thanks, bro," Luther said and looked admiringly at the hoard of attractive men and women standing around the Tiki Bar. "She was my life coach," he said.

"But how can you live here for free?" Robert asked. "What does that mean?"

"It means there isn't any income tax in Florida," he said. "This place costs me less than I paid in income tax to Utah," he said. "How cool is that?"

"Very cool," Robert confirmed.

"And the real estate taxes I don't pay by not owning a home in Salt Lake City are enough to buy us dinner at Nobu every night! We've been living on black cod and spicy rock shrimp!"

"It sounds like you've really figured out the system," Robert said.

"Everything in life is a trade," Luther said. "I went short my job and long my life. I just wish I'd figured it out thirty years ago when I was a bit more vigorous."

"You look pretty vigorous to me," Robert said.

"Thank you," Luther said.

When Robert looked into the canvas cave from which Luther had emerged, he spotted the red herring for the Viking Tankers IPO. The waterlogged document was sitting on the low teak table next to an asthma inhaler, a tiny syringe and a white ceramic ashtray in which two of Luther's fat cigars sat smoldering.

Even from a distance, Robert noticed that there were dozens of tiny multi-colored plastic flags attached to the various pages of the swollen offering memorandum. Judging from the volume of flags Robert figured Luther was going to have a lot of questions about the deal.

"I see you've been doing your homework," Robert said.

"I'm probably the only human being in the world who has read your entire prospectus other than you and the lawyers," the old man laughed as he tossed his robe over a teak lounge chair and stepped out of his slippers. "I bet even your mommy hasn't read that term paper."

"I really appreciate your taking the time," Robert said.

"It's nothing. Actually, the steroids keep me up at night," Luther said. "I picked up your prospectus thinking it would put me to sleep but that sucker read better than a John Clancy novel."

"I'm glad you enjoyed it."

"It was awesome. Now come with me, Bobby," Luther said and motioned toward a pair of chaise longue chairs submerged in the shallow end of the swimming pool. "We're taking a voyage together."

"Pardon me?" Robert asked unsteadily.

"Get in this pool right now or I won't give you any of the Church's cash…which means you'll spending the rest of your roadshow in the back of the airplane with the screaming babies," the old man barked.

"I'm all yours," Robert laughed as he kicked off his loafers and peeled off his black socks. "Just be gentle."

"And what better place is there to talk about a maritime deal than in a swimming pool by the sea? I even noticed some tankers out there," Luther added and pointed toward the empty bulk carriers on the horizon. "I bet those babies are making money as we speak. This is perfect."

"It sure is," Robert agreed, "except that I'm wearing a wool suit."

"We both know you've suffered far greater indignities working for me than this," Luther chuckled. "Besides, that's the beautiful thing about Miami Beach," Luther said as he waded toward the furthest chair and sat down. "Nobody cares what you do down here as long you got the scratch – especially a couple of old guys like us."

"Us?" Robert choked. That an octogenarian included him in his generational peer group did little to ease Robert's anxiety about turning forty in less than two weeks. Then again, Luther seemed sharper and more physically fit than Robert was at thirty-nine, so maybe he could learn something.

Once he had removed his shoes and socks and rolled- the pants of his suit above his knees, Robert waded fully clothed across the shallow end of the pool. Sure enough, not a soul at the crowded Tiki Bar looked twice; not even Luther's new bride.

"So why don't you tell me about this little offering of yours, Robert," Luther said as he splashed water over his crispy red flesh and lovingly admired his bouncing pectoral muscles.

"With pleasure," Robert said, relieved to finally be getting down to business. "Viking Tankers is one of the largest owners of…"

"Bobbie, did you know I've made money for those Lutherans in almost every distressed industry in the world – coal, steel, telecoms, mining, autos, pulp and paper…you name it and I've tamed it, but reading the Risk Factors in your prospectus was more exciting than watching *Argo*."

"Um, thanks," Robert said. "We tried to articulate the risks and opportunities associated with…"

"Tanker shipping is a spicy dish in a world of bland investments," Luther interrupted. "I don't think I've ever seen an industry where rates can quadruple one month and drop almost to zero the next."

The psychotherapist who worked on the institutional sales and trading desk at Haakon Gate Capital had counseled Robert about how to deal with American investors who were nervous about the inherent volatility of tanker shipping.

"And that's the beauty of this deal, Luther," Robert said. "We were able to lock in very high time charter rates on the ten vessels at a time when the supply and demand for ships was imbalanced in our favor. That's how we've been able to get the risk out of the deal."

"Zip it, Fairchild," Luther buzzed.

Robert glanced down at his suit pants and said, "It is zipped."

"Look, I know you shipping guys are used to buttering up your bankers by telling them there's no risk in your business, but I'm an equity investor, kid; you need to tell me a different kind of story."

"I do?"

"For the true equity investor risk isn't something to be ashamed of, Fairchild, risk is something to be embraced – something to be celebrated! Risk on, bro! The way I see it, this is a business where you hit a homer or you strike out, which is perfect because I'm looking for a double," Luther said.

"Huh?" Robert said, unable to follow the mix of metaphors.

"I want a two-bagger in three years or I want to lose all my money and the supertanker business appears to be one of the few that is sure to provide me with that."

"Okay, so you are looking for an investment that will double your money or wipe you out?" Robert asked slowly as he struggled to process Luther's line of reasoning.

"Just between you and me," Luther said, "the Lutheran investment committee is going to take back all the un-invested money in my Distressed Opportunities fund at the end of the year."

"Why?" Robert asked.

"Because they think there are no more Distressed Opportunities left," Luther said, "which is why I've decided to give all my money to you."

"Wow," Robert said. This was, literally, a gift from God. "Just out of curiosity, Luther, how much un-invested money do you have left in your Distressed Opportunities fund?" Robert asked gently and stroked the string of worry beads that were in his pocket.

"About $125 million," he said, "but I want twice that much."

"You want $250 million worth of shares in Viking Tankers? But that's half the deal."

"You always were good at math," Luther said. "Your deal is a no-brainer, right? Here's how I see it; I can get a 50% margin loan from a commercial bank which costs 4%. I can use that money to buy twice as much Viking Tankers which is going pay me a guaranteed yield of 14% thanks to those time charters you have with American Refining Corporation."

"Okay," Robert said slowly. He hadn't even considered the idea of an investor putting leverage on the already highly leveraged shares of Viking Tankers; maybe Luther really was a shipping man after all, Robert thought.

"By the way," Luther said, "those charters to ARC are rock solid, right?"

"Of course they are," Robert scoffed.

"No chance of default?"

"Less than zero," Robert confirmed.

"Good, that means that for every dollar I invest in Viking Tankers I get twenty-eight cents of dividends minus four cents for the cost of the margin loan. That means I make twenty-four cents on every dollar, every year, which is a 24% annual dividend and it's secured by your leases to American Refining, a company that has bonds that yield about three percent. This deal is easy money."

That was when Robert realized that he had been right all along; Luther really was investing in the dividend and not the actual value of the ships themselves. And he didn't even seem to mind the fact Viking Tankers wasn't amortizing much of its bank debt or that half of his coupon was a return of his own money while the other half was a return on his money; God bless America.

"And here's the kicker," Luther said. "I only have to pay 15% tax on my turbo-charged dividend thanks to George W. Bush," Luther shouted. "What am I missing here?"

What Luther was missing, of course, was that the initial valuation of the IPO was double the value of the ships which meant that if anything went wrong with the time charters to ARC the value of the company would plummet to the value of its old tankers – and Luther's church would lose 50% of his money overnight.

As Robert stared at the nearly naked Luther Livingston, an inconvenient moral dilemma formed in his mind: was there any sort of ethical issue associated with selling $250 million worth of shares in Viking Tankers to a religious organization whose investment manager was clearly in the throes of a personal crisis? Given more time, Robert might have written an anonymous letter to Randy Cohen, who wrote "The Ethicist" column for *The New York Times*, to seek an answer to the moral quandary.

"Hey turkey brain," Luther said and slapped Robert on the back. "Did you hear what I just said?"

The combination of Luther's reprimand and his spanking caused Robert's philosophical questioning to yield quickly and completely to the most powerful and basic of human instincts – job preservation and shelter for his family – in the form of a $3 million sea captain's house on the island of Martha's Vineyard.

"Thank you for the order," Robert replied. "I'll put you in the book for $250 million."

"Now let's go have a high-protein strawberry daiquiri," Luther said as he rose from the sunken chair. "I want to introduce you to my new wife."

"I'm buying," Robert said.

"Great," Luther said. "There's just one little detail I forgot to mention."

"What's that?" Robert asked.

"The only way in Hades I will invest a single penny in Viking Tankers is if Mr. Jacobsen agrees not to take any money out of the business until I have received my entire $250 million back in the form of dividends," Luther said. "And if Viking Tankers gets liquidated by its lenders, God forbid, I want to get paid back in full before Coco sees a nickel. Got it?"

"Hold on a minute," Robert choked. "Are you saying you want preferred shares in Viking Tankers?"

"Of course I want preferred shares; do you think I'm some kind of doped-up dummy, Fairchild? I have no idea what this company is really worth which means my best chance of success is by putting the man in charge, Coco Jacobsen, underneath me in the cash flow waterfall. The less I understand an investment, the more I demand from it."

And the more you demand from it, Robert thought, the less likely you are to actually get it.

"So do we have a deal?" Luther asked.

Nothing was easy in the deal business. Robert knew that Coco was going to be furious when Robert told him what Luther was demanding, but he also knew shipowners rarely turned down the offer of a huge pile of money irrespective of the terms. It was like Coco Jacobsen always said: possession was nine-tenths of the law and when it came to ships and money, shipowners possessed both.

"It's a deal," Robert said and shook Luther's soft hand.

Chapter 15

The Scream

One of three known paintings of "The Scream" by Norwegian Edvard Munch was purchased in 1937 by Thomas Olsen, whose grandfather founded the shipping company Fred Olsen & Co. Thomas had known Munch through his childhood days learning to sail in Hvitsten, Norway where Munch was establishing himself as a painter. Munch even painted Olsen's wife in the summer of 1932. When Munch's work was labeled as degenerate by the Nazis, Thomas Olsen struck a deal with the Germans in 1937 to save seventy-one pieces of Munch's work and hid thirty-five of his personal Munch paintings in a hay barn until the end of the war. Thomas' son Petter Olsen has continued preserving the artist's work and legacy and purchased Munch's property in Hvitsten and plans to turn it into a museum.

Coco Jacobsen downed a pair of double espressos without taking his eyes off the uniformed police officers standing at the entrance of the duty free lounge in Oslo's Gardermoen Airport.

As confident as the shipowner was in the talents of Wade Water and his army of legal eagles in London and New York, he couldn't help but wonder if he was about to be arrested, publically lambasted – and handed a bill for $50 million to get out of jail.

"Relax, Coco," Wade Waters said when he observed his client looking exceedingly tense. "You are safe here in the Duty Free Zone."

"Ja, but Wade, are you absolutely certain this legal theory of yours will work," Coco whispered with an unsteadiness that was not characteristic of the hard charging tanker tycoon. "I am too good looking to spend time in a Norwegian jail."

"I, um, I think so," Wade stammered.

"You *what!*" Coco exploded with such fury that the two officers each involuntarily reached for the most deadly weapon in their possession – their walkie-talkies. "What do you mean, *you think so*! You told me this plan was bulletproof!"

While experimenting with any new legal theory was stressful, the process of beta testing Coco's groundbreaking tax mitigation strategy was downright torturous.

"Coco, we both know that nothing in this world is certain except death and…" Wade paused when he recognized his poor judgment in selecting that particular quote from Benjamin Franklin.

"…Taxes!" Coco wailed the final word of the famous sentence and threw his head onto the table. "Argh!"

Although Coco's taxation predicament wasn't unusual among shipowners, his strategy for dealing with it was. Although he had often overheard his mentor, Hilmar Reksten, bemoaning Norway's tax rates – as high as 65% when you tallied-up income tax, property tax and wealth tax – Coco had never paid much attention. Taxation, even excessive taxation, didn't matter much to a seventh-grade dropout who earned minimum wage for sweeping telexes off the floor at night.

But ten years later, after Coco had started chartering-in ships for his own account at age twenty-five and using them to fulfill the Contracts of Affreightment he'd arranged with hardscrabble oil companies in fringe nations, Coco's fortunes changed. Coincidental political instability in Iran, Nigeria and Syria caused charter rates to soar and Coco made his first $100 million in profit almost overnight by trading the rented tankers in the blistering spot market. Without a moment's hesitation, the Norwegian deployed the freshly minted cash by buying the eighteen-vessel fleet of the Latvian national oil company.

The bold acquisition of the Latvian fleet proved woefully ill-timed. In fact, before Coco had even accepted delivery of the final ship the charter market had cooled and tanker values had plummeted. Just as Coco was sifting through the wreckage of the deal, trying to figure out what to do with the tankers he had been forced to lay-up in the fjord near Molde, the Norwegian taxing authority presented him a bill for $50 million.

Although Coco had not reported the offshore income earned during the short-lived tanker boom, his arch-rivals at Knut Shipping in Bergen graciously had. They supplied the government with a tidy dossier of forensic evidence that documented Coco's gains – from vessel sale and purchase reports to a list of charter fixtures on the Viking Tankers fleet.

"Ja, but this makes no sense!" Coco shrieked when he opened the certified envelope while still in the presence of the courier who handed it to him at the bar of D/S Louise. "How can I possibly owe taxes if I don't have any money?"

Coco had been guided by the faulty, albeit reasonable, logic that reinvesting profits into more ships was the same thing as spending money on deductible business expenses. Once the relevant accounting principles had been explained to him, that items added to the balance sheet as assets could not be considered expenses, Coco found himself in an unpleasant situation shared by many shipping men: long on iron, short of cash and unable to sell ships because their value had slumped below their loan balance.

After two years of unsuccessfully attempting to collect Coco's unpaid tax bill, the Norwegian government undertook an intense forensic investigation into the long strand of offshore "mailbox" companies that formed the DNA of Viking Tankers. The formal report presented to the country's Parliament concluded precisely what the taxing authority had feared; Coco Jacobsen had not only replicated the spot market chartering strategy of his mentor Hilmar Reksten, he had adopted the man's byzantine corporate structure as well.

The clarity about Coco's opacity brought to light a dark period in the history of Norwegian taxation of shipowners. Thirty years earlier the government had charged Hilmar with eight counts of tax fraud and went to work hunting down the $500 million Kroner that they believed he had collected from British Petroleum in the form of time charter payments.

After nearly twenty years of fruitless searching the government finally made a deal with Hilmar's estate. In exchange for sixty million Kroner in cash and the title to a health center on the Canary Island of Lanzarote worth just twelve million Kroner the charges would be dropped. Challenging the notion that you can't take it with you when you go, the legendary shipowner, who had amassed more wealth during his lifetime than any Norwegian in history, was declared bankrupt after his death – leaving behind more buried treasure than Captain Kidd.

Loath to repeat the embarrassing Reksten Incident the Norwegian taxman made Coco Jacobsen an offer he literally couldn't afford to refuse; the constitutional monarchy agreed to forgive the $50 million unpaid tax bill provided that Coco agreed to publicly renounce his citizenship. The Norwegians were sorry to lose the revenue but almost everyone agreed it was a small price to pay for ridding their mostly peaceful, oil-rich kingdom of an economic de-stabilizer like Coco Jacobsen.

That Coco's subsequent success would cause him to become one of the single largest employers of Norwegian people, and account for a whopping 5% of Norway's GDP, was an irony that went unnoticed by almost everyone, including Coco.

The major only problem with Coco's devil's bargain was that he was permitted to spend no more than sixty days in-country or be subject to the unpaid tax – and sixty days wasn't enough time to satisfy his love of country. He longed to spend time in the lovely port town of Bergen where he had first worked for

Hilmar. He dreamed of being back in the mountains of Geilo where his mother had taught him to cross-country ski under the light of the full moon and ached to return to the west coast village of Ostervold where he had said goodbye to his papa when he set out on that ill-fated pelagic fishing trip. He also loved the beautiful village of Oslo, which was still one of the best places in the world from which to run an oil tanker empire thanks to a robust community of highly talented shipping professionals. The $50 million tax bill hung over Coco's head like the Sword of Damocles, suspended by a single strand of horse hair.

Never to be vanquished, Coco mushed Wade Water and his legion of lawyers like a team of sled dogs to locate a loophole in his plea bargain that would allow him to be present in Norway for more than sixty days without being liable for tax. Working around the clock for weeks, his legal team reached an elegant if unproven solution; if Coco were to conduct his business meetings in the Duty Free area of the Oslo International Airport, the Norwegian customs officials wouldn't stamp his passport. If the Norwegian customs officials didn't stamp his passport, his counselors advised, Coco couldn't officially be deemed to have been in-country. *Voila.*

Coco was now one hour into testing out the novel legal theory and so far things were going to plan. When the Twitter message went out that Coco's G-5, an aircraft festooned with an image of Norwegian explorer Thor Heyerdahl, was approaching Oslo more than one hundred shipping professionals had shuffled into the Centrum station and boarded the Flytoget train to the airport clutching budget tickets to Stockholm they would never use; they bought the tickets purely so they could pass through passport control and enter the lounge in which Coco would be doing his wheeling and dealing.

Just when Coco thought his stress level couldn't get any higher one of his tiny cell phones began chirping and flashing the name "Kraken" as it sat among the dozens of tiny espresso cups and empty bottles of Ringnes lager. Rocky DuBois was calling Coco directly for the first time in a decade and the tanker boss didn't need to answer the phone to know he was about to get royally hosed.

As he stared at the phone with eyes bulging and mouth agape, neither Coco nor any of the advisors that fed off him like pilot fish on a whale failed to recognize his resemblance to the most famous of Norwegian paintings, *The Scream* by Edvard Munch. And while thoughts of fine art might have been soothing to some the thought only stoked Coco's fury as he recalled the evening a decade earlier when another Norwegian (a twenty-five-year-old supply boat princeling from Ålesund, no less!) had outbid him for the particular painting at a Sotheby's auction.

Before Coco had reached for his cell phone, Magnus Magnusen quickly refilled the tanker king's aquavit and Peder Hansen pushed a bottle of Ringnes toward him as a chaser. It was the work of an experienced triage team and the moment the magnate refused to take a sip of either beverage the men exchanged the shared concern of medical professionals faced with a grim prognosis. Something must be seriously wrong with the patient.

"Rocky, my friend," Coco cried out with false enthusiasm and a psychotically exaggerated smile. "How are you?"

"Call me Mr. DuBois," Rocky said into the speakerphone as he collapsed onto the Italian leather bucket seat of his new navy blue Mercedes sedan and closed his eyes – a vehicle with the license plate IGOTGAS.

The CEO of American Refining Corporation had enjoyed two Mt. Gay and tonics at lunch and was feeling nicely buzzed. Consuming hard alcohol during the day was an indulgence he rarely allowed himself, but Rocky figured it was time to start easing into the rituals that would become so important in his upcoming retirement. He had five decades' worth of unwinding to do.

"What do you want?" Coco snarled at the Houstonian.

"Looks like you got yourself between a Rocky and a hard place," the Texan laughed over the sound of "My Way," the Frank Sinatra anthem to self-reliance drifting from the network of twenty-eight German speakers.

"Don't frack with me," Coco replied.

"Good one," Rocky said. "But we got a real problem."

"There's no such thing as a problem, only an opportunity," Coco replied through grinding teeth even though he knew exactly what the oilman was referring to; Rocky was losing his shirt on the ten ships he time chartered from Robert Fairchild now that the tanker party was over.

"I'm afraid it's not that simple, son," Rocky said.

"Of course it is," Coco said. "Shipping is a very simple business and my vessels are all performing to the specifications in the time charter agreements."

"Yeah, well I'm afraid we're going to have to frustrate those charters," Rocky said as he adjusted several air-conditioner vents to cool the sunburn he'd gotten on the back nine at River Oaks.

"You can't just walk away from the charters," Coco said.

Coco's already dark face ripened to the color of a plum while he listened to Rocky. First the man had tried to cheat him out of $64,000 of charter hire in Nigeria. Then he'd falsely accused him of crimes that prevented him from entering America. Now he was mugging him again! If Rocky defaulted on the ten time charters not only would Coco have forfeited the earnings he *would have* made during the tanker party, his IPO would be dead and he wouldn't have the $500 million he needed to give the Greek.

"And why's that, son?" Rocky laughed.

"Because those are legal obligations," Coco said.

"Ha," Rocky snorted. "Since when are you so concerned about the law?"

"Since you put me on the run from it," Coco replied.

"You're right, boy, those ten time charters are legal contracts but the only problem is that ART is very close to running out of money," Rocky explained. "I don't even know if ART has enough cash to make the next charter hire payment to you."

"ART? Who is ART?" Coco asked and looked around but the team of advisors orbiting around him just shrugged their shoulders and exchanged puzzled glances. "And why does it matter if he's running out of money; American Refining Corporation is an investment-grade company," Coco said, repeating Robert Fairchild's words even though he didn't know exactly what they meant. "You're a member of the Poor Standard!"

"Let's be clear on something right now," Rocky said. "American Refining Corporation *is* an investment-grade company and it *is* a proud member of the Standard & Poor's 500 but the guarantor on your little time charters isn't ARC...its ART."

"Then get him on the phone!" Coco screamed. "I want to talk to ART!"

"I'm afraid that's not possible," Rocky said.

"Why?"

"Well, because ART doesn't have any employees," Rocky laughed. "ART stands for American Refining *Transportation* and it's just one of those mailbox companies with no assets. It's domiciled on some crazy little Caribbean island called St. Christopher. You ever even heard of that place?"

"No," Coco said.

"Surely Mr. Fairchild analyzed the risk associated with having a counter party such as American Refining Transportation," Rocky said. "Everyone knows I never offer a full corporate guarantee on shipping deals; there's too much risk."

"Mr. Fairchild did not mention that," Coco said. He had assumed Robert Fairchild was smart enough to make sure the time charters were guaranteed by the same legal entity that held title to ARC's assets; it was an exercise even a kindergartner would have known to perform and Fairchild missed it.

"Then it looks like I gotcha," Rocky said.

"That's just not right, Rocky," Coco said, shaking his head back and forth. Like most people who made their living from the business of transacting, the Norwegian had a highly developed sense of what was fair. "You can't just walk away from a deal without having a real reason."

"Oh, I have plenty reasons," Rocky said.

"Like what?" Coco challenged.

"Like the fact that my superintendent said the oil water separator on the *Viking Alexandra* has been disabled. And he said the engine room on that ship has more flashing lights than Las Vegas."

"That's not true!" Coco wailed like a wounded animal.

"My man said the *Alexandra* is real a pig," Rocky added.

In a fit of love-struck bravado six months earlier, Coco had changed the name of his newest vessel to *Viking Alexandra*. It was the first time he'd ever broken the pattern of naming ships after characters in Homer's *Odyssey* – an arrangement he and the Greek had dreamed up one night in Monaco – and he had clearly jinxed the ship.

"Ja, but this is just fair wear-and-tear," Coco proclaimed, laboring to push any thought of Alexandra Meriwether out of his mind. "And this type of thing is permitted according to the charter party. You can put her off hire while we make the necessary repairs," Coco said, meaning that Rocky would not be responsible for paying the daily charter hire while the ship was out of commission. "I believe she's in the Caribbean right now so I can have her in and out of the Cuba dry dock in two days."

"Whoa!" Rocky laughed. "Did you just say *Cuba*? You're not trading with the enemy again, are you pal? I might just have to make a drop a dime on that one. I bet OFAC's got you on their speed dial by now."

"I said Curaçao," Coco seethed.

"Doesn't matter," Rocky said. "Those boats may have your little Viking rowboat painted on the smokestack, but if the media finds out I put ARC's crude oil on a broken down oil tanker owned by a guy who's on INTERPOL's "Most Wanted" list, I'm going to be treated like a cross between Tony Hayward and Joe Hazelwood," Rocky said.

"I'll substitute another vessel in for *Alexandra*," Coco said. "I have plenty of others."

"I bet you do," Rocky said, "especially these days. Listen Coco, we both know those charters are finished. The only thing left to talk about is whether or not I'm going to kill your little IPO," Rocky snickered.

Rocky DuBois hadn't been happy that Coco had forced him into swallowing fifty years' worth of time charters just so he could move thirty million barrels of lousy crude oil over the course of a few weeks, but when the old oilman read in

TradeWinds that Viking Tankers was in the process of raising $500 million on the back of those usurious time charters, he was irate.

"I would be happy to cancel those time charters," Coco said. "We can just pretend those charters never happened and you can wire me the $75 million that you *would have* paid me if you had taken those ships from the spot market during my tanker party," Coco said.

"Are you suggesting that I'm a back-trader?" Rocky asked with righteous indignation. "I would never ask you to do such a thing. What I really need from you, Coco, is your expertise," Rocky said. "I need your help."

When his former roommate from University of Texas, Piper Pearl, called Rocky DuBois earlier that day and told him about Mr. Xing's unusual condition precedent to closing – that ARC somehow gain control of fifteen gas carriers currently under construction at Regal Shipbuilding in South Korea – Rocky's initial reaction had been to panic. He had tried to charter-in a few LNG carriers six months earlier and failed miserably.

After working with a team of shipbrokers in New York and London he learned there had been a shortage of such ships ever since Japan began systematically switching its source of power from nuclear to natural gas after the Fukushima meltdown in 2011. The Germans had also decided to switch from nuclear power to gas and the French were threatening to follow suit.

The problem was that the fleet of high-specification LNG carriers was small to begin with and most vessels were purpose-built to serve specific long-term contracts. The so-called "spot market" for the LNG ships was virtually non-existent so when demand for the ships increased charter rates jumped by five hundred percent almost overnight.

But a few minutes after Piper told Rocky the nature of Mr. Xing's pre-closing requirement, the old Texan felt a warm rush of pleasure; he had been looking for a way to get even with the Coco Jacobsen before he retired and now he had it. Piper had offered to task his colleague Alexandra Meriwether with finding the ships, but Rocky was going to take matters into his own hands as well; he would simply threaten to cancel ARC's ten time charters from Viking Tankers unless Coco found the ships for him. It would be the knock-out punch that would finally end Rocky's sparring matching with Coco.

"You want my help?" Coco asked. "Is this some kind of joke?"

"It is my understanding, Coco, that there is a series of fifteen state-of-the-art LNG carriers currently under construction at a place called Regal Shipbuilding in Korea," Rocky explained. "*South* Korea that is," Rocky chuckled, "just in case you're getting any funny ideas about dealing with Pyongyang."

Coco didn't know how much Rocky knew so the Norwegian decided to play dumb. "What does this have to do with me?"

"I need your help to figure out who owns them."

"That's the help you need?" Coco asked. "You just want to find out who owns those vessels?"

"Apparently they were sold recently and the new owner has remained completely anonymous, which I assume means it's some scary government that an American like me isn't allowed to do business with. And since you don't seem to have any problem dealing with scary governments, I figure you are the right guy to negotiate terms and get a deal done for ARC to buy them," Rocky explained.

"But why do you want to buy fifteen new LNG vessels, Rocky? You always told me that you hate owning ships," Coco said as if they were an old married couple. "You told me you didn't need to own a garbage truck just because you had to get rid of some trash every now and then."

"There's a bit more to this story, and in the spirit of working together on this, I'm willing to tell you what's going on here," Rocky said. "But you must agree to keep it confidential."

The Texan knew full-well that he should keep his mouth shut like he always did when it concerned sensitive commercial matters, but the two glasses of Barbados rum combined with his potential cash windfall made him unusually chatty.

"You have my word of honor," Coco replied as he crossed his fingers, a gesture that elicited considerable laughter from his team of advisors.

"The Minister for Natural Resources for the People's Republic of China, a man named Mr. Xing, has agreed to buy my little business," Rocky said.

"Why would they do that?" Coco asked as he wrote down the man's name on a napkin – *Mr. Xing, PRC.*

"Because they're hungry for my shale gas and I'm hungry to cash out while I still can," Rocky said.

"Wow," Coco said as he smiled, "it sounds like you and Mr. Xing really needs those LNG ships."

"Big time," Rocky said.

"I'll really miss having you in the business, Rocky," Coco said with the hollowness of a sibling who learns his brother is going away to school. "Shipping may not be a team sport when we're in the heat of battle, but we're all friends in the locker room," Coco said. "We all sustain the same injuries."

"I appreciate the towel snapping, Coco, but if I don't get my hands on those fifteen LNG carriers then Mr. Xing won't buy ARC," Rocky said.

"Does that mean we are finally on the same team?" Coco said with an insidious smile as rubbed the evil eye charm against his unshaven face.

"For once, it appears our interests are aligned," Rocky said. "So here's the deal, Coco, you find me those ships and I will keep paying on those lousy time charters for the next five years."

"I will try to help you," Coco said, "but this will take some time."

"How much time are we talking about?" Rocky asked. Both men knew exactly what was going on: the longer Coco dragged out the process, the more charter hire payments Rocky would be forced to make.

"A month," Coco offered.

"You got ten days," Rocky said. "After that I start handing back your lousy VLCCs in the most wretched ports in the world," Rocky DuBois said and hung up.

Chapter 16

A Fragile Market

My grandmother had a simple saying about the cycles: "98 ships and 101 cargos equals boom, 101 ships and 98 cargos equals bust." Bearing in mind my grandfather was a Captain and shipowner and she had travelled under sail with him on a small schooner from Kassos Island in Greece to the Black Sea, Marseilles, Casablanca, Buenos Aires, Boston and Liverpool over eight years, it came from the lips of a lady who had personal sea experience and had learned well what she taught.

Mr. Nicholas A. Pappadakis, CEO, A. G. Pappadakis & Co. and Chairman, Intercargo

It was the kind of day when absolutely nothing could go wrong Robert Fairchild thought as he emerged triumphantly from the back of the black Lincoln Town Car in front of Malone Academy, the private elementary school where Oliver attended third grade.

After the chauffeur slammed the door behind him, Robert paused on the Upper East Side sidewalk, looked up at his beautiful wife standing in front of his stately alma mater and savored the prosperous residential surroundings. He felt bittersweet as he admired the hosed-down sidewalks and the rows of neat, four-story brownstones dotted with flower boxes thick with orange and red mums.

Robert had never felt better about the current state of his life, which made him question his decision to change it by moving his family to the island of Martha's Vineyard and away from the richness of opportunity on offer in New York City. Then he remembered the objects of his desire: the backyard, the minivan, the dock, the hose, the garage, the sidewalks, the bikes – and maybe even the dog Oliver wanted.

On the business front, everything was going almost to plan. The roadshow had gained momentum thanks to the $250 million cornerstone order for preferred shares he'd received from the muscle-bound Luther Livingston. During the past seventy-two hours, the rented Hawker 900 had jumped like a grasshopper between Miami, Dallas, Denver and Detroit as Robert pitched twenty-six hedge funds and "soft circled" orders for another $325 million of preferred shares.

So confident was Robert about the success of the IPO that he'd instructed his teenage rent-a-pilots to return to Teterboro Airport in New Jersey so he could spend a couple of hours participating in "Career Night" at Oliver's school before returning to Chicago where he had an investor breakfast in the morning. Although taking a break during an IPO roadshow was as advisable as taking a break during childbirth, Robert had always been guided by one simple principle that always trumped everything else: family first.

"For God's sake, honey, will you please button up your shirt?" Grace Fairchild said as her husband ascended the stately stone steps of the elite Manhattan school – an institution so hard to be admitted to that Robert had actually fallen to his knees and begged the admissions officer. "You look like Johnny Depp in *Pirates of the Caribbean*."

"I know you love Johnny Depp," Robert said as he kissed her lips.

"Yes, but the feelings I have for Johnny Depp have no place in an elementary school and neither does your slightly hairy chest and unshaven face," Grace said as she went to work tidying-up her husband's disheveled and quickly-graying hair. "And will you please put away those worry beads; people are going to think we're *Catholic*."

"What's the matter with being Catholic?" Robert asked as he slipped the worry beads Spyrolaki had given him at the Marine Club in Piraeus back into his pocket.

"Oh gee, honey, I don't know," she said as her husband took her hand and they crossed the stone threshold leading into the building, "how about the lack of *birth control?*"

"Then let's try to have another one," Robert whispered into her ear as they walked down the hallway. "Maybe this is a sign."

After he made the proposal, the rhythmic clicking of his wife's high heels stopped. She grabbed Robert's arm and spun him toward her. "*Another one?*" she gasped.

"I think it would be fun." Robert shrugged his shoulders, "and I know Oliver would enjoy it," he added.

"You won't let the kid get a *dog* and now you want to give him a baby?" Grace said.

"We can't bring a dog into Il Cantinori," Robert smiled. "*Capische?*"

"Don't take this the wrong way, sweetheart, but your income isn't reliable enough for us to have one kid in this city, never mind two," Grace said.

"Which is why we're moving out to Martha's Vineyard," he reminded her.

"You are truly crazy," she said, shaking her head back and forth, "which is why I love you."

"I know," he smiled, "and I'm grateful."

"By the way, I just got your paycheck." she said. "It looks as though charter rates have taken a turn for the worse."

"Welcome to shipping," Robert said. "Once the market learned how high charter rates were, every ship in the world that could carry oil rushed back to the Arabian Gulf just when OPEC reduced production by a million barrels to try and increase the price of oil."

"What about your little tanker party?" she asked.

"The lights have been switched on, the parents are home and the punch bowl has been taken away," Robert said. "The party is over."

"That didn't last long," she said.

"It rarely does, but don't worry honey, once I get this IPO wrapped up we'll never have to worry about the volatility of the marketplace again," Robert took her arm and guided her down the hall toward Oliver's classroom. "This deal is going to change our lives forever," he added and immediately regretted his fateful choice of words.

"That's good, Robert, because a loan officer from the Bank of Martha's Vineyard called today and they want us to document the source of our $1 million down payment for the Captain Fisher House by the end of next week," Grace laughed.

"Why?"

"Because apparently there is someone else that's keen to buy the house if we aren't able to close the deal," she said, "and the sellers don't want to lose them."

"Don't worry," Robert said. "We'll close the deal."

"Okay Aristotle, it's time for you to button up your shirt, put away the rosary beads and make Oliver proud," she whispered after the soft jingle of the teacher's bell summarily silenced the group of gregarious parents.

When Robert Fairchild stepped inside his son's classroom, he was dazzled by the richness of the surroundings. From a chart of the human genome to a diagram of aquifers, from an outline of photosynthesis to an explanation of Penicillin and digestion, the small classroom was a place of worship for the inexplicably complex miracles that enabled even the simplest forms of daily life. The shelves were sagging with books and games and puzzles and blocks and even the floor was covered with information like maps, geometric shapes and various calculations of distances and angles.

As Robert waited for Career Night to kick off, his eyes moved slowly over walls covered with butterflies and African masks, paper mâché animals from Australia, cloud formations, rainbows, spiders and sea creatures. There were Native American tools, beaver pelts, bird nests and snakeskins. A twenty-foot fish made from garbage the kids had found in Central Park hung from the ceiling and one entire wall was devoted to "*365 Ways to Reduce Your Carbon Footprint.*"

When Robert scanned the litter of little children lying on the floor in the front of the classroom, it didn't take him long to spot Oliver. His son was the only child wearing a black patch over his left eye, a clip-on gold hoop dangling from his ear and a red bandanna tied pulled tightly over his head – an unusual outfit considering it wasn't Halloween.

As boys of that age sometimes do, Oliver Fairchild had become totally, utterly, encyclopedically focused on a singular subject. In his case the object of his obsession wasn't baseball statistics or types of heavy machinery or railroad schedules or even state capitals – it was piracy. The boy loved pirates.

Robert had attempted to explain to his son what piracy actually involved in the modern age: desperate people in destabilized countries that robbed, tortured and killed innocent seafarers as their ships passed by – but that wasn't enough to unwind the romantic notions of piracy that had been drilled into him since birth. Robert even shared with his son the story about his own experience with piracy when his bulk carrier *Lady Grace* was attacked by a longboat loaded with machine gun-toting Somali pirates in the Gulf of Aden, but the anecdote did nothing to diminish the lad's penchant for privateering.

Robert had no one to blame but himself. His boy's love for pirates was an unintended consequence of Robert's own unbridled enthusiasm for all things maritime and was supplemented by his nightly reading aloud of *Treasure Island* by Robert Louis Stevenson. The classic pirate story was just one of the many sea-related books that Robert had shared with his son since he became involved in the shipping world a year and a half earlier and Oliver ended up catching a boy's version of the "shipping bug."

"Good evening!" an indefatigable third-grade teacher named Mrs. Martha boomed to the large group of children and parents packed into the classroom. "I want to thank all of the parents for coming in tonight," she said. "The children are as proud of you as you are of them. We are very fortunate to have Mr. Robert Fairchild, Oliver's father, as our first presenter tonight," she said and began to scan the room expectantly, hoping he had arrived.

Grace squeezed Robert's hand, "I'm so proud of you, too."

His wife's breathy voice whispered directly into his ear made Robert want to go back to their apartment after Career Night and not back on the tin can of a rent-a-jet. Then he reminded himself that there would be plenty of time to relax when the IPO was done and they were living on "island time."

"Thanks, Grace," he said.

"And I know how hard you are working to *protect* Oliver and me," she added. "I want you to know how grateful I am that you are so *careful* with us."

Grace's eerie choice of words made Robert's heart flutter. In his mind, he had neither protected them nor been the least bit careful. In fact, he had recklessly wagered Oliver's shares in Viking Tankers, the family's only meaningful asset, *double or nothing*, on a harebrained shipping scheme cooked-up while drunk in a London pub. Unlike most shipowners who spread their bets among different ships and markets, Robert Fairchild was all-in.

"Mr. Fairchild informed me that he has just come in from the road in a private jet to be with us tonight," Mrs. Martha giggled.

Robert was instantly embarrassed that the teacher had repeated the Wall Street lingo that he had thoughtlessly emailed her while still high from a successful investor lunch at the Four Seasons Hotel in Dallas. When the teacher spoke the words "private jet" Robert watched every head, large and small, instantly crane around to examine him. Their facial expressions ranged from curious to contemptuous. Never in history had a mode of transportation been as pregnant with images of malfeasance as private air travel.

"Mr. Fairchild is in the shipping business," she added while waving him up to the large oak teacher's table in the front of the classroom. "Take us away, Mr. Fairchild. Take us on an exciting adventure!"

The third-grade classroom was silent as Robert made his way to the chalkboard at the head of the class. Just as he cleared his throat and prepared to speak a tiny girl sitting next to Oliver thrust her arm high into the air. "Oliver's daddy," she said as Robert strained to read the paper nametag stuck to her pink sweater. "Are you a pilot?"

"Am I a *what*, Daisy?" Robert laughed.

"Mrs. Martha said you are in the business of shipping and she said you just flew here on a private airplane. We're learning how to make predictions and based on the information we have been given, my prediction is that you are a pilot for FedEx," Daisy said.

"That's a very astute prediction, Daisy," Robert said, "but I'm not a pilot, which is a very important job by the way."

"Are you a trucker?" a boy asked. "Since Mrs. Martha said you came in from the road."

"Another insightful deduction," Robert said. "But no, I'm not a pilot and I'm not a truck driver, but I *am* in shipping. Can anyone guess what my job is?"

Robert gazed across a sea of blank faced children and their parents. To him, this was the amazing thing about America; not only had ships carried most of the kids' great grandparents to the New World, ocean shipping was also one of the most fundamentally important components of the U.S. and global economy. It was the critical link when it came to the import, export and prices of everything from energy to building materials to consumer products to food. It was everywhere, but it was invisible.

"I am in the ocean shipping business," Robert finally said and prepared for a robust reaction that never came. To compensate for the appreciable lack of interest in his confession, Robert picked up a stub of white chalk from the tray behind him and wrote the word *shipowner* on the chalkboard.

"I am a shipowner," he announced dramatically even though, technically speaking, he wasn't a shipowner at all; he was a shipowner's bagman. Coco had put the 10% of Viking Tankers in Oliver's name which meant the miniature pirate in the front row was actually more of a shipowner than he was.

"Oliver's daddy," Daisy said as she raised her hand, "I just don't think shipowner is one word."

Robert was stunned; the precocious little tyke had instantly seized on one of the fundamental questions that had always puzzled him, too. Even having looked up the word in the dictionary and searched for it on Google he still didn't know if "ship owner" was one word or two – or maybe even hyphenated.

"That's a good question, Daisy," the teacher said delicately. "But this is Mr. Fairchild's profession so I imagine he knows how to spell it."

"But truck owner isn't one word," Daisy said.

"Either is train owner," added the little boy sitting on the other side of Oliver. His son's face was red with embarrassment.

"How about this?" Robert Fairchild said as he erased the word "shipowner" with his now sweaty palm and replaced it with the words "*Shipping Man.*"

"No," the boy said.

"No?" Robert asked.

"No, because oilman is one word," a boy said. "Are you really sure Shipping Man isn't one word? And why do you capitalize it?"

"Besides, Oliver's Daddy, aren't there any *women* in your business?" Daisy asked.

"Of course there are women, just not as many as I'd like, as *anyone* would like," Robert stammered when he noticed Grace's elevated eyebrow. "I mean, um, Shipping Man is just an expression. It's old-fashioned. I think it's Norwegian. There are women in Norway. They are mostly blonde and very tall. I guess maybe it doesn't translate because…"

"Now children, let's give Mr. Fairchild a chance to talk about his career," Mrs. Martha laughed and gave him a consoling look. She urged him to press on with a fluttering of her hand.

"Thank you," Robert said and demonstrated his relief by pretending to wipe the sweat from his forehead. "You guys are tougher customers than the Iranian National Oil Company," Robert laughed.

"Did you just say Iran?" one of the fathers probed in a deep voice. Robert ignored him.

"The first thing I want to tell you kids is that 97% of all international trade is carried on ships," Robert said after ignoring the father's comment.

Robert was hoping this mind-blowing statistic would amaze the children as much as it had amazed him when he first learned it, but when he surveyed the crowd all he saw were slack jaws, glazed eyes and a robust bloom of stifled yawns. Then a hand went up – Daisy's hand.

"Oliver's daddy, what are you doing to reduce its carbon footprint?" She asked.

"What am I *what*?" Robert said.

"Your carbon footprint," she said "What are you doing to make it smaller?"

"That's a great question," Robert said. "I am proud to say that shipping is the most environmentally efficient form of transportation in the world. Ships contribute just 5% of all emissions even though they carry 97% of trade," he said. "That's less than one-third of what trucks produce in terms of CO2. And air freight pollutes more than *forty times* as much as ocean shipping."

"That wasn't my question," she said.

"It's wasn't?" Robert asked.

"No," she said. "Please focus. My question was what are you doing to *reduce* your emissions. Everyone in Mrs. Martha's class is making an effort to reduce their carbon footprint, so I was just wondering what you're doing to reduce yours? We can all do better, Mr. Fairchild."

These little kids were hitting all the hot buttons, Robert thought. He wouldn't have been surprised if one of them asked him about the impact of fracking on the tanker market. The truth was that whether by modifying the hull configuration of a vessel or using smaller, fuel-injected engines, the development of ships that produced fewer emissions was an important one in the shipping industry.

The sad part for Robert was that as important as the issue was, it wasn't particularly relevant for a cash-poor shipowner like Coco. The Viking Tankers fleet was a fuel-thirsty one, built at a time when oil was $20 per barrel and when the world was more terrified about the impact of global cooling than global warming.

Just as Robert was preparing to update the children and parents on the subject of "eco-ships," despite the fact he didn't even know if the pre-fix "eco" was short for "ecological" or "economical," he felt his telephone ring inside the pocket of his suit jacket. He pulled out the device out and silenced it without looking down to see who was calling.

"Where was I?"

"I believe you were about to tell us about doing business with *Iran*," the baritone in the back said.

"No," Daisy said, "he was about to tell us about how he is reducing the environmental impact of his vessels," Daisy said. "Are you using renewable resources like wind turbines or kites aboard the ships? Have you looked into solar power?"

"The shipping industry has entered a revolutionary new phase in which shipowners are working hard to reduce the…" Robert stopped midsentence when he heard the distinctive bark of Oliver's iPhone.

Despite criticizing his father for using his BlackBerry at inappropriate times – including soccer games, during meals, while walking down the street, in church, in bed and even in the delivery room of his only child's birth – his son didn't hesitate to answer his own device during Career Night. Had Robert Fairchild's life been set to music the opening chords of Harry Chapin's haunting hymn *Cat's in the Cradle* would have begun playing softly in the background.

"*What* are you doing, Oliver?" Robert finally said.

"It's Uncle Coco," Oliver said and moved the phone away from his ear. The Norwegian's booming voice was so loud that Robert could hear it from ten feet away.

"Please tell Uncle Coco that I'll call him back later," Robert said calmly but sternly.

"He doesn't want to talk to you, Dad," Oliver said. "He's calling because he wants to tell Mommy something," Oliver said and added, "something urgent."

Robert reached forward to snatch his son's phone but Grace Fairchild, driven by the mysterious and preternatural instincts that come along with motherhood, fluidly maneuvered through the scrum of children and plucked the device from Oliver's hand.

"What's so urgent, Coco Jacobsen," Grace snapped, "that you have to call a third-grader's cell phone during career night?"

Robert heard only Coco's "Ja, but…" before his wife disappeared into the deserted hallway and he continued his remarks. After he had provided a two-minute explanation of the various ways in which the international shipping industry was trying to reduce its emission of particulate matter (by slowing down, burning higher-grade fuels like LNG, and using more efficient, fuel-injected engines), Mrs. Martha said "thank you" and welcomed the next parent. Daisy had no further questions for the witness.

By the time Robert tiptoed out of the classroom and into the hallway to find Grace, her conversation with Coco had just ended. "What did he say?" Robert asked his wife.

As he waited for her reply, Robert looked back into the crowded classroom and watched as the next presenting parent, a neurosurgeon, brutally excised the word "Shipping" from the chalkboard and leaving behind only the emasculated residue of the word "Man."

"I can't tell you what it means," Grace said, "but I can tell you what he said."

"Okay," Robert said slowly, "what did he say?"

"He said that someone named Rocky DuBois has threatened to default on all the time charters to Viking Tankers and start redelivering ships. He also said that your IPO is on hold and Magnus Magnusen wants you to stop the roadshow," she said. "They are giving back the airplane tonight and they will leave your luggage at Teterboro."

Coco asked Grace to deliver the dramatic message to Robert even though she had no idea what it meant or why he wanted her to be the bearer of the bad news. All she knew was that judging from the withering expression on her husband's face, the parroted words had dealt him a crushing blow.

"But how can Rocky just default on the charters?" Robert complained. "We have *contracts!*"

"Coco said that you entered into those contracts with an undercapitalized subsidiary called American Refining Transportation and not with American Refining Corporation," Grace said. "That's why Coco is upset; he said you didn't even read the documents. Is that true, honey? Did you really not even read the documents?"

The funny part was that Robert *had* read the documents. He had to read them since Coco didn't want to pay a London lawyer to perform the task. Poring over the papers, Robert had learned that like so many of the traditions that still governed shipping deals the time charter of ten supertankers to American Refining for five years, an agreement worth $900 million of gross revenue, had been documented on twelve pages of eighteenth century boilerplate with more fill-in-the-blanks than a *Mad Libs*.

Robert clearly remembered reviewing the English Law documents while sitting in the Starbucks on the corner of 51st and Park Avenue, trying to read the lines of legalese that had been redacted and added by hand. He had been curious about the reference to an entity called American Refining Transportation but his analysis was forever suspended when he answered an urgent call from Alistair on an unrelated topic.

"If what you are saying is true, Grace," Robert said quietly, "I am ruined."

"It will be okay, honey," she said and rubbed her husband's shoulder.

"No, really, *we* are ruined," he said to his shoes. He was too ashamed to even look his wife in the eye. Robert Fairchild was suddenly face-to-face with the thing he feared most in his life: doing something patently stupid that adversely affected people who were counting on him.

"Come on, Robert," Grace said, "we can always find a way to work things out and we don't really need a $3 million house on Martha's Vineyard; after all, I'm not even sure if we can get the good kale out on the island year round," she added.

In order to get his wife's complete attention, Robert knew it was time to drop the O-bomb. "Oliver is ruined," Robert said softly.

"*WHAT?*" his wife snapped and leaned-in to shoot him a soul-piercing glare.

"I think I went a little too far this time," Robert said as he resumed staring at his loafers. "This is my fault," Robert groveled as he wandered down the deserted hallway trying to locate locker number 333, the same one he'd been assigned when he attended Malone Academy three decades earlier. He longed to go back to that simpler period of his life.

"You didn't play around with the shares Coco gave Oliver, did you?" she asked. "I sure hope not because the children of shipping men need nest eggs!" Robert thought briefly of telling Grace the joke about how you make a million dollars in shipping, by starting with a billion, but thought the better of it.

"Did Coco say anything else?" Robert replied.

"Yes," Grace said and Robert froze with his back to her. He slowly ran his hand over the air vent on the top of the maroon locker as he waited for his wife's next words. "He said there's still a way you can get everything back on track," she said. "He said there's still a chance to make things right."

Robert exhaled two lungs full of stress and turned around to face Grace. "I knew we could find a way out of this. So what did he say? What do we need to do?"

Grace pulled the leopard-covered iPhone from the back pocket of her Levi's and began to read the notes she'd jotted down during her call with Coco. "He said Rocky DuBois needs to get an MOA signed for a fleet of fifteen high-spec LNG tankers under construction at a shipyard in Korea."

"Excuse me?" Robert said. He was startled to hear the commercial jargon coming out his wife's lovely mouth; it was as if she'd been possessed by the spirit of a shipbroker.

"Coco said that if you can broker a deal for Rocky to get control of these fifteen LNG tankers, then he will keep paying for the time charters and you can finish the IPO," Grace repeated Coco's words. "Does that make sense?" she asked.

"Nothing in the shipping industry makes sense," Robert said, "but that's what makes it so exciting!"

When Robert recalled the conversation he'd had with Prasanth aboard the *Viking Alexandra*, the one about shale gas and the super-cooled ships needed to transport it, Rocky's request did make sense. Once again, the shipping industry had pushed Robert Fairchild to the brink of emotional and financial disaster and then carried him up to a euphoric high – all within the span of a few short minutes; it was like bungee cord jumping.

Robert reached into the pocket of his jacket pocket and pulled out his telephone. He didn't know if he and Coco would be successful in their quest to gain control of the fifteen coveted gas carriers but at least he now had hope for the future – and hope for the future was precisely what kept people interested in the shipping.

"Just what do you think you're doing?" Grace said as she seized his forearm and held it, as if practicing a martial art.

"What does it look like I'm doing?" Robert said. "I am calling Coco."

"Oh, no you're not," Grace said as she yanked the telephone from his hand.

"Give me that thing back, Grace!" Robert barked, searching her eyes for an explanation. "What are you doing?"

"Coco said he won't take your calls anymore," she said.

"What do you mean he won't take my calls?" Robert laughed.

"That was the last thing Coco said," Grace replied. "He said, 'Ja, but little Fairchild is the one who got us into this mess and little Fairchild is the one who get us out,'" Grace said with an adorable attempt at imitating Coco's never-ending Norwegian laugh.

"Really?"

"Yes, and he also said not to bother looking for the answer on the computer. He said "the Google" won't save you on this one."

"Are you being serious?"

"Yup," she inhaled and smiled at her husband. "It looks like you're on your own this time." Grace raised her hand to her forehead and saluted. "It's your ship now, captain."

"Don't be ridiculous, Gracie," Robert laughed, "I don't know the first thing about buying LNG carriers. This is absurd."

"There must be someone who can help you, honey. I mean, you really shouldn't rely on just Coco; what if something were to happen to him some day?"

"But I don't know anyone else in the shipping business, Grace," Robert said. "I'm focused on the money people, not the shipping people," Robert said.

"But you bought your own bulk carrier last year," she said. "Surely you met some shipping people."

Just before Coco had ended the phone call with Grace, the Norwegian had instructed her to make sure Robert went to Greece immediately to meet with Spyrolaki Bouboulinas. Although she didn't understand why, she agreed to use her charms to get him there.

"I guess I could call Spyrolaki," Robert said.

"That's a great idea, honey, but I thought you always told me that shipping deals were best done face-to-face," she reminded him. "That's why you told me you have to go to Europe every other week, remember?"

Grace Fairchild suppressed a giggle when she hugged Robert. If she had learned anything about managing her husband and son over the years it was this: if she wanted either male to do something, *anything*, she had to make sure they believed it was their idea.

"Wait, I have an idea," Robert said. "If the roadshow is on hold then maybe I should go *see* Spyrolaki. I just so happen to have my passport in my jacket pocket," He said and patted the inside pocket of his suit jacket.

"Do you really have your passport?" Grace said and moved toward him with outstretched hands. "You are so smart."

"Maybe I can spend the night at home tonight," Robert said with a wink, "and catch a flight to Athens in the morning."

"You know what I love about you?" she said. "You are a man of action…a man who seizes opportunities when they are presented and doesn't just sit around talking about them."

"I have another great idea," Robert said as he swelled with confidence for the future. "Maybe I could catch the Delta flight to Athens tonight; I think it leaves in ninety minutes. I won't have time to go home and get clothes but…"

"…But Jack Sparrow sure looked good in dirty old clothes in *Pirates of the Caribbean*," Grace finished his sentence.

"I'm on a course for adventure!" Robert said as he took his wife in his arms, dipped her back and kissed her.

Chapter 17

The Century of Gas

Sitting in his office overlooking the Saronic Gulf in the southern suburbs of Athens, a large map of the globe lined with sea routes on the wall beside him, the forbidding Prokopiou remembers how he got into the LNG game. "The idea of transporting liquefied natural gas was droning around in my brain since 2003. I could see that this would be the century of gas. There are plentiful supplies, it is half the price of oil and it is also a quick fix for pollution and CO_2 emissions. This is particularly important for the cities of China and India as they expand, to keep pollution under control," he tells TIME in a deep, gravelly voice.

George Prokopiou, Dynagas

"I am finally going home," Alexandra Meriwether tingled with excitement as she surged past the iconic brass clock in the center of Grand Central Terminal. That she was now six months pregnant was obvious from the shape of her body but not from her brisk stride as she moved fluidly through a clutch of rush-hour commuters.

Alex's plan was simple; after she'd purchased her ticket, she was going to buy a stack of trashy tabloids and board the 8:07 p.m. Metro North train to New Haven, Connecticut. Once she reached New Haven two hours later, she would transfer to the "Clam Digger," a dimly-lit two-car diesel train that rumbled across the sluices and salt marshes of Connecticut's eastern shore. She would probably be the only passenger to get off in the sleepy village of Stony Creek where she would walk down an unlit street until she saw the red and green running lights on her father's Boston Whaler waiting to pick her up take her out to the island.

Alex was unsure how her dad would initially react when he first noticed her swollen body emerge from the foggy darkness, but she wasn't worried about it. She knew any potential misgivings he might have would evaporate when she shared the news that his only child was going to keep the family alive.

She couldn't wait to get home. It was time to go off the grid and there was no better place to do that than her dad's ten-acre mound of granite – thick with cedar trees and alive with nature. It was the perfect place to exchange Chanel suits for flannel pajamas, trade wasabi-crusted sushi tuna for a big bowl of Cheerios and replace the nocturnal noise of garbage trucks and ambulances with the sound of gulls laughing and waves breaking on the rocky shore below her bedroom.

The only problem with her plan was that this trip would be a quick one, Alex thought, as she stepped into the back of the ticket line behind three little boys engaged in a spirited three-way thumb war. She had to be back in New York the following evening to join a client's gastronomical marathon at Per Se, the French restaurant in the Time Warner Center. But once she collected her $8 million bonus in a few months and summarily retired from investment banking, she would move out to the island full time.

To help celebrate all the good news, Alex had entered the train station on Lexington Avenue and passed through Grand Central Market. Slowly strolling through the gauntlet of gourmet grocers, she had tossed a collection of her dad's favorite items into the LL Bean tote bag she'd handed out as a closing gift for the Clear Sky IPO, a badge of honor for investment bankers and corporate lawyers.

By the time she reached the opposite end of the European-style market, the white canvas bag with long leather handles was weighed down with everything from caviar to fresh *cavatelli*, paper-thin *Jamon Serrano* to olive oil so green it was opaque. Earlier in the day, she'd also visited her neighborhood *négociant* in Chelsea and picked up two bottles of her dad's preferred red – 1999 Chateau Petrus Grand Cru from the sun-soaked eastern shores of the Gironde River. At $250 per bottle, the inky Bordeaux was an extravagance that she was happy to shower upon her father before her income dramatically dried up.

"Ma'am, can I help you?" snapped a woman's voice from the opposite side of a glass window striped with brass bars. "Do you want to buy a ticket or not because there are a lot of people behind you who do."

"I'd like to go home," Alex said softly to the woman in the pale blue-striped uniform.

"Join the club," the clerk said as she looked down at her oversized watch and rolled her eyes. "Only six more hours until this girl will have her pajamas on," she sighed.

Alex collected her round-trip ticket from the cool stone countertop, stepped out of line and gazed around the concourse. Ever since she was child visiting the city with her parents, she'd been overwhelmed by the majesty of the train station. It wasn't just the soaring neoclassical architecture or the field of astrological constellations illuminated in gold against the vast canopy of fern green that moved her; it was the human energy. Alex could feel the profound residual energy left behind by the one billion human spirits that had rushed through the three-acre portal since its construction a century earlier.

As Alex moved toward the gate for track 25, she felt her shoulders drop; it was the first sign that the multi-step process of disconnecting from her job, and Manhattan, had begun. It would take time, maybe even weeks or months, to detox from her dependence on overstimulation, but she had to start somewhere.

Just as Alex was walking past the information kiosk in the center of the train station, the place of so many liaisons, the jingle of her BlackBerry stopped her in her tracks like a dog whose electronic collar had beeped. Alex reflexively dropped her bag on the floor, opened the handles and spotted the device sandwiched between a wax paper envelope of prosciutto and a wedge of St. Auger cheese. The name "Pearl" was buzzing on the screen like an angry insect.

Alex took a steadying breath and remembered that absolutely no good could come from answering the incoming call – particularly as she was preparing to visit her father to tell him the biggest news of her life. Enough was enough, she decided as the phone rang again. Her work was done for the day. It was time to put her feet up, read *Us Magazine* from cover to cover and decompress as the train moved toward the delightful darkness of the eastern shore of Connecticut.

Then Alex remembered the money; she thought about the $8 million bonus and considered how much freedom, security and opportunity for advancement such a substantial sum could provide for her unborn child. As she listened to the phone ring again, she recognized that her life wasn't just about her anymore. It was about her child too and that meant there were going to be some things she would do even if she didn't want to – like answering the telephone at that moment.

"To what do I owe the pleasure," Alex cooed as she shot a glance at the departure board and confirmed her fear; the train she was about to board was the last one that connected with a Clam Digger that day. If she missed this train, she wouldn't be able to make it out to the island that night and if she didn't make it out to the island that night, she had no idea when she would be able to.

"They want to do it!" Piper sang out merrily. Alex could tell from his labored breathing and the sound of an ambulance in the background that Piper was walking down a city street.

"That's great; do you mean the Brazilian oil rig guys?" Alex replied with feigned enthusiasm. "I'm glad all that time we spent in that churrascaria in Rio paid off. Of course, I never want to see another piece of steak as long as I live."

"What are you talking about?" Piper snapped.

"Oh," Alex said and paused. Piper had sent her on more fool's errands than she could remember and she was scrambling to recall some of the deal pitches they had made together. "Has Mr. Zuckerberg decided that he wants to buy the…"

"No," he cut in, "which is too bad because I really like that kid," Piper said with fatherly affection. "Remind me to buy some hoodies for myself."

"Oh, I know," Alex said. "The Saudi sovereign wealth fund has finally agreed to ease up on the Sharia Law restrictions and…"

"Guess again," Piper said. "Please follow up on that because I completely forgot about that deal. I love those Arabs. They are just so cool," Piper riffed.

"Are you talking about the Russian timber guys?" Alex asked. She was becoming increasingly frustrated by wasting precious time playing this ridiculous guessing game with Piper as the last train of the evening was preparing to depart. "But I thought Putin insisted that…"

"It's not Putin," Piper whined like the overgrown baby that he was. "I can't believe you don't even know what I am talking about. Don't you take my ideas seriously?"

"Of course I do," she said; dealing with Piper Pearl was good training for motherhood. "It's just that you have *so many* good ideas," Alex said tenderly. She was always careful not to bruise his sensitive ego.

Alex was only tenuously in control of her temper as she watched the minute hand on the brass clock click one step closer to her missing the last train. If she walked down the ramp toward the track, she would drop the call and risk the $8 million. If she stayed where she was, she would miss the last train of the night; either way, Piper would make sure she lost. She was trapped.

"You have to kiss a lot of toads if you want to find a prince," Piper said.

"Who's the toad *du jour*?" Alex asked as she watched a few stragglers rushing to board the train.

"American Refining Corporation," Piper said.

"You can't be serious," Alex laughed as she remembered the disastrous five-minute pitch they'd made in the bar of the Four Seasons Hotel. She was absolutely stunned. Of all of Piper's stream-of-consciousness deal ideas, selling a domestic-American oil and gas producer to the government of China was just about the most ridiculous she'd ever witnessed.

"I am serious, Alex, but the buyer has a substantial condition precedent to the purchase that's going to require some heavy lifting," Piper said slowly.

Alex shook her head back and forth bitterly as she realized there was no way she was going to make her train. "What is it?" Alex challenged. "What is the heavy lifting?"

"Your buddy Mr. Xing said that unless ARC gets its hands on some ships they won't buy the company," Piper said.

Alex didn't yet understand exactly what Piper was talking about but she sure didn't like the idea of ships steaming back toward her life. After that final night she'd spent with Coco on St. Bart's the closest she wanted to come to the insane world of international shipping was her dad's Boston Whaler.

"And how, exactly, does this involve me?" she asked even though she knew the answer.

"You, my darling, are the firm's resident shipping expert," Piper said, "which means you are the one who will be doing the heavy lifting."

"Piper, Allied Bank of England has an entire shipping department in England," Alex protested. "Alistair Gooding has been financing the shipping industry for thirty years! Let's call him."

"Yeah right," Piper scoffed. "Do you really think I'm going to share our M&A fee with the London office?"

"But isn't finding the ships ARC's problem?" Alex asked.

"Actually, it's your problem," Piper said.

"*My* problem?" she asked. "How is that my problem?"

"Because if you don't find the ships for my old roommate, Rocky DuBois, you can kiss your big fat bonus goodbye," Piper said.

"What?" Alex protested despite even though she'd seen Piper motivate many of her colleagues in precisely the same manner over the years. "I earned that money fair and square."

"Alexandra, let's just say the firm's Compensation Committee would not be pleased to learn that you have carnal knowledge of a client – a client I've recently learned is under federal investigation for doing business with some very bad people," Piper said patronizingly. "I suppose that's why you 'forgot' to do a Kroll Report on that big boy before we agreed to underwrite his disaster of a junk bond deal?"

Alex was confused by the sound of Piper's voice; not only had the background noise vanished, but it also sounded as though his words were coming from over her shoulder – not just from the tiny speaker on her BlackBerry. When she instinctively spun around to investigate, Alex was face-to-face with her demanding boss.

"This is real simple, Alex," Piper said as he put his hand on her shoulder. "All you have to do is call your Viking boy toy and ask him to figure out who owns those fifteen LNG boats. What's the big deal?"

"The big deal, Piper, is that I haven't spoken with Coco in months," she said. "I don't even know where in the world he is these days."

"I do," Piper smiled devilishly as he handed her a folded section of the *Financial Times*.

Alex accepted the orange newspaper and studied the large photograph appearing below the fold. The enormous caption read "Energy Kings" and the photo showed Coco on a Swiss ski slope with a posse of familiar faces. His arm was draped around a famous Mexican-American actress who was wearing a revealing Bogner ski suit.

"Why on earth would Coco Jacobsen attend the World Economic Forum?" she asked. A socio-corporate boondoggle like Davos was about the last place in the world that she would have expected to find a free-trading lone wolf entrepreneur like Coco.

"You can ask him when you get there," Piper said.

"What do you mean 'when I *get there*'?" she choked.

When Alex woke up that morning, she'd been planning to spend the evening in front of a crackling fire on her father's island sipping peppermint tea and reading *What to Expect When You're Expecting*, not eating shrink-wrapped cheddar cheese in a business class lounge at JFK while waiting for a flight to Switzerland. She had been hoping to enjoy the security of being in her only true home, not experiencing the anxiety she always felt before leaving on an overseas trip; the fear that she might never come home.

But even as she was shaking her head back and forth, Alex realized it was probably a good idea to make the trip to Davos. As unadvisable as it was for a six-month pregnant woman to travel internationally, she knew it was time to apologize once and for all – and at least let Coco know that he was going to be a daddy before he actually was.

"My secretary's secretary took the liberty of booking you a first-class ticket on the last flight to Zurich tonight," Piper said.

"Okay," she sighed. "I'll go."

"I know you will," he smiled.

Piper Pearl looked down into the canvas bag full of epicurean delights that she'd set on the ground between them. "The TSA will never let you through security with all this dangerous stuff," he said and heaved the bag over his shoulder.

"*Bon appétit*," Alex said as she watched the red lights of the last train to Stony Creek disappear into the tunnel below Park Avenue.

Chapter 18

The Greek Shipowner's Grandmother

Listening to Nikolas Tsakos, one of Greece's leading shipowners, talking about his grandmother reveals much about why his compatriots control such a high proportion of the world's ships. Even as she neared her death aged 98 in 2001, Tsakos recalls, Maria Tsakos continued to believe there was no higher calling for a man than that of a sea captain – a role which in her formative years also equated with being a shipowner. It reflected the value system during her childhood on the Aegean island of Chios in the early 1900s. "When you would introduce her to someone who was a doctor or a lawyer, she would say, 'Oh dear, the poor man couldn't become a captain,'" Tsakos recalls.

Robert Wright, Financial Times, 2008

Robert Fairchild was carried on a river of pedestrian traffic as he moved down the Akti Miaouli searching for the offices of Blue Sea Shipping & Trading – and Spyrolaki Bouboulinas.

As he passed by an unlikely mix of coffee shops and storefronts and crumbling office buildings comingled with modern ones, he experienced an arousing blend of jet lag, hyper-caffeination, déjà vu and anxiety. Despite having just nine days to somehow gain control of the fifteen LNG carriers under construction in Korea, being back in Piraeus, the port of Athens, made him feel surprisingly optimistic.

Nearly a year and a half had passed since he signed the MOA to purchase the elderly bulk carrier *Delos Express* from

Spyrolaki over lunch at the Marine Club of Piraeus – a remarkable clubhouse for Greek shipping tycoons located just one block from where he was standing. That was the day Robert's life had changed forever. It was then that he began living dangerously: eating fried minnows like they were French fries, drinking foreign tap water, smoking Marlboros with abandon and even drinking white wine at lunch.

Robert's excitement wasn't surging purely because the Akti Miaouli was the nerve center of the world's biggest shipowning community – its sprawl of buildings occupied by a multitude of companies ready to provide hundreds of local shipowners with everything from Filipino crews to Liberian ship registrations to Swiss banking services all at a moment's notice. Nor was he stimulated by his presence in a port that had been in service since 517 BC and through which nineteen million people and countless vessels passed each year. No, what moved Robert Fairchild as he strolled down the famed Piraeus street was the novel *Zorba the Greek*.

Spyrolaki had given him a well-worn paperback copy of the magnificent book written by Nicos Kazantzakis in 1946 as a "closing present" and it hadn't taken long for Robert to understand why. The Olympic Airlines flight back to New York had barely crossed the Ionian Sea before Robert recognized his similarity to the protagonist, Basel. He read the novel non-stop during the eleven-hour flight back to New York, hoping for a happy ending that would mirror his own fate.

The book tells the story of a naïve and restless intellectual who takes a break from his schooling in England to move to Crete and learn about the grit of the "real world" by attempting to restart his father's abandoned lignite mine. When a storm prevents him from boarding a ferry in Piraeus, Basel goes to a café on the Akti Miaouli where he meets Alexis Zorba, the *bon vivant* who ends up changing Basel's view of life; he teaches Basel about the importance of being free and bringing passion to whatever he does. In the closing moments, as Basel and

Zorba confront their failure to restart the mine, Zorba teaches Basel to dance the sirtaki and they laugh and sing.

Robert was suddenly alert when he spotted the number "93" etched above the doorway of a modest, 1970s-vintage glass-front building on the Akti Miaouli. Still wearing his outfit from the roadshow because he didn't have anything else to change into, he tightened his necktie, patted down his hair and entered the lobby.

"*Kalispera*," said the attendant who was smoking a cigarette and watching television on a small black and white monitor.

As Robert approached the desk, his attention was immediately drawn to a wall covered by a mosaic of rectangular brass placards each engraved with the name of a different company; there must have been a hundred of them. As his eyes moved across the wall, he was struck by the names appearing on the plaques: Kardamyla Chartering, Chios Shipping, Aegean Carriers, Mastic Management, Bat Man Navigation and Barbie Shipbrokers. Although Robert didn't notice it, the spot where the *Delos Express* placard had resided for twenty years was now occupied by the shiniest, newest, plate of them all – Treasure Island Navigation.

During the transformative eighteen months he had spent in the shipping business, Robert had learned it was customary for shipowners to set up a special purpose corporation (SPC) for almost everything they owned – or did. Motivated by a variety of factors from tax efficiency to insulating one ship from the liabilities of another to enhancing confidentiality, even a reasonably active career in shipowning could produce dozens of offshore companies in nearly as many jurisdictions – the names and locations of which even the shipowners could sometimes not recall as their memories began to flicker and grow dim with age.

"*Kalispera*," Robert replied to the male receptionist through the smoky haze. "I am here to see Spyrolaki Bouboulinas."

"Eight," the man said in English before lighting a fresh cigarette from the glowing embers of another.

When the gray sheet-metal doors opened onto the unoccupied reception area of Blue Sea Shipping & Trading, Robert felt as though he'd been transported into a museum of maritime ephemera. As he stepped out of the elevator on the spongy Oriental rug in the deserted foyer, he felt a warm sea breeze on his face.

Directly in front of him was a highly detailed scale model of a ship called *Blue Dream*, its brass fittings shining and its deck thick with a forest of derrick cranes. Next to the model was a four-foot-high Chadsburn & Sons ship's telegraph that had been removed from a vessel before she had been scrapped. As a person prone to nostalgia, Robert gravitated toward the mahogany paneled wall packed tight with black-and-white photographs.

It didn't take the American long to realize he was looking at a generation of family photos – and that every one of them involved a ship. He couldn't help but smile at the first one he saw. Its corners yellow with age, the overexposed image showed a mostly toothless young Spyrolaki holding a soccer ball over his head and laughing as two jovial African men in white T-shirts hoisted the boy onto their shoulders.

As he leaned in to study the photo more closely, Robert noticed a soccer goal in the background that had been fashioned from giant burlap sacks, one marked "Cocoa" and the other "Coffee." While a seven-year-old Robert had been playing soccer with a bunch of boys on the Great Lawn in Central Park, Spyrolaki had been playing soccer in the hold of a cargo ship in Africa.

In the next photo, Robert saw a smiling little girl waving from her father's lap as he drove a now-antique, right-hand-drive Mercedes Benz over the stern ramp of a ship toward a primitive, desert seaport. Below that photograph was one of a beautiful and vaguely familiar-looking woman cutting the hair of two young children as they sat on stools on the poop deck of a cargo ship surrounded by a vast expanse of glittering sea.

Another photo showed the same elegant woman, presumably Spyrolaki's mother, holding a giant fish in her arms as she stood in a ship's galley surrounded by a team of Filipino seafarers who were triumphantly gripping fishing rods. Next to that one was another photo depicting an improbably young-looking ship captain with mutton chop sideburns wearing an oversized white uniform and pointing to the words "Full Ahead" on a shiny telegraph – a device that looked exactly like the one Robert was leaning against.

During the ten minutes Robert Fairchild spent inspecting the dozens of photographs in the foyer of Blue Sea Shipping & Trading, he had learned an irrefutable truth: Greeks weren't in shipping – shipping was in Greeks. Now it was time to get down to business; it was time to find Spyrolaki and ask him to help Robert find the owner of the LNG ships.

Chapter 19

The Resilience of Greek Shipping

In the beginning of the First World War, the Greeks had 475 steamers and 884 sailing ships of 1,001,116 gross tons. At the end of the War, they had just 205 vessels. After the Second World War, the Greek government gave certain guarantees, so that 100 Liberties and 7 T2 tankers could be given to Greek owners. This was the beginning of the latest re-vitalisation of the Greek merchant marine, and in the 30 or so years that followed, they reached the highest peak yet in their very long maritime history of over 54,000,000 gross tons in 1981, the largest fleet in the world.

Mr. Spyros Polemis
The History of Greek Shipping

"I have excellent news, Dad!" Spyrolaki Bouboulinas proclaimed, his words causing the thirty human beings wheeling-and-dealing on the shipping company's open trading floor to suddenly fall silent.

"Save your breath, tiger," his twin sister laughed. "Daddy's still on the phone in the conference room with the Far East."

While Spyrolaki waited for his father to break free from another one of his endless conference calls, he mopped his forehead with his blue shirt and wandered over to the wall of glass that separated the Blue Sea Shipping & Trading chartering room from the busy harbor below. Pressing his hands up against the glass, he leaned forward and watched a pair of bunker barges fueling a cruise ship a few feet away from the towering white *Minoan Lines* ferry that was easing out of a berth to begin her weekly run into the forest of Aegean islands.

"*E'lla!*" Captain Spyros Bouboulinas boomed a few seconds later as he dramatically pushed through the double doors of the conference room and entered the trading floor. He pulled off his telephone headset like a football player removing his helmet at halftime and tossed it onto the workstation that he shared with his son and daughter.

"Is everything okay, Dad?" Spyrolaki asked his father.

"Yes, yes, we are just working out some of the final details. There are always more details in this business," the stout old man replied.

"Thank you for supporting the project," Spyrolaki said.

"It is my pleasure," the old man replied with a smile on his face and a flash of excitement in his copper eyes. "Now please tell me your news!"

Like many fabulously successful first-generation Greek shipowners Captain Spyros Bouboulinas's happiest moments were not the ones spent lounging at his apartment in Paris or hopping around the Aegean on his yacht or touring his half-million-acre sheep farm in New Zealand by Land Rover. What the old man loved most in life was the thing he was lucky enough to do almost every day – sitting in the midst of his chaotic international shipping company teaching his only two children the multi-generational Greek art of making money with cargo ships.

The Captain, as he was known the world over, was so engaged in the day-to-day business of shipping that he had designed his office so that his own desk was sandwiched between the commercial department (which found cargo for his ships) and the technical department (which was responsible for ensuring that the cargo was loaded, carried and discharged safely and efficiently). Over the course of his long career, the Captain had learned that making money in shipping required an unusual combination of micromanagement alongside expansive thinking – and never, ever being out of the marketplace. That was why he liked having his ships in the spot market, because it put him in the middle of the information flow all the time.

"*Blue Horizon* was just cleared to discharge in Buenos Aires," Spyrolaki replied with pride. "That puts her three days ahead of schedule."

"Bravo!" The Captain smiled. "With China buying all of the soybeans the Argentines can grow, the South American farmers will be happy to have 27,000 tons of good Canadian potash to make more fertilizer," his father said. "Without ships, half the world would starve."

"I think you mean 29,500 tons of good Canadian potash," Spyrolaki corrected him and savored the look of pleasure blossoming on his father's face.

Growing up as the son of a sea captain-turned-shipowner, Spyrolaki knew how much his father appreciated the art and science of getting a little extra cargo safely onto an already loaded ship. "The base cargo is the meat and potatoes in this business," his dad had been telling him since he was in third grade at Athens College, "but the extra stowage…is the gravy."

"Magnificent," the Captain said with a variety of admiration usually reserved for artistic or athletic achievement.

"Let's hope the charterers thank us with some repeat business," he said.

"He's going to need it," Aphrodite laughed under her breath.

"But how did you do it, son?" The old man asked eagerly. "How did you manage the extra stowage?"

"We had a full moon and a very high tide in Vancouver which allowed us the extra draft we needed to load the bonus cargo," Spyrolaki said. "We were lucky."

"Luck is what happens when you pay attention," the Captain said. "But if you had such a full load, how did the ship make good speed?"

"La Nina," Spyrolaki said. "She gave us a following current all the way to Tierra del Fuego which allowed us to make an average of speed fourteen knots from pilot station to pilot station."

"Yes, fine," the Captain laughed, "but then how much extra fuel did she burn?"

"None," his son replied. "We used an average of twenty-two metric tons per day." There were 383 gallons to the metric ton which meant the *Blue Horizon* had burned 8,500 gallons of fuel at a cost of $16,000 each day – which was about the same as the charter rate for the ship.

"In this business, every voyage presents its own set of unique circumstances," the Captain said with a sense of wonder that had not diminished during his decades in the shipping business.

"And who was the captain on that ship?" the old man asked.

"Captain Gyftakis," Spyrolaki said.

"Harris or Nico?" the Captain asked.

"Nico," Spyrolaki said, "the older one."

"Ah, but they are twins, just like you two," the Captain laughed as he looked down at his glamorous daughter as she carefully examined the Disbursement Account associated with a cargo of salt she had recently discharged in Peru.

"They may be twins but Nico is two minutes older and we all know the older twin always runs a tighter ship," Aphrodite said as she fluttered her mascara-caked eyelashes at her "baby" brother.

"Yes, but the younger one takes more chances," Spyrolaki said.

"And makes more mistakes," Aphrodite retaliated.

"But tell me this, son," the Captain asked as he examined the 10 x 15-foot map on the wall next to his private office. "How can the ship possibly be at the discharge port today when she hasn't even cleared Tierra del Fuego?"

"Oh, that," Spyrolaki said sheepishly as he moved toward the map.

"According to the position map she is still off the coast of Santiago which is another three days steaming to BA," he said. The old man used the word "steaming" as many shipowners did; it was one of the many references to the old days when ships were still powered by coal-burning steam engines.

Spyrolaki looked over at the pushpin-speckled map that was supposed to show the approximate location of his family's dry cargo ships at any given moment. Each of the pushpins was festooned with a tiny paper flag that denoted the name of the particular vessel.

There were more than a dozen solitary red flags showing the ships that were making long voyages across the oceans of the world – carrying grain from New Orleans to Rotterdam, briquettes of HBI from Venezuela to Houston, metallurgical coal from Richards Bay, South Africa to Rotterdam for the German auto makers, salt from Mexico to Japan, iron ore from Brazil to China for steelmaking, cement from Asia to West Africa, aluminum ingots from Malaysia to Japan, coffee and cocoa from Africa to America, bauxite from Port Kamsar, Guinea to Texas and dozens of other "minor" commodities that most people had never heard of – but were essential to the products they used every day.

The majority of the Blue Sea fleet, though, was clustered around the chokepoint of global shipping – the antiquated and often congested seaports that strain to handle the endlessly increasing demands for loading and discharging bulk cargo.

"Don't look at me," Spyrolaki laughed and flashed the same mischievous smile that had landed him on the cover of countless Greek tabloids over the years. "It was Aphrodite's job to move the pushpins," he said.

"What a load of bullshit," she sang out rhythmically without looking up.

"I do not like that language young lady," the Captain cautioned his daughter.

Despite their constant bickering, Captain Spyros couldn't help but smile when he looked at his children. They were the accomplishment of which he was most proud. That was why he was feeling uneasy about the changes that were about to occur at Blue Sea Shipping & Trading. Deep down the Captain knew it was time for his traditional Greek shipping to evolve. His fleet of dry cargo ships was approaching the end of their useful lives and his children believed the business needed to adapt if it was going to thrive in the future.

"But daddy," she said and flashed a reef of dazzlingly white teeth. "My language was not bad; I was just referring to Spyrolaki's cargo of fertilizer," she explained. "It really was an impressive load of bullshit he was able to carry. Good work, brother."

"The important thing now is that we are about to have an open ship in Buenos Aires," the Captain said as he pulled out the pushpin representing the vessel *Blue Horizon* and jabbed it into the pockmarked port of Buenos Aires. "So kids, tell me what she's doing next," he demanded.

"Why don't you ask the boy with the golden pajamas," Aphrodite quipped as she carefully drew a ruler-straight red line through a fraudulent $495.50 invoice for waste oil disposal. "I believe he is still looking for a cargo," she tattled.

"What?" the Captain gasped and turned to his son.

"Thanks, Aphrodite," Spyrolaki said.

"Is this true?" the Captain asked with horror. "Are you really still looking for a cargo for a ship that is about to begin discharging? She will be open in a matter of days."

"I told him he should have fixed her last Friday," Aphrodite interjected as she got up from her chair and tugged down on the leopard print skirt. "But Romeo over there decided to go SCUBA diving off Chios with his new girlfriend," she added and began walking away from the trading desk in her high heels. "Now if you will excuse me."

"Where are you going?" the Captain asked his daughter.

"To the elevators," she said. "Uncle Vassilis just called from the lobby. Apparently Mr. Robert Fairchild has finally arrived from New York and I am going to give him a *proper* greeting," she said and curtsied.

Chapter 20

The Volatility of Shipping

After operating expenses, a Panamax bulk carrier trading spot would have earned $1 million in 1986, $3.5 million in 1989, $1.5 million in 1992, $2.5 million in 1995, and $16.5 million in 2007! A new Panamax would have cost $13.5 million in 1986, $30 million in 1990, $19 million in 1999 and $48 million in 2007.

Dr. Martin Stopford, Maritime Economics

Coco Jacobsen gazed out the frost-covered window of the Grand Hotel in Davos, Switzerland. Watching the snow fall softly on a forest of cedar trees made him ache to be back in the mountains of Norway where he always spent Christmas when his parents were still alive.

As the shipping magnate stared through the grid of leaded panes, he was irritated by his malaise. Here he was on the brink of completing the biggest deal of his career with the Greek and preparing to harvest a banner crop of free money on Wall Street, yet for some reason he didn't feel happy.

The better his life became, and the more of his problems he solved, the more apparent it was that he lacked the most fundamentally important thing of all – a family. He didn't have Alexandra Meriwether and he didn't have children. He was all alone; he was nothing but a big boy with a lot of toys.

"Bring me the Aalborg!" Coco cried out to the Swiss barmaid, sounding like a rowdy pirate.

The tanker tycoon knew it may not have been a good idea to drink Aquavit before doing a billion-dollar deal with the Chinese government, but that didn't stop him. The fact was that Coco missed Norway and when Coco missed Norway, he craved drinking aquavit and singing haunting and emotionally-charged Norwegian folk songs. He just wished *Smalahove* – severed sheep's head – was on the menu of the Swiss restaurant to further enhance his visceral experience.

As he waited anxiously for the patriotic elixir to arrive, Coco took out the tiny pink iPod that Alex had given him during the enchanted week they spent together as the *Kon Tiki* plowed through the gray water of the North Atlantic en route from Cap Ferrat to St. Bart's.

Although the miniscule machine held hundreds of Alex's favorite songs, songs she'd once wanted to share with her new lover, Coco had never moved past the first one. He had listened to the same song repeatedly since their final encounter on St. Bart's and rarely was he able to resist singing it out loud; the song had become a battle cry to all he had lost.

Coco stuffed the tiny white buds into his giant brown ears, pressed the play button, cleared his throat and began to wail.

"She's got a smile it seems to me, reminds me of childhood memories, where everything was as fresh as the bright blue sky."

The modern day Viking screeched the Guns N' Roses heavy metal ballad from his overstuffed embroidered couch in the corner of the bar room, his pitch hauntingly high for a man of his girth.

"Oh, oh, oh, sweet child o' mine," he continued.

Coco's emotionally charged vocals immediately captured the attention of a huddle of Silicon Valley plutocrats, a too-casually dressed group of zillionaires for whom the leverage-funded binge of the early twenty-first century had resulted in more than steadily declining income, higher taxes, damaged psyches and upside-down mortgages on their homes.

One bottle of Aalborg led to another as Coco watched an endless parade of politicians, industrialists and financiers come and go from the hotel bar. Most of the ones who hailed from oil-producing nations stopped to thank Coco, offering him drinks and kind words for using his giant ships to miraculously transform their mud into money.

It was just after 11:00 p.m. when the person he had traveled to Davos specifically to see finally arrived. Because the cheery man was as nearly intoxicated as Coco, and never passed up a chance to sing karaoke, it took little effort for the Norwegian to persuade his future charterer to join him in singing an encore of Guns N' Roses.

After the odd couple had completed the rousing song with the back-up support of some gregarious Dutch bankers, Coco finally opened his eyes. When he did, he was stunned by an image that he believed existed only in his imagination: Alexandra Meriwether floating through the doorway of the bar room, the candelabra illuminated above her head giving her the ethereal appearance of St. Lucia.

Chapter 21

A Family Business

*Most if not all Greek shipping companies are family firms.
When people said during the buying spree that everybody and
his brother were ordering ships, it might have been true.*

Fortune Magazine, 1974

Robert Fairchild drew-in a fortifying breath of salty air and
marched toward the doorway that he assumed must lead into
the office area. Just as he began to round the corner leading
into the chartering room, Robert was startled to find himself
nose-to-nose with another person – the same statuesque siren
that had tempted him into putting his life at risk at the Astir
Palace Hotel a year and a half earlier. The mysterious
Aphrodite was so close to him that Robert could smell the
primal musk of leather, tobacco and Channel No. 5 on her
skin.

"Hello, Mr. Robert," Aphrodite greeted him, pronouncing his
name like a growl. "I am feeling so happy to see you again."

The combination of Aphrodite's aroma and the sultry sound of
her voice brought back a tsunami of visceral memories of
Robert's lost night at the Astir Palace Hotel. He remembered
her hair so panther black that it reflected the full moon, eyes so
dark they appeared wet and skin so impossibly tan that she
seemed to disappear into the night. The large golden hoops
hanging from her ears were the same ones she had been
wearing that night in Greece as they stood together high above

the shimmering Saronic Sea – the shiny bling had attracted Robert like a bluefish to a reflective lure.

As Robert continued to stare silently at Aphrodite he remembered the words she had spoken to Spyrolaki when the three of them were standing at the bar next to a swimming pool illuminated by a thousand floating candles. "Will this one buy the ship," she'd said without even looking at Robert. "Or should we offer it to the other American who is sitting in the bar waiting for us." After issuing the challenge, she placed her bejeweled hand on her hip and awaited his reply. Her words and actions had been a Circe's invitation that Robert simply couldn't resist.

"Let's do it!" Robert said spontaneously in the same manner he had agreed to accept the time charters from Rocky DuBois, gamble his son's shares on the IPO and buy the $3 million house on Martha's Vineyard even though he didn't have the cash. "I will buy the *Delos Express!* I will be a shipowner!"

It wasn't until he woke up in a fog the following afternoon, after a long night of celebrating in a beachfront nightclub in Glyfada, that Robert considered the consequences of his impulsive act; he had signed a legally binding document that committed him, personally, to purchase a thirty-five-year-old freighter sight-unseen from the Greek for $4 million.

"What are *you* doing here, Aphrodite?" he asked after snapping out of his flashback. Before he had received her reply, Robert Fairchild felt a pair lips press against his face – he also felt the stubble of a beard.

"Hello, my friend!" Spyrolaki exploded after he had aggressively pushed Aphrodite aside and pecked the startled American once on each cheek. "I always knew you would come back to me," the Greek added in his smoky Greco-British accent. Even though it was a customary greeting among adult men in Greece, Robert Fairchild would never be truly comfortable being kissed by any man that wasn't a blood relative.

"Well I sure didn't," Robert laughed. "In fact, when I finally managed to unload that old bulk carrier you sold me, I prayed I'd never see you again."

"Yes, but this is the shipping business," Spyrolaki said and raised his hands into the air. "Whether you are in London or Oslo or Hong Kong or Piraeus you will see the same people over and over. Shipping is the original global village."

"I know," Robert said sadly as he momentarily thought of the feud between Rocky DuBois and Coco Jacobsen, "for better or worse."

"Did I just hear you ask what Aphrodite is doing at Blue Sea Shipping & Trading?" Spyrolaki said with a smile.

"You sure did," Robert said and waited for the reply. "I am very curious."

"Then allow me tell you. She is not as much as she should!" The Greek slapped his thigh and roared with laughter before wrapping his arm around Aphrodite's neck and dropping her into a tight headlock.

"That doesn't mean much coming from a grown man who had to have his *daddy* find him a grain cargo out of Argentina!" Aphrodite grunted as she jabbed her elbow into Spyrolaki's stomach and broke free from his grip. Then she stomped on his foot with the stiletto heel of her black shoe and he howled with pain.

"At least I'm not the *malaka* whose ship ran out of lube oil in the middle of the Panama Canal last week," Spyrolaki fired back, "just because you wanted to buy them for a few dollars cheaper in Port of Balboa on the other side."

"A shipowner who watches the pennies doesn't need to worry about the dollars," she said sweetly as she fixed her hair. "Besides, you know full-well that the gauges don't work right on those old French built ships."

Before Spyrolaki had the opportunity to retaliate, an old man's voice roared from the opposite side of the wall with such fury that it instantly silenced Spyrolaki and Aphrodite. "Children!" the man bellowed. "Enough is enough!"

Robert dropped his head, opened his eyes wide and said, "Did that man just say '*children*'?"

"Sadly," Spyrolaki said with solemn nod.

"Wait a minute," Robert gasped as he tried to think through what this new information actually meant to him. "Are you telling me you two are *brother and sister*?" He didn't know whether to laugh or cry.

As the American's brown eyes moved between the smirking Spyrolaki and the smiling Aphrodite he answered his own question. All at once, he saw the resemblance in the almond shape of their eyes, the proud slope of their noses and even the contour of their cheekbones. Their hair may have been a different color and each may have spoken with a different accent, since Spyrolaki attended high school at Eton and Aphrodite at *Institut le Rosey* in Switzerland, but Robert had been a fool not to have noticed their many physical similarities when they were together at the Astir Palace.

"Twins," Aphrodite added. "And I'm the elder."

"By *two* lousy minutes," Spyrolaki interjected.

"I can't believe this," Robert said. "Is this what children of Greek shipping magnates do for fun on a Saturday night? You go down to the Astir Palace Hotel and hustle an American hedge fund rube like me into buying an old cargo ship?"

"Only on special occasions," Aphrodite said.

"Haven't you ever heard of going to the movies, or maybe bowling?" Robert asked.

"Can you believe my sister made me pay Barbie Shipbroking a 1% commission just for standing around while I pitched you," Spyrolaki said without looking at Aphrodite. "That was forty thousand dollars."

"Barbie Shipbroking?" Robert asked, recalling the placard he had seen with that name in the lobby of the building.

"Our father gave us our first Liberian companies when we turned ten and he let us name them," Spyrolaki said. "She picked Barbie."

"Oh yeah, well you chose *Bat Man!* And did you just say I did nothing but *stand around?*" Aphrodite laughed with disbelief. "If I hadn't created a sense of urgency, Fairchild would never have bought the ship. He would have said he needed to think about it and woke up in the morning thankful he hadn't made a terrible mistake; there are some risks that can only be undertaken at night. And don't forget, little brother, I'm the person who invented the recipe for 'Shipowners' Punch,'" she laughed.

"I knew Greeks were into shipping, but I didn't know I was up against Apollo and Artemis. In fact, I…"

Before Robert had finished his sentence a barrel-chested old man charged around the corner like a bull. Then he stopped. Robert's first impression of the thick man breathing hard in front of him was that he looked like he'd been cut from stone. He was not finely crafted with precise lines of a Roman sculpture but instead hewn from a boulder with just a few rough chisels. His hairless head appeared almost rectangular beneath his navy blue Greek fisherman's cap, his nose was a thick triangle and his massive ears were like squares that had been appended to the sides of his head. But what struck Robert more than the collection of basic geometric shapes was the brightness of his copper eyes – they flashed like a pair of freshly minted pennies.

"Robert," Spyrolaki cleared his throat and spoke with sudden formality. "I would like to introduce you to our father, Captain Spyros Bouboulinas."

"*Ti kanis*, Robert Fairchild," the old Greek smiled warmly as he raised one of his rough mitts and offered it to Robert.

"It's a pleasure to meet you, Captain Bouboulinas."

When Robert took the old man's hand he was surprised more by thickness of the man's calluses than by the stump of his missing index finger – caught in the winch of a crane loading bananas in the Congo fifty years earlier.

"I am so glad to finally meet you as well, Mr. Fairchild," the old man said softly. "The children have enjoyed your company very much and I am also happy to have this opportunity to congratulate you on the *Lady Grace*. She was a good ship."

Good for you, but not for me, Robert thought.

"Thank you," Robert said.

"We are all so happy that you were successful with her in the end," he smiled. "It is like I tell the children, if you take care of the ship, the ship will take care of you."

"Well I'm glad my folly into shipowning provided some entertainment to you and the *children*," Robert said and then flashed a wry smile at Aphrodite and Spyrolaki. Now that it was over, Robert couldn't help but feel amused that he'd been hustled by the Greek twins. "That was quite a learning experience."

"No it wasn't," the Captain said and shook his giant head back and forth. "Not really."

"Excuse me?" Robert laughed.

"There are few things more dangerous to a career in shipping than early success, Mr. Fairchild. In this sense, I suppose it resembles life," he added thoughtfully.

"There's nothing wrong with beginner's luck," Robert mused.

"In shipping there is," the Captain corrected him again.

"What's that?"

"The child who never falls off the bicycle will become reckless," the Captain said. "The gambler who wins the first time he places a bet will become reckless and the person who makes money on their first shipping investment will also become reckless," the Captain said. His words echoed the ones spoken by Coco Jacobsen at Brown's Hotel in Mayfair three months earlier. "Beginner's luck can be a curse."

"You're probably right," Robert sighed as he thought about the foolish double or nothing bet he'd made with Oliver's 10% of Viking Tankers.

"But don't worry," the Captain said as he laid a fatherly hand on Robert's shoulder. "You are not alone. Shipping is the second-oldest profession in the world and yet for some reason people make the same mistakes."

"So what brings you back to Greece, my friend?" Spyrolaki asked.

"I need your help on a deal," Robert confessed.

He had just nine days to get his hands on the LNG ships and save the IPO of Viking Tankers and he had already wasted enough time on pleasantries. Now it was time to sit in a conference room and start working the telephones to figure out who owned the ships – and what it would take to get them to sell them.

"Oh," Aphrodite said and struggled to hold back her laughter, "are you considering the purchase of another old bulk carrier?"

"No," Robert said, "I am here because I need to buy some very special tankers."

"This is perfect," the Captain said as he began to move toward the elevator. "It is five o'clock which means we can discuss your tankers over a nice lunch."

"You want to go for *lunch*?" Robert asked. "But this is an urgent matter of tremendous importance," Robert stressed.

"So is lunch," the Captain replied with a smile. "We must never forget to enjoy the simple pleasures."

Chapter 22

The Jim Tisch $5 Million Test

*And what is the Jim Tisch $5 Million Test, you may ask?
While on the ship, you look to the front and then you look to the
rear...then take a look to the right and then to the left...then
you scratch your head and say to yourself — "Gee! You mean
you get all this for $5 million?!"*

James Tisch, CEO, Loews Corporation
2006 Commencement Address, Columbia University

Once the foursome had boarded the freshly-washed black
Cadillac Escalade idling on the sidewalk in front of 93 Akti
Miaouli, Robert Fairchild was anxious to get back on the grid.
He hadn't checked his email for more than fifteen minutes and
he was eager to see if there was any update on his fate.

Moments after the vehicle lurched forward and made an
abrupt left-hand turn onto a steep hill called Skouze Street
Robert lowered his head and placed his hands together. While
some observers in the Orthodox country might have assumed
the man in the middle row of the SUV was praying, he was, in
fact, just carefully inspecting his BlackBerry.

Robert Fairchild furtively scanned the forty-three messages
he'd received during his short time in the offices of Blue Sea
Shipping & Trading as he searched for one in particular. He
was anxious to know from Oddleif if ARC had paid the $7
million of freight they owed to Viking Tankers every two
weeks for the time charters (10 ships x 14 days x $50,000 per
ship per day = $7,000,000).

Robert was disappointed the harvest didn't yield a single one from Oddleif. Then he noticed the tiny red star illuminated on his infrequently used text message inbox. He dragged his thumb across the keypad, made a few clicks and spotted a message that had been sent from one of Coco's mobile phones – as always, it was written in the truncated style of a shipping man nostalgic for the bygone days of the telex machine:

"Bad news…Stop…we r in rcpt of termination notice and redelivery instructions from ART…Stop…Nine days left to sign MOA on LNG vssls…Stop…Oliver and I r counting on u…So is Grace. Brgs…Ends."

Just as Robert finished reading the text message he felt his breath leave his lungs – not from Coco's haunting message but because the huge American car began free-falling down Koumoundourou Street. When Robert jolted his head up to see if he should lower his head to prepare for impact he was startled to find that the chaotic urban density of Piraeus had been replaced by a beautiful Greek harbor loaded with boats. When the vehicle reached the bottom of the steep hill, the driver finally tapped the brakes, lit a fresh cigarette and began to creep slowly along the traffic congested harbor-side road.

Robert marveled at the tiny seaside village through the giant tinted windows. The right-hand side of the street was lined with dozens of tavernas that opened onto the sidewalk. To the left of the vehicle were an equal number of waterfront dining rooms served by the restaurants across the street. A man wearing a white apron stood in front of each of the establishments vigorously encouraging passersby to come in for lunch.

"Welcome to Mikrolimano," the Captain said warmly from the front seat of the vehicle as they stopped in front of a restaurant called Jimmy the Fish.

"It is lovely," Robert said. He was disoriented that they had been transported from hot and chaotic urban sprawl to a fragrant harbor in the time it took to check his email.

"Many of the shipowners have moved their offices out of Piraeus so they can be closer to their homes in the north of Athens," the Captain said, "but to me, the magic of shipping will always be here in Piraeus. Did you know this port was used by Themistocoles?"

"Mikrolimano means tiny harbor," Aphrodite whispered into Robert's ear.

Not to be outdone, Spyrolaki chimed in from over Robert's shoulder, "We have three harbors in Piraeus. The third one is called Zea."

When they were just six-years-old the Captain had forbidden Aphrodite and Spyrolaki from sitting in the same row of the car as a result of their incessant roughhousing – and the rule remained in effect almost thirty years later. They weren't even allowed to sit together when they travelled on the family airplane.

"It is absolutely stunning," Robert marveled.

When Robert stepped down from car, he felt instantly refreshed. The sky was deep blue and cloudless and the light breeze blowing off the water lowered the heat he'd experienced on the Akti Miaouli to an energizing seventy degrees. The temperature and lack of humidity reminded him of his favorite time of year – the first warm spring days in New England – which reminded him of how far he was from his family and his home.

There were captivating things to look at in every direction; multi-colored fishing boats bobbing on moorings, hulking white mega-yachts tied up to the stone bulkheads on the opposite side of the harbor and loads of stylish and happy-looking young Greeks sunning themselves in the outdoor cafés and restaurants. It was a workday in a European capital city, yet the harbor of Mikrolimano felt like a resort town in full swing. It was a far cry from buying food wrapped in plastic and eating it at a desk in the company of a computer screen, a

BlackBerry and a telephone as he had done for so many years in New York. The Southern Mediterranean may not have the economic strength of America or Northern Europe, but there was a lot to learn from its way of life.

Once they had climbed down from the car, Spyrolaki, Aphrodite and Robert trailed the patriarch like obedient pets as they walked across the street onto the pebble-covered patio of the restaurant. As if scripted, they all marched across the uninhabited dining room and directly to the large round table positioned next to the harbor. Only later would Robert learn that the table was the equivalent of the "Owner's Cabin" on a ship; always reserved for the exclusive use of the Captain whether or not he happened to be.

A few feet away from the table, the swell of the emerald green Aegean Sea gently lifted and dropped a floating dock on which a dozen fishing skiffs of various colors and sizes were made fast. After the waiter delivered a basket of warm bread, Spyrolaki began lobbing pieces into the water creating a frenzy of fish boiling on the surface.

"As our guest, we would like you to select the fish, Mr. Fairchild," the Captain said as he gestured with his damaged hand toward the fish that were battling for bread next to an outboard motor.

"Um, what?" Robert asked.

"What my father is saying," Aphrodite explained, "is that he would like you to pick the fish that we will eat today."

"This is an important tradition at a Greek taverna such as Jimmy the Fish," Spyrolaki added. "First you must select the fish that you would like to eat and then the chef will catch it and cook it for us."

"Not today," the Captain said solemnly as he wagged the stump of his finger.

"Oh," Robert said hopefully, "are we having Gyros instead?"

"No, today is a special occasion because you have come a long way to be with us. Therefore, today we will have the fish Sashimi style," the Captain said and smiled. "We will just slaughter the beast right here at the table," he said and lifted a butter knife from the table. "And we will eat it raw."

"I'm allergic to fish," Robert blurted out.

After what seemed like an interminable silence the Captain raised his arms into the air and proclaimed, "Bravo!" Then each member of the Bouboulinas family exchanged congratulations for their successful gag; it was their signature joke when entertaining visitors from aboard. So far only their Japanese visitors had embraced the idea. "Come with me, Mr. Fairchild."

Once again trailing the Captain, the "children" retraced their steps under the canopy of the outdoor restaurant, ambled across the narrow street and stepped into the cool concrete building where the restaurant's kitchen was located. As they entered the building, a portly chef burst through a set of doors carrying a sickle-shaped knife and wearing a white apron splattered with blood.

"Kapetanie!" the chef sang out, brandishing the stainless steel scalpel high in the air as he approached them. After the chef had kissed Bouboulinas family on each cheek, Robert quickly backed away.

"*Ti kanis,*" the Captain said with a warm smile.

"Come with me," the chef said in clear English and ushered them toward the door at the back of the restaurant from which he had emerged. "We have some very nice things for you today."

Robert followed the Greeks into the frigid chamber where hundreds of fish, lobsters, crabs and a variety of more exotic and less identifiable species of seafood were embalmed on drawers packed with shaved ice. "Tsk, tsk, tsk," the chef said to Robert when he caught him watching a fish that was twitching on a stainless steel tray.

He pulled the American by the sleeve toward a rack on which several large, coral-colored fish were laying in varying states of death and dying. After a rapid fire exchange of Greek the Captain firmly pushed his index finger into the eyeball of one particular fish and then nodded. The Greek shipping magnate lowered his nose until it was almost touching the fish, closed his eyes and inhaled as deeply as a man preparing for an underwater swim.

"She's the one," the Captain said dramatically as though choosing a life partner and not ordering lunch.

"Always the red snapper for you," the chef marveled.

When they arrived back at their seaside table, the Captain folded his nine-and-a-half fingers together. "So," he sighed, "please tell us a little bit about the tankers that you need our help with."

As the Captain waited for Robert's reply, Spyrolaki poured straw-yellow white wine from a carafe into four tiny stem-less glasses that reminded Robert of the recycled jelly jars he drank milk from as a kid.

"First of all, I need to know if you are comfortable being taken over the wall?" Robert asked.

"I know Aphrodite is," Spyrolaki laughed just seconds before his sister kicked him in the shin with her sharp-toed shoe.

"Over what wall?" the Captain said, working hard to ignore the rancor of his twins. "This may be a problem because my knees are not so good anymore."

"Don't worry," Robert smiled. "That just means that everything I'm about to tell you is confidential because it relates to the public offering of securities regulated by the United States government," Robert said.

"I may be just a simple shipowner from a small island in north Aegean Sea, but I do know how to keep a secret," the Captain said and looked at his children. "Isn't that right, children?"

"Yes, Captain," Spyrolaki and Aphrodite said with one compliant voice.

"After I sold the *Lady Grace*," Robert said, "I went to work for a company called Viking Tankers. We are in the process of raising $500 million through an IPO in America."

"I am very sorry to interrupt your very nice speech, Mr. Fairchild," the Captain said after taking a tiny taste of the wine, "but can you tell me what "IPO" stands for? I very much hope it doesn't stand for International Pollution Organization. There is no nation more careful or respectful of the sea than Greeks, but enough is enough with all these different regulations."

"IPO stands for Initial Public Offering," Robert explained slowly. "It means that Viking Tankers is selling some of its shares to investors in America and those shares will become freely traded on the New York Stock Exchange."

"Yes baba, this is what the Tsakos Family has done so very successfully. Will you be the CEO, Robert?" Aphrodite asked with a flash of excitement in her anthracite eyes.

"Actually, I already am," he said. He decided not to mention the detail that he would be demoted to unlicensed third-mate on the *Viking Alexandra* if he didn't get control of the fifteen LNG carriers, somehow convince Coco to subordinate his shares to Luther Livingston's and successfully conclude the IPO at a valuation of 200% of asset value.

"I see," the Captain said. "And who owns this Viking Tankers? Is that a Swedish company? They were Vikings, right?"

"Bite your tongue," Robert laughed. "It is owned by Coco Jacobsen and he is very much a Norwegian."

"I am sorry to say that I have never heard of that lady," the Captain said. "However, I wish to say that I think it is wonderful that we have more women shipowners like Ms. Jacobsen these days."

"Dad," Spyrolaki laughed, "Coco is a man and he's one of the biggest tanker owners in the world."

"Okay, but if Ms. Jacobsen is such a big fish and you are her big CEO then how can a small Greek family shipping company like ours help you?" the Captain asked. "As you know, we are just simple shipowners from a small island in the…"

"I know," Robert cut in, "a small island I the north Aegean Sea. I get it."

"We are like the dump truck drivers of the oceans," the Captain added.

"It's Mr. Jacobsen," Robert stressed, "and while I understand that you are just simple shipowners you are also my only hope."

"Really?"

"I'm afraid so," Robert sighed. "Let me tell you what's going on here; the only reason the American investors will buy shares in Viking Tankers is because ten of our ships are on five-year time charters to a subsidiary of a large corporation called American Refining Corporation at very good rates."

"Very good rates for whom?" the Captain asked; it was yet another haunting echo of Coco's sage words at Brown's Hotel.

"Very good rates for us, of course," Robert said.

"Ah, so then your customer is suffering because of these very bad rates for them," the Captain said using the same frustratingly simple logic that Coco used when faced with complex fact patterns.

"The point is, sir, that our time charters to ARC generate the free cash flow we need to pay our American investors a 14% dividend," Robert said.

"I know I never had the opportunity to attend a fancy university as you three have," the Captain said, "but I have never understood why shipping companies pay dividends that are so high."

"Because we can," Robert laughed.

"Not for long," he said.

"What's that supposed to mean?" Robert asked.

"Mr. Fairchild, removing the cash from a shipping company is like removing the blood from a body – you can't take too much too quickly – and you always have to be ready to put it back in if necessary," he said.

"We just need the dividend to be high when we first do the IPO. After that, our share price will go up and down as investors re-price the risk of our company relative to what's happening in a broader context. In other words, the shares become like a hot potato."

The Captain's copper eyes lit up as he finally appeared interested in what Robert Fairchild had to say. "Potatoes? Would you like some potatoes, Mr. Fairchild?" The Captain asked. He just loved it when his children and their friends were hungry. He immediately began waving his hand in the air to alert the waiter that he needed a plate of *pommes frites* pronto. "I think that is an excellent idea!"

"It's just a figure of speech, baba," Aphrodite whispered to her dad.

"Oh," the Captain sagged as he lowered his arm. "Now let me guess what happens next. The market has dropped and the charterer wants to get out of the deal."

"Sort of," Robert said and took a sip of wine.

"Shipping, like history, repeats itself," the Captain said, "but each time it's dangerously a little different."

"I need a cigarette," Robert said to Spyrolaki. "Can I bum one?"

The Captain shot a searing stare at his only son. "But this is impossible! My little Spyros does not smoke cigarettes. Isn't that right, Spyrolaki?"

"Of course not, Captain," Spyrolaki said sheepishly and slipped his nicotine-stained fingers under the table.

"Instead of a cigarette, Mr. Fairchild, may I offer you some advice?" the Captain said.

"Sure."

"Time charters may be acceptable for part-timers who would otherwise get slaughtered like lambs in the spot market, but they are often a losing bet for a shipowner who is in the market place every day," the Captain said.

"But don't time charters offer security?" Robert asked.

"Unfortunately, the higher the time charter rate the less likely the time charterer is to pay," he said. "A shipowner who does not wish to be in the market should not be in the market."

"But I just don't understand how charterers can get away with defaulting on contracts whenever the market drops," Robert said. "That doesn't happen in any other industry unless the company files for bankruptcy."

"Shipping is a mysterious business," the Captain reflected. "Anyway, what does this American oil company want from you now?" the old man asked again. "Do they want a lower rate on your tankers?"

"Actually," Robert said, "they want more ships."

"More ships," the Captain laughed. "That's an unusual request."

"Different ships," Robert clarified. "ARC is demanding that we gain control of fifteen highly specialized LNG carriers that are presently under construction at Regal Shipyard in Korea," Robert said.

The Captain whistled. "That is a very good shipyard. Along with Samsung and Hyundai Mipo, Regal is one of the finest in Korea – which means it's one of the finest in the world."

"Robert, why don't they just call a good sale and purchase broker?" Aphrodite asked. "We have a cousin in America named Christolakodakis who would be more than happy to help you."

"Because they want to keep it quiet," Robert said.

"I can understand that," the Captain replied.

"I should warn you, Robert," Spyrolaki chimed in without looking at his dad. "I do not think my father knows what an LNG carrier is never mind how to go about buying fifteen newbuildings. He is from the old school of Liberty Ships and T2 Tankers."

"Thank you for your confidence," the Captain said modestly and patted his son's hand. Then the old man reached for the iPad that Spyrolaki had placed on the brightly varnished table.

"Mr. Fairchild, it really doesn't matter what kind of ships they are or where they are being built," the Captain said as he began swiping the screen with the stub of his severed index finger. "The first thing you need to do is figure out who owns those ships and the best way to do that is with this," the Captain said and pushed Spyrolaki's iPad across the table toward his guest. "In the old days it would have taken six months and a harrowing transatlantic journey to get this information, but now it appears on the screen like magic."

"What?" Robert gasped.

"Is something the matter, Robert?" Aphrodite asked.

Robert was so disgusted with himself that he couldn't even look down at the screen. "I flew all the way from New York City to find out who owns these ships and now you are pointing me to a website!"

"Of course," the Captain said.

"But I thought this industry was all about secret information and personal relationships," Robert said.

"It is about those things, but *Fairplay Solutions* is a database that catalogues the owner of almost every ship that is currently under construction," Spyrolaki said. "This is not the answer to your problems but it can be a very useful place to start."

Spyrolaki leaned over to see what was on the screen but Aphrodite quickly pulled it away before he could see it.

"Voila!" she said. "Here are the ships you are looking for – 174,000-cubic meter LNG carriers currently under construction at Regal Shipyard. There are fifteen sister ships and they will start to deliver next month," she said and pointed with a slender finger.

"Great Dane Shipping in Copenhagen, Denmark," Robert said with excitement. "Is that the owner?"

"Yes," she confirmed.

"Do you know them?"

"Don't you?" Spyrolaki laughed.

"Great Dane is one of biggest and most successful shipping companies in the world," the Captain said.

"And they didn't get that way by being stupid or generous," Aphrodite added. "I once spent $176,000 and two years arbitrating a claim over some bad chain worth $14,000."

"If you are trying to buy ships from those guys I think you have your work cut out for you, shipping man," Spyrolaki said. "They are neither willing buyers nor willing sellers."

"Mr. Fairchild, it appears that you will be leaving us now," the Captain said and whistled with his fingers to rouse the driver who was taking a nap in the driver's seat of the Escalade.

"You want me to leave now?" Robert asked just as the waiter approached them carrying a salad of tomatoes and feta and a plate piled high with fried minnows. Robert was eager to meet the owner of the vessels in Denmark, but he was also starving.

"Business before pleasure," the Captain said. "There is only one more flight to Copenhagen today, it goes through Zurich and leaves Venizelos in one hour. Don't worry, there will be plenty of time to eat, drink and be merry once you've gotten your hands on those ships."

"That's right," Spyrolaki laughed. "I bet the world will feel like a party once you've gotten control of those vessels."

Robert rose to his feet, said goodbye and began walking toward the car. When he was about halfway across the dining room, he felt a hand on his shoulder. He turned around and saw Aphrodite. "Listen to me, Robert, and listen carefully," she said.

"What is it?" Robert replied.

"Always remember that in the business of shipping, when you are ready to give up you must hang on a little longer," she said. "If you can do that, you will almost always be okay."

Chapter 23

John Pierpont Morgan

In 1902, J.P. Morgan & Co. financed the formation of International Mercantile Marine Company, an Atlantic shipping combine which absorbed several major American and British lines – and owned the RMS Titanic. Morgan hoped to dominate transatlantic shipping through interlocking directorates and contractual arrangements with the railroads, but that proved impossible... Analysis of financial records shows that IMM was overleveraged and suffered from inadequate cash flow that caused it to default on bond interest payments.

Robert Fairchild spent his first seven hours in Copenhagen, Denmark sweating beneath a puffy white duvet in the Karen Blixen suite at the posh Hotel D'Angleterre. The Captain's long-serving personal assistant had made the last-minute hotel reservation while Robert was en route to Denmark via Zurich and the opulent accommodations were apparently the only ones available on such short notice.

Although Robert had been granted the "Seaman's Book" discount rate (an age-old concession still offered to shipping companies when relocating their crews), the nightly rate was still 6,000 kroner, which equated to about $1,100. It was a princely sum for a bad night's sleep and Robert knew Coco Jacobsen would surely reject it when he submitted his expense report by way of the embarrassing *vive voce* ritual at the end of the month.

Sitting like a supplicant at Coco's desk aboard the *Kon Tiki*, Robert was forced to defend every item for which he was seeking reimbursement from his boss. His chances of recouping more than $1,000 for a single night's stay in a hotel room were slim. "Ja, but Fairchild," Coco would groan as he jammed another load of Snus into his upper gum, "this fancy hotel room of yours costs more than the daily time charter rate on our VLCCs some days."

When Robert finally climbed out of the enormous Danish bed at 11:00 a.m. he was in that state of disorientation that comes after the first hard sleep on a different continent. Two cups of instant coffee and an ice-cold shower later he had finally worked up the courage to check his email and text messages. Yet again there was just one of substance, a text message, and it was highlighted with a red, sad-faced emoticon:

8 Days Left… Love, Coco. Ends.

With his anxiety now awake, Robert Fairchild pulled his wrinkled blue Brooks Brothers shirt over his head and stepped into the now shabby looking grey-flannel suit he had been wearing since he left the Delano Hotel three days earlier.

Although he was certainly not dressed for success, Robert was nonetheless feeling confident about his game plan while in Denmark; he was going to locate the offices of the Great Dane, pay an unannounced visit to its CEO and major shareholder, Mr. Cornelius Juhl, and make the man an offer on his fleet of fifteen LNG carriers that he simply couldn't refuse.

Rocky DuBois had apparently demanded that Viking Tankers gain control of the gas tankers, but he'd said nothing about the price or terms so Robert was going to use the *carte blanche*. If he had learned anything about shipping during his eighteen months in the business, it was this: ships were commodities that could be easily replaced with an equivalent one. That meant every ship was always for sale at the right price.

Robert Fairchild was feeling so optimistic about his strategy to acquire the vessels that he had already checked out of his fancy accommodations and booked himself on the SAS flight from Copenhagen to Newark that evening. There had been a flight to JFK, the airport of choice for residents of the Upper East Side like him, but that one required a stopover in Oslo and Robert didn't want to chance it. Coco had told him about Wade Waters' "tax management" strategy and Robert was deathly afraid that he might bump into Coco and his posse of professionals holding court in the airport's Duty Free Zone.

Between Coco, Magnus Magnusen, Peder Hansen, Alistair Gooding, Wade Waters and the rest of the professionals who had something riding on the success of the Viking Tankers IPO, Robert would fear for his personal safety until the listing was closed. If Robert wasn't successful in his quest, he figured he might have to go into hiding in a rented cottage on Martha's Vineyard, change his name and hope the shipping mafia didn't track him down to collect the $1 million of bills he'd racked-up preparing for the deal.

When he finally walked outside his hotel, Robert was greeted by yet another beautiful day in Europe. But like anyone with a life-altering transaction hanging in the balance, he had no interest what-so-ever in seeing the sights of Copenhagen. All he really wanted to do was offer Mr. Juhl whatever it took for him to sign the MOA, fax the document to Coco and hope he could revive the slumbering roadshow before it was too late.

Although Robert didn't plan to take any interest in Copenhagen, when he stepped onto Kongens Nytorv that morning and made a right onto Strøget, the world's longest pedestrian walkway, he couldn't help himself; he was stunned by the clear autumn sky, the invigorating ocean breeze and the prairie of salt water surrounding the city. Robert wandered aimlessly as he took-in the sights and sounds of the lovely city.

After half an hour on foot, he came to the conclusion that Copenhagen was a picture of perfection. There were children riding to school on their father's shoulders, well-dressed women briskly walking the cobblestone streets and an orderly fleet of cyclists hauling everything from babies to groceries as they moved past the neat and brightly colored buildings lining a canal packed with boats. Copenhagen's distinction as the capital of the "happiest" country in the world was easy to understand.

But as always, Robert's reverie was tempered because Grace was not with him. He'd had the privilege of traveling to so many interesting places around the world thanks to his chance encounter with the shipping industry, but yet he could never fully enjoy them – not the cafés and restaurants, not the museums and not the hotels – without his beautiful wife. In fact, the beauty of the city only made him feel farther from home. He knew it was time to finish the crazy deal he'd started in Brown's Hotel in London that snowy night all those months ago – and go home.

As he formed his plan while in the throes of insomnia the previous night, Robert figured it would take at least an hour to find the headquarters of Great Dane Shipping. The Greek had told him that the company was large, but since it was a shipping company its office was probably tucked away in some back alley near an industrial seaport. So it was with considerable surprise that Robert suddenly found himself standing in front of the headquarters of Great Dane Shipping, a structure as big as the Pentagon that was prominently positioned in the center of town.

Fortified by two lungs full of clean Baltic air and a double macchiato from a café called Baresso, Robert confidently strode into the lobby of one of the world's biggest shipping companies. It was time to play *Let's Make a Deal* for the fifteen LNG carriers.

Robert quickly learned that the shipping centers of Piraeus and Copenhagen were distinctly different environments. While Piraeus was gritty and chaotic, Copenhagen was spotless and orderly. And while the offices of Blue Sea Shipping & Trading were rich with ephemera and nostalgia, crammed with family photos and ship models, the offices of Great Dane Shipping were modern and austere. The crystal-clear plate-glass windows and pale hardwood floors made the place feel more like an Ikea showroom than a one-hundred-year-old shipping company. The only evidence of shipping, in fact, was the pair of modest sized ship models in the center of the lobby.

"*Godmorgen!*" Robert sang out manically after he'd passed through the freshly squeegeed plate glass doors and approached the receptionist. She was a well-maintained woman in her fifties wearing a plaid skirt and crisp white blouse. Her blonde-gray hair was pinned back neatly with a pair of bobby pins.

"Good morning," she replied skeptically, her perfect English carrying the hint of her British education. "How may I help you?"

"My name is Robert Fairchild and I am from New York City."

"That's nice," she said.

"I am here to see Mr. Cornelius Juhl," Robert said.

"Do you have an appointment?" the woman asked after stifling a laugh at the mere suggestion of having a walk-in meeting with one of Denmark's wealthiest men.

"No," Robert said, "but I *do* have something very important to discuss with him."

"I'm sure you do," she said gently as she slowly opened a huge leather datebook. She was buying time as she considered whether or not to press the red *panik* button beneath her desk to alert the *politiet* about the delusional American dressed like a vagrant who was loitering in Great Dane's offices.

"I'm here to buy some of his ships," Robert offered, "the big ones." When the woman appeared unimpressed, Robert added in an unintentionally menacing voice, "And I'm not going home without them." That was when her slender finger moved toward the red button.

During the thirty-five years that Ida Bonnesen had been manning the reception desk at Great Dane Shipping she had seen it all; Greeks looking to buy ships, Koreans looking to sell ships, French looking to charter big, new ships, Swiss-Italians looking to charter small, older ships. She'd met Chinese looking to build ships and more American investment bankers offering money than she could remember. There had been thousands of hopeful visitors to the understated global headquarters of Great Dane Shipping but Ida could not recall a single one showing up in country with a wrinkled suit and no appointment.

"Well that certainly sounds exciting," she said absently as she pushed down on the red button. Before she set off the alarm, she took a moment to adjust her hair knowing that the drama that was about to unfold would likely be featured on the evening news – and she wanted to look her best.

But just as Ida prepared to unleash a silent distress beacon summoning no less than one hundred police officers who would come to the rescue of Mr. Cornelius Juhl, the pale pink steel door next to the bank of elevators on the opposite side of the lobby slowly creaked open. An instant later, the bushy-haired head of an old man popped out like a puppet appearing on stage. His body followed close behind clad in a disarming outfit of blue corduroy trousers, brown suede Hush Puppies with Velcro straps and a red cardigan sweater over a blue button-down shirt. The understated Danish magnate looked more like Mr. Rogers than Mr. Onassis.

"Ahoy there, matey!" he sang out in a strained but merry voice to the utter shock of Ida Bonnesen who slowly removed her finger from the alarm button.

"Ooh, hello Mr. Juhl," she cooed.

"Ida, my darling, good morning!" he said smoothly to the star-struck receptionist. "You are looking as fresh and lovely as this beautiful autumn day."

"Why thank you, Mr. Juhl," she blushed at the silver-tongued octogenarian.

"The pleasure is mine, Ida, always mine." he said.

"Mr. Juhl, this gentleman's name is…"

"Mr. Fairchild," Mr. Juhl finished Ida's sentence. "Mr. Robert Harrison Fairchild, Harvard University class of 1994. I know all about him. Please come with me," the old man said to Robert and with a wave of his hand summoned him through the pale pink door from which he had magically emerged two minutes earlier.

For the second time in twenty-four hours, Robert Fairchild found himself trailing in the wake of a living shipping legend. He had to work hard to keep up with Mr. Juhl who was skipping every other step as he bounded briskly up the five flights of stairs to his penthouse office.

Robert's breathing was labored by the time he followed Mr. Juhl into his office. It was a spare room furnished only with a small wooden desk, a tan modern couch, a pink rug decorated with a white emblem and a wall of windows facing a beautiful Sound known as Øresund. On the side of the office opposite the sea was a massive expanse of white wall that was completely bare but for a small black-and-white photograph hanging smack in the center. Robert was drawn toward it.

"Did you know that I have owned and operated more than five hundred vessels in my lifetime," Mr. Juhl said, "but the one in that photograph is the one of which I am most proud – it is also the smallest."

"What is it? I mean…" Robert corrected himself as he moved closer to the grainy image, "I mean who is *she?*"

Not until Robert was a few feet away did he realize the photograph had been clipped from an old, brittle newspaper and lacquered onto a piece of wood that appeared to have been a strake of a vessel.

"Ships have been heroes for thousands of years, Mr. Fairchild, and that one is no exception. On October 1st, 1943 a small group of Danish shipowners were informed that Nazi forces were coming to collect the 7,000 Jewish people residing in Denmark at the time," Mr. Juhl said as he joined Robert staring at the photograph. "That ship, and few others like them, carried almost every one of those people to safety in Sweden."

"Wow," Robert said and lowered his head respectfully.

"Helping save those people will always be my proudest moment and that little vessel will always be my favorite," he said and then dramatically fell onto to the long, modern crème-colored couch.

"Ships have been helping people since the beginning of time," Robert said. "Ships have created opportunity, provided freedom from persecution and carried food and goods from faraway lands to the people who need them; even Noah used a ship."

"What you say is very wise, Mr. Fairchild," Mr. Juhl smiled. "And there is my second favorite vessel," the man said, pointing toward the harbor. "That is my yacht."

Robert looked through the panorama of freshly washed floor-to-ceiling windows and scanned the beautiful body of water spread out before him but he was unable to locate a yacht. In fact, the only vessel he could see was a small boat, no more than thirty-five feet in length, tethered to a large blue and white mooring ball directly in front of the office.

"I don't see a yacht," Robert said after unsuccessfully searching for a vessel akin to Coco's 200-foot Feadship, a migratory beast that moved between St. Bart's and Cap Ferrat and carried a larger crew than a VLCC. "The only thing I see is that boat over there."

"Yes, and she is my little baby," he said as he looked admiringly at the small boat. "Did you know that vessel costs me just 3,000 kroner per year to keep up? That's less than half of what some people spend on a fancy hotel room for a single night," he said, winking at Robert. "Can you believe that?"

"That's a very good value," Robert said, deliberately invoking the one word that every successful shipowner, large or small, lived by.

"Ida was about to call the police on you," Mr. Juhl laughed as his faded blue eyes twinkled.

"Really?"

"Oh yes," he said and then blew his nose into a pink and white striped handkerchief. "She actually had her finger on the panic button."

"She did look a little uncomfortable," Robert said.

"It's okay," he said. "The event provided her with some excitement."

"So why did you take the meeting with me?" Robert asked.

"Because I have a security camera above Ida's desk and when I heard you say your name I Googled you," he said and added slyly, "I am very good with the Google."

"What did you read about me on Google that you found so compelling?" Robert laughed. "That I was captain of the chess club at Harvard?"

"As a matter of fact, that did interest me because I am also a competitive chess player," he said and pointed to a small table on the opposite side of the room with a hand-painted chess board on its surface. "But you did not come here to play chess, am I correct?" Mr. Juhl asked.

"You are correct," Robert said.

"The thing I found even more interesting than your chess ability is that you are apparently the financial mastermind behind *Coco Jacobsen*." The old man spoke the Norwegian's name as though it were a curse. "I assume you are the brains behind Coco's brawn."

"Oh," Robert smiled, "do you know Coco?" Robert was flattered to be referred to as a mastermind and not just a bagman CEO.

"Let me tell you something, Mr. Fairchild; anyone in the shipping industry who tells you they don't know Coco Jacobsen isn't telling you the truth," he said. "That man is in every market, all the time."

"I'll keep that in mind," Robert said.

"As a matter of fact, Mr. Jacobsen is the main reason we have remained a private family-owned shipping company at the expense of some growth and risk-sharing with outside investors," he added.

"And why is that?" Robert asked.

"Because my father built this company from scratch, starting with nothing but a leaky rowboat and a pair of broken oars," he said. "This is our family legacy and I never wanted it to get caught in the middle of one of Mr. Jacobsen's violent feeding frenzies. I assume you know what he did to Knut Shipping?" the old man asked.

"I have seen the cufflinks," Robert replied respectfully.

"And I assume you know why Coco launched his hostile takeover of Knut Shipping?"

"Probably to get even with them for turning him into the Norwegian taxing authority," Robert said.

"No."

"Maybe because Coco believed the company's assets were undervalued relative to other investments," Robert said.

"Some people believe it was because the heir to Knut Shipping, Knut the Fifth, teased Coco because his parents couldn't afford to buy him a decent pair of boots when they were schoolboys in Bergen; Coco wore sneakers all winter. Apparently that's why Coco dropped out of school and went to work for Hilmar Reksten. He wanted to learn the shipping business so he could beat Knut at his own game."

"That's crazy," Robert laughed.

"Other people believe your employer is a modern-day Viking who is now attacking companies in the countries that have attacked Norway over the last 2,000 years – just to get even."

"That seems a bit far-fetched," Robert said.

"Does it?" Mr. Juhl said. "Did you know that Coco Jacobsen is singlehandedly responsible for the extinction of Swedish tanker shipping? That is a fate that I do not want the Danish people to suffer."

"But Mr. Juhl, if you think Coco is your sworn enemy and you think I am his mastermind, then why did you invite me up to your office?" Robert asked. "Why didn't you allow Ida to press the panic button and send me to a Danish jail for the rest of my life?"

"Because I have grown more curious and less disciplined in my old age, Mr. Fairchild," he said. "And now I am interested in knowing exactly how you and Coco are planning to victimize an old man like me."

"I don't want to victimize you," Robert said. "I want to make you rich."

"I am already rich," he said plainly. "My family's main objective now is just to keep things the same. That is the guiding principle behind every decision we make: the preservation of the status quo."

That sounds exciting, Robert thought.

"Mr. Juhl, you've been direct with me so I'll be direct with you," Robert said. "I am here to make you an all-cash offer on the fleet of fifteen LNG carriers you are currently building at Regal Shipyard in Korea." As Robert spoke, he watched the old man's eyes widen theatrically.

"You do know those are brand new vessels," Mr. Juhl said.

"Yes," Robert confirmed.

"But I should think these would be the last vessels in the world a man like Coco would want to buy," Mr. Juhl said.

"Why?"

"Because I thought he could only afford the old vessels like the ones he bought from me."

"Which vessels were those?" Robert asked.

"A few years ago I placed an order with my old friends at Regal Shipbuilding to build twenty new VLCCs to replace my entire fleet," he said. "Every time a new ship was delivered I decided to sell an older ship to a scrapyard in Bangladesh. The older ships were not at the end of their life, and could have been sold for more money for further trading, but I sold them to demolition in order to keep the supply and demand of ships in balance."

"That sounds rational," Robert said.

"Yes, I thought so, too," he said, "but then a funny thing happened. After I thought I'd sold the first twelve vessels to the scrapyard I noticed that the ships I thought were dead kept coming back and offering very low rates for cargoes in the Arabian Gulf."

"That's surprising," Robert said.

"So is Mr. Jacobsen," he said. "As it turned out the scrapyard in Bangladesh wasn't a scrapyard at all," he said. "It was Mr. Jacobsen. He used my old ships to compete with my new ships for another ten years!"

"Look Mr. Juhl," Robert said, "I understand that you and Coco have a history, everyone in the shipping industry seems to have a history, but I am here to make you a very generous offer on your LNG ships," Robert said.

"There is no such thing as generosity in the shipping business," Mr. Juhl said. "There is only a rapid re-pricing of risk, which is exactly why the market is so active. By the way, did you know that people ridiculed me when I ordered those LNG carriers?" he said.

"Why?" Robert asked.

"Because they said those vessels cost too much to build, and until recently, they generated very modest financial returns. But ever since the Fukushima incident last year and the discovery of U.S. shale gas everyone in the world now seems to want them."

"That must have been a pleasant surprise," Robert said.

"Let me give you some advice, Mr. Fairchild; if you built a good ship at a low cost, as I did with those vessels, then almost every surprise is a pleasant one," he said. "But if you pay too much for a ship, you will be disappointed until the bitter end."

"I am here to offer you a very good price on those vessels," Robert said.

"You should also know, Mr. Fairchild, that you are not the only person in the world who is interested in those particular ships," Mr. Juhl said and closely studied Robert's face to gauge his reaction.

"I can believe that," Robert said.

"In fact, there is another American coming this afternoon to make me an offer on the vessels," he said. "And she had the decency to make an appointment with Ida."

"Have you Googled her, too?" Robert asked.

"I sure have," the old man smiled boyishly and raised his eyebrows.

"Then let's go have lunch and make our deal," Robert said, rubbing his hands together. "Let's do it – shipping style."

"I am not sure who you have been talking to, but here at Great Dane Shipping everyone eats lunch at their desk," he said, "including me."

"Do you want to hear my offer or not?" Robert asked. There was almost nothing more demoralizing than trying to buy something from someone who didn't need to, or want to, sell it.

"Not really," he said.

"But you have a duty to your shareholders to explore…"

"I am my shareholders," he interrupted. "Besides, Mr. Fairchild, I simply cannot sell those vessels to you."

"But you haven't even heard my price?" Robert whined.

"It doesn't matter; I can't sell them to you Mr. Fairchild because they are gone," the old Dane confessed as he shook his head back and forth. "They are gone and I will never get them back."

"What do you mean they're gone?" Robert pleaded. "I mean I already sold them, to someone else," he said.

"But why? Why did you sell them?"

"For the same reason anyone sells anything; I had a higher use for the money."

"What did you do with it?"

"I donated the $750 million profit I made on those vessels to create a cancer hospital in France," he said. "If I have learned anything during my lifetime it's that there's no better value than using money to help people, but you won't see that on your fancy little calculator!" he said and shot a glance at the HP 12C cradled in Robert's palm.

Robert had learned during his short time in the industry that if you needed a calculator and a lot of time to analyze a shipping deal, it was probably a bad deal; all the best ones seemed to be done on napkins.

"But you are still listed as the registered owner in *Fairplay Solutions*," Robert said. "I just saw that on the internet yesterday!"

"Yes, that's because technically I am still the owner since we sold the ships to the new owner using the Norwegian Sales Form. In our case, the buyers gave us a sizable deposit when they signed the MOA and they will pay the rest of the money when they vessels start delivering," Mr. Juhl explained.

"Fine," Robert said with irritation. "Then can you at least tell me who you sold the ships to, so I can make *them* an offer?"

Robert was profoundly disappointed that he would not be going home on the SAS flight that evening, but he knew that no good would come from returning to his apartment before he'd made a deal to buy the LNG ships and rescued his IPO and Oliver's shares from ruin.

"I'm afraid I have absolutely no idea who the buyer was," he admitted. "Sorry about that."

"What do you mean you have no idea?" Robert protested. "That was a multi-billion dollar deal! How can you not know who you sold them to?"

"Because this is shipping, Mr. Fairchild," he said. "The buyer was a nominee company based in the Marshall Islands that was represented in the negotiations by a shipbroker in London," he said. "That's all I know and that's all I *need* to know."

"Then can you *at least* tell me the name of the Marshall Islands holding company that bought the ships?" Robert begged. "Maybe that will give me some kind of clue as to who the actual owner is."

"That I can do," Mr. Juhl said happily and walked over to the wall on the far end of the room that was packed from floor to ceiling with hundreds of three-ring binders containing the key documents associated with individual vessel transactions.

"Thank you," Robert said.

"LJS Holdings," he read loud. "The nominee company that bought the fifteen LNG carriers under construction at Regal Shipbuilding is called LJS Holdings."

"What LJS does that stand for?" Robert asked.

"It stands for Long John Silver," he said.

"Long John Silver Holdings?" Robert repeated slowly. It was yet another oddly coincidental reference to *Treasure Island*, his son's favorite book. Maybe this was a sign from above that it was time to give up and go home tonight, he thought.

"That's the one," he said.

"So what am I supposed to do now, call Blackbeard?" Robert blurted out. "I need your help, Mr. Juhl, please," he begged, "I have a lot at stake here."

"Everyone always has a lot at stake in this business each and every day," Cornelius Juhl said. "That's why it is so intense. The truth is, Mr. Fairchild, there's only one thing you can do."

"Give up and get a real job?" Robert asked.

"Oh no, never give up," he said. "Your only hope is to follow the money back to where it came from."

"Follow the money back to where – to the Marshall Islands?" Robert choked. "I don't even know where the Marshall Islands are!"

"They're located in the South Pacific Ocean and they are absolutely lovely by the way. But no, my recommendation is that you pay a visit to the shipbroker in London that represented LJS Holdings," he suggested. "Surely he will be able to tell you who his client is."

"What's his name?" Robert asked and put pencil to paper.

"Nicholas Eaton-Hardy," Mr. Juhl said.

"Do you think he'll be willing to meet me?" Robert asked.

"Shipbrokers are always happy to take a meeting. They are one of the single best resources in the entire shipping industry," Mr. Juhl said. "They are generous with information, willing to share their knowledge and almost always happy to have a beer."

"I could use a few of those," Robert said.

"Then I will phone him right now and let him know you are coming to visit him tomorrow," Mr. Juhl said.

"Tomorrow?" Robert said as he stood up. "I can't wait until tomorrow. I need to go to London right now!"

"Well done," the Great Dane said as he lay down on his couch for his first of two daily naps. "I hope to see you again very soon."

Chapter 24

The Baltic Exchange

Founded in the mid-1700s in a coffee shop near the Royal Exchange in London, the Baltic Exchange is the world's only independent source of maritime market information for the trading and settlement of physical and derivative contracts. The 550 members of the exchange are responsible for a large proportion of all dry cargo and tanker fixtures as well as the sale and purchase of merchant vessels.

The black handsome cab inched off the choking traffic and stopped in front of the single most important address in international dry cargo shipping – 38 St. Mary Axe.

After Robert had disembarked from the iconic vehicle he stood on the ancient corner of St. Mary's Axe and Threadneedle and he savored the thick mist blowing off the nearby River Thames. As he looked at the low ceiling of grey-green clouds, the neoclassical buildings darkened with one-hundred-year-old coal soot and the red phone boxes, he felt as though he'd travelled back in time. To Robert, there was simply no city in the world in which it was easier to imagine life in the nineteenth century.

"Seven days and counting," he muttered to himself like a lunatic as he pulled open the impossibly heavy door of the church-like structure at 38 St. Mary Axe, the address where Mr. Juhl instructed him to meet Nicholas Eaton-Hardy. "I have just seven days to find out who owns the fifteen LNG ships and get an MOA signed so I can resume the IPO roadshow before it's too late." If the IPO wasn't successful, Robert knew his career in shipping, and Oliver's 10% of Viking Tankers, would both be gone – forever.

When he entered the building where he was supposed to meet the legendary shipbroker, Robert once again wondered if he was in the wrong place. The stone foyer was dead quiet and based on the bustling chartering desk he had witnessed at Blue Sea Shipping & Trading it just didn't seem possible that he could be in a global shipbroking house. In fact, his only company in the room was a ghostly old black-and-white photograph from which a group of men in top hats and tails were sternly staring down at him.

"You must be Mr. Fairchild," a raspy British accent broke the heavy silence. The voice belonged to the man slowly ambling in his direction with the assistance of an intricately carved wooden cane.

Robert had plenty of time to observe the aristocratic and arthritic gentleman making his way toward him – the wisp of his long gray hair, his once towering frame, his ruddy cheeks and an otherwise proud nose slightly crooked to one side. The man looked like Peter O'Toole out for a walk on the Dartmoor: green flannel trousers, a tweed sports coat and a green knit tie all wrapped in a brown Barbour oilskin jacket.

"It's nice to meet you," Robert said as he took a few steps toward the man and gently shook his cool and translucent hand.

"Sir Nicholas Eaton-Hardy at your service," he said. "But please, call me Sir Nicholas."

"You want me to call you *Sir Nicholas*?" Robert asked with a disbelieving chuckle. "Are you serious?"

"I think that's only appropriate considering I was knighted by the Queen in 1988 for exceptional service to the crown for promoting London as a maritime center," he said with a dramatic flair. "This is one of our country's highest honors you know. It is the same one that was bestowed upon Sir Paul McCartney a few years ago."

"Sir Nicholas it is," Robert said as he reflexively fished around in his pocket for his BlackBerry.

As Robert began to withdraw the electronic device, Sir Nicholas jabbed his twisted wooden walking stick into Robert's hand. The assault caused the American to fumble the machine back into his pocket and recoil with pain.

"What was that for?"

"The smarter the phone, the dumber the man who operates it becomes," he said. "That little poke was to teach you some manners."

"You call that *good manners*?" Robert laughed.

"Yes, and next time you whip that thing out I'll jab you six inches to the left," he threatened with a chummy wink of his rheumy eye.

"Would you care to tell me why?" Robert asked.

"It may be among the last of them, Mr. Fairchild, but ocean shipping is still a proper business of manners here in the City of London; ladies and gentlemen should not refer to their gadgets when they are having a conversation with another human being. In this business a person should look another person in the eye and listen to what they have to say."

"Your country, your rules," Robert said and smiled. "Thanks for taking the time to see me today, Sir Nicholas."

Once the pain and surprise of Sir Nicholas's nearly neutering assault had dissipated, Robert felt grateful to be exactly where he was. Between Mr. Cornelius Juhl, Captain Spyros Bouboulinas and Sir Nicholas Eaton-Hardy, he'd had the good luck to spend time in the company of several of the world's greatest living shipping legends – men with nearly three hundred years of front-line shipping experience between them. Robert knew he had a lot to learn and he couldn't ask for more experienced teachers.

"The pleasure is mine Mr. Fairchild. There isn't a shipbroker in the world that isn't tickled pink to meet an American investor these days," he said.

"And why is that?" Robert asked.

"Because it seems as if American equity capital is behind the purchase of almost every modern vessel nowadays," Sir Nicholas said and coughed violently into his a pocket square. "I never would have never thought it possible, but even the most traditional private shipowners seem to be working with large investment funds from your country."

"I appreciate you sharing your insights," Sir Nicholas said.

"Is this place your office?" Robert asked as he peered up at the photograph of stern-faced men long since deceased looking down at him.

"Unfortunately I was born one hundred years too late for that," Sir Nicholas said. "My office is in a modern tower along the River Thames. This place is called the Baltic Exchange and it is where merchants and shipowners began coming together in 1744 to drink coffee, share the overseas newspapers and make charter parties for the carriage of goods by sea. I asked you to meet me here because I just finished a meeting upstairs."

"The New York Stock Exchange started as a coffee house, too," Robert said, unaware that he had just wandered into the place that was responsible for his discovery of shipping. A year and a half earlier Robert had accidentally typed BDI, shorthand for Baltic Dry Index, into Google instead of his stock quotation box on his Bloomberg – and the rest was history.

"Most of the world's greatest endeavors began with a coffee and a handshake," he said, pointing to a wooden plank into which four words were carved.

"*Our word, our bond,*" Robert read the words aloud.

"That's the shipbroker's motto," Sir Nicholas said and looked up at the grainy black-and-white photo. "At least it was when those gentlemen were still alive; before people came along who believe a bond is something that exists to be restructured, or bought back at a discount."

"You European as so sentimental about capital," Robert said.

"Those men lived through the glory days, Mr. Fairchild," Sir Nicholas sighed wistfully as if reflecting on his own personal experience in the eighteenth century. "The days when The River Thames was thick with ships and the British Navy still ruled the sea. The days when cargo ships moved by sail to the Baltic Sea and your Virginia Colony to collect the only commodities that mattered – pitch and pine timbers to make the masts of sailing ships," he said dramatically.

"What goes on in here now?" Robert asked.

"The same thing that goes on in your trousers," the old man said slowly and without the hint of a smile.

"Excuse me?"

"Electrical impulses," he winked. "I'm sure technology has changed every business but the availability of information has totally transformed the international shipping business."

"There is no shortage of information available," Robert said as he thought about his fruitless visit to Copenhagen, "but a lot of it is out of date, wrong or incomplete."

"Back in the old days, having information that no one else had the way to make money. Before the internet, the email and the fax machine, all we had were expensive and unreliable transatlantic cables. That was when a few shipbrokers around the world controlled the market. They were the only ones who knew how much a ship cost to build, how much an oil company might pay to charter her and on what terms a London bank would provide financing. The people who had the information made a fortune in this business…sometimes paying off an entire vessel on just one voyage."

"What is it like now?" Robert asked.

"Now it's the organizations that can gather and process the overwhelming amount of information and manage a massive number of relationships that dominate the business now."

"Is there still a trading floor here at the Baltic Exchange?" Robert asked as he peered deeper into the building in search of the soaring marble ceiling portrayed in the photograph looming above him. "I'd love to see it."

"A trading floor?" Sir Nicholas laughed. "The closest thing we have to a trading floor is the snack bar."

"So where do shipping people come together nowadays to make their deals?" Robert asked.

"Today they will come together over lunch at Harry's Bar," Sir Nicholas said as he opened the heavy wooden door and motioned for Robert to walk outside.

"Harry's Bar?" Robert asked.

"Yes, that's where I'm going to trade you two bottles of Domaine de la Romanée-Conti for the information you need," Sir Nicholas said.

Chapter 25

Sammy Ofer

Sammy Ofer (1922-2011) was an Israeli shipping tycoon, businessman and philanthropist. He was one of the wealthiest people in Israel, although most of his time he spent abroad, and managed his businesses from Monte Carlo in Monaco. Ofer was born in Romania and two years later, his family immigrated to Mandatory Palestine. After Ofer finished elementary school in Haifa, he started working as delivery boy for a shipping company. In 2008, Ofer donated $33 million to fund a new wing at Britain's National Maritime Museum, which observers said was the largest private donation ever made to a British cultural institution. He was subsequently awarded an honorary knighthood.

Robert Fairchild held Sir Nicholas' arm as the shipbroker limped around the corner of St. Mary Axe and Threadneedle Street, howling in pain whenever he put even a modest amount of pressure on his left foot.

The men moved slowly for another half block, battling the wet wind blowing-in from the Thames before cutting across a small cobblestone courtyard to Harry's Bar. Once they were inside the restaurant's foyer, Sir Nicholas smoothed his mane of windswept gray hair. He drew-in a breath, peered grimly down the dark stairway that led to the dimly lit basement dining room and sighed, "This is going to be truly excruciating."

"I've heard arthritis is tough," Robert offered.

"Arthritis!" the old shipbroker roared as he turned to face Robert and lifted his cane as if preparing to whack the American again.

"They say it's a very common condition," Robert replied. "And it's not your fault. The humidity in this city must be brutal," he added as he took a step back from the shipbroker.

"I don't have arthritis!" Sir Nicholas said. "I've got the gout, boy!"

"The gout?" Robert asked with grave concern. "What's the gout?"

"You call yourself a shipping man and you don't know about the gout?" he coughed.

"I've heard of it," Robert said, "but I thought that was something sailors got in the seventeenth century, like scurvy."

"That's almost right," he smiled. "I got mine from spending seven days on a shipowner's yacht during the Rugby Sevens in Hong Kong; I had been living on nothing but shellfish and lager which is exactly what causes the uric acid crystals to get stuck in the joint of the big toe."

"Sounds like an occupational hazard for a shipbroker," Robert said.

"You're quite right," he laughed. "I flew home to London with a swollen toe and a 1% commission on eighteen new bulk carriers worth $360 million," he smiled.

"I bet thinking about that commission makes you feel better," Robert said.

"Spoken like a true deal man," Sir Nicholas smiled.

"Maybe should we try to find a more accessible restaurant, perhaps one with a ramp?" Robert said. The shipbroker would have preferred a ground-level restaurant, but that wasn't an option; he had strict instructions to bring the American to Harry's Bar.

"You listen to me, Fairchild," he admonished. "I've been buying and selling ships since Andi Case and Richard Fulford-Smith were in diapers and I'll doing it when they're back in diapers," Sir Nicholas said as he heaved his inflamed toe down the first step. "I do not need a ramp!"

When they finally arrived at the bottom of the stairs, the hostess moved quickly across the dining room to greet them. "Nico!" said warmly and kissed him once on each cheek. "How's the toe?"

"It's still angry as an alligator, Julia, but better than yesterday," he said and handed her his cane and green tweed hat.

"Don't worry," she said and spun around. "I'll bring you a glass of fresh squeezed cherry juice straightaway."

Like so many things about the City of London, the cellar dining room of Harry's Bar made it easy for Robert to imagine life as an eighteenth century shipping man; the massive stone hearth, the candle-dim lighting and the rough-hewn beams holding up the horsehair plaster ceiling appeared unchanged from the days when tallow and timber were the cargoes of interest and the world was fueled by whale oil and hard labor – instead of leverage and carbon.

Despite claims that the shipping business was moving to the Far East to serve China, and that capital was coming primarily from America, Robert learned that London's multi-century role as the epicenter of the international ocean shipping industry was unlikely to change – at least in his lifetime.

With its storied maritime history dating back to when England traded with her colonies, twenty-first century ocean shipping still employed half-a-million professionals who generated more than $30 billion of annual revenue. A staggering 50% of tanker and dry bulk chartering, along with vessel sale and purchase, was concluded in the City of London thanks to the roughly 2,000 shipbrokers who operated in the city twenty-four hours a day. Shipping was important to London and London was important to shipping. Full stop.

While a diaspora of shipowners would forever wander the world in search of the ideal balance between maximum lifestyle and minimum taxation, the largest and longest standing ship financiers in the industry were rooted in London. The city was also home to the ship finance industry's best known graduate school, Cass, which produced a guild of professional talent that ensured the specialized knowledge of ship financing would passed down through the generations.

Just as he and Sir Nicholas sat down at the corner table, Robert was startled by the explosion of laughter that erupted on the opposite side of the room. He turned around expecting to find a pack of intoxicated twenty-five-year-old bankers in the midst of a liquid lunch. Instead, he saw a dozen well-dressed older gentlemen packed tight around a round table.

"Who are those guys?" Robert asked.

"Take a guess," Sir Nicholas asked as he raised his arm in what looked like a type of tribal greeting. "Let's see how perceptive you are."

"They look like bankers with a generous expense account," Robert replied.

"You have a keen eye, Mr. Fairchild," Sir Nicholas said without peering up from the leather-bound wine list.

"But I thought London bankers were all depressed because they don't get bonuses anymore," Robert said.

"The Dippers are different," he said as he peered over the rim of the tortoiseshell reading glasses perched on the tip of his crooked nose. He slammed closed the leather bound wine list as though it were a form of emphatic punctuation.

"The what?" Robert asked with a laugh.

"The Dippers," Sir Nicholas repeated as he used the cryptic hand signals of a baseball catcher to communicate his indulgent selection to the sommelier. "It's a very special organization."

"What makes it so special?" Robert asked.

"That small group of men and women control more than $150 billion of ship loans," he said. "That's nearly 50% of the entire global market for debt secured by ship mortgages."

"Wow," Robert asked. He was stunned that such a massive industry, the single largest asset class on the planet, was controlled by the handful of people sitting around a round table having lunch.

"The Dippers got together in 2009 after Lehman Brothers collapsed and the shipping market went into a terrible slump when Letters of Credit dried-up. They had to repossess hundreds of vessels, but they couldn't afford to sell them because the losses would have made the banks insolvent. So instead of selling the ships at the bottom of the market and taking the losses, they formed a shipping company and named in DIP Shipping."

"DIP Shipping?" Robert asked.

"It's short for Debtors in Possession," he laughed.

"How did that work out for them?" Robert asked.

No more than two minutes after the shipbroker had hand signaled his desired vintage, a solicitous sommelier had peeled the crimson foil from the neck of a green bottle and was screwing an opener into the cork. After he'd filled the bottom of Sir Nicholas's large wine glass for his pre-purchase evaluation, the broker closed his eyes and rolled the Burgundy around with a look of ecstasy on his face. Then he lifted his glass in front of a nearby wall sconce, closed one eye and studied the streaks of residual alcohol.

"Quite well actually," Sir Nicholas broke the silence and lowered his nose into the wide bowl of the glass and took a sniff.

"Really?"

"Some people accused them of kicking the can down the road, the people who didn't really understand the peculiarities of shipping, but their patience proved to be the right strategy; it saved the shareholders of their bank from massive losses."

"Just when you're ready to give up you need to hang on a little longer in this business," Robert said.

"Indeed," Sir Nicholas said. "The DIP fleet is not only profitable in its own right, but has now become a place where banks voluntarily put their ships; the pooling of tonnage is the future."

"Sounds like they are really stick together," Robert said.

"That is the code of the sea, Mr. Fairchild," he said, "and it extends to shipping people on land as well," Sir Nicholas said.

"I'll drink to that," Robert said and raised his empty glass. The American was praying he would be able to preserve his position at Viking Tankers and not be forced back into the real world; even when shipping was bad it was still pretty good.

"Oh my," Sir Nicholas said suddenly with a look of concern suddenly spreading across his face.

"What's the matter?" Robert asked. "Is the toe flaring up again?"

"This is worse," he said. "There appears to be a new Dipper at today's lunch: Alistair Gooding."

"Alistair Gooding?" Robert cranked his neck around to confirm the presence of Viking Tankers' largest lender. "Why is he at the Dipper lunch?" Robert asked. "I always thought Allied Bank of England had the cleanest portfolio in the industry."

"He's probably looking for a place to park Coco's ships," the old broker said casually and popped a morsel of brown bread into his mouth.

"That's ridiculous," Robert laughed.

"Oh please," he said as he aggressively refilled his own empty glass while ignoring Robert's. "Everyone knows that Coco Jacobsen and Alistair have been sharing the same leaky lifeboat for years. When Coco goes down, Mr. Gooding will be forced to take possession of an ungodly quantity of crude oil tankers."

"But why would Alistair repossess Coco's ships?" Robert asked.

"You would know better than I," Alistair said. "Broker gossip says that the end is near for Mr. Jacobsen. Apparently he chartered-out quite a few ships to those blokes at American Refining Corporation and now they are in the process of handing them back."

"But that makes no sense," Robert said. "Even if ARC, I mean ART, does default the spot market for VLCCs is still about $25,000 per day; Viking Tankers can squeak by with rates like that."

"Actually, the spot market has been firming nicely during the last few days," Sir Nicholas said.

"It has?" Robert asked. He had not been keeping track of the tanker market since he started the roadshow and then began his global scavenger hunt for the LNG ships. "What's going on?"

"What's going on is that the pundits got the market wrong," Sir Nicholas said. "A lot of people just assumed that the tanker market would crumble because the U.S. is importing less crude oil; a lot of people were wrong."

"How could they be wrong about that?" Robert asked. "It couldn't be more obvious."

"The movement of commodity is a complex organism," the shipbroker said. "As it turned out, the barrels of light, sweet crude that America stopped buying from West Africa are now going to China which is *twice* as far as the U.S. Gulf and – that is very good for crude oil ton mile demand. In fact, the future for crude oil tankers has never looked brighter."

"Holy smokes," Robert said softly. "Coco was right."

"He usually is."

"That's great news," Robert said. "Because if the spot market is stronger, then Viking Tankers will be okay even if ARC, I mean ART, does default."

"I'm afraid it's not that simple," he said.

"But you said the spot market is looking robust," Robert said.

"The spot market isn't the problem," Sir Nicholas said.

"What's the problem?"

"The problem, boy, is that Rocky DuBois has apparently threatened to file a complaint with the U.S. Coast Guard alleging that Viking Tankers has been ordering its crew to pump oily water in the ocean."

"But that's absolutely not true!" Robert cried. "No one is more careful about that than Coco; he spends a fortune on oil-water separators."

"Perception is reality," Sir Nicholas said. "If ARC makes the allegation nobody will charter *any* of his ships; Coco Jacobsen could be blackballed in the Arabian Gulf."

"Oh no," Robert finally said slowly, his head spinning with vertigo; he had never even considered the possibility that ARC could permanently damage Coco's ability to trade his ships. He hadn't thought about the fact that in a small business like shipping, reputational risk was one of the biggest risks – bigger than storms at sea and bigger than pirates and even bigger than the market itself; a ship that couldn't earn money was nothing but a liability. In trying to protect Coco with the time charters, Robert had actually put him at greater risk.

Just as Sir Nicholas raised his arm, Alistair Gooding rose from his chair, placed a neatly folded cloth napkin on the table and marched aggressively toward Robert. "What on earth are *you* doing here?" the British banker demanded after failing to acknowledge Robert's outstretched hand.

Robert wasn't sure if the banker knew about ARC's threat to default on the ten time charters, and its demand for the fifteen LNG carriers, and he wasn't about to tell him. "I'm just having a nice lunch," Robert smiled. "Just like you and the Dippers."

"Unfortunately, I am doing business," Alistair snarled. "Shouldn't you be on the IPO roadshow?"

"Now Alistair," Sir Nicholas said in a soothing voice, clearly trying to calm the enraged banker. "Take it easy on Fairchild, he's just a boy."

"He's not a boy, Nico, he will be a forty-year-old man in just a few days and I want to know why he's not out raising the equity that he promised he would raise for Viking Tankers," the banker demanded again.

"Because I…"

"Follow me," the normally genteel banker growled through his gritted teeth. "We have to talk."

Robert Fairchild reluctantly rose from his seat and slowly followed Alistair like a man marching to his own execution. Once Alistair was satisfied that no one in the dining room could see them, he grabbed Robert by the collar of his wrinkled blue button-down shirt and pushed him up against a wall paneled with the wood of old French wine cases.

"What's the matter with you?" Robert croaked as he unsuccessfully attempted to remove Alistair's hand. "You're hurting me, Allie."

"Not as badly as you're hurting *me*! You may have free money on Wall Street, Mr. Fairchild, but money is most certainly *not* free at the Allied Bank of England!" He shouted into Robert's face.

"But, I…"

"Do you know what will happen if I have to repossess the entire fleet of Viking Tankers, because no one will charter them from Coco?"

"No."

"Then let me tell you. My bank is leveraged twenty-to-one and that means if I write off half that $1 billion loan my bank will lose $20 *billion* of economic capital. Do you happen to know what the market capitalization of my bank is?"

"Less than $20 billion," Robert said in a small voice.

"*Substantially* less," he said, lowering his voice to a muffled shout. "I will be *nationalized*!"

"But those ships are cougars," Robert said. "They are beautiful and nicely-maintained."

"Who told you that?" he laughed bitterly.

"A Chief Engineer," Robert replied in a small voice.

"Trust me, nobody will think they're beautiful and nicely-maintained when they get arrested and auctioned in every backwater port in the world," he said. "I'll have every keel-kicker and scallywag in the world lowballing me on those ships. I am going to have to make a credit bid and put them into the Dipper."

"Well…"

"Do you understand the gravity of this situation, Fairchild? I gave Coco Jacobsen an amortization holiday because *you* promised to get that IPO done and pay down my loan," he said.

"I thought you gave him the holiday in exchange for the $5 million amendment fee," Robert said.

"Now you listen to me and you listen closely," he whisper-shouted. "I haven't the foggiest notion why you are in a London pub drinking wine in the middle of the day with a retired shipbroker who is suffering from early stage dementia – a man who just last week told me his mum was the Queen of England – but you had better get back onto that roadshow in America *post haste*!" Alistair spat as he released his grip on Robert.

"I'll do what I can, Allie," Robert said stiffly. He decided it was probably not a good time to share the news about Luther's draconian demand for preferred shares.

"You had better do more than that, Fairchild," Alistair said. "You had better get that IPO done on terms acceptable to Coco."

Robert was visibly shaken when he returned to the table where he found Sir Nicholas sheepishly sipping his wine. Robert's suit was rumpled, his hair was messy, his skin was pale and his eyes were darting quickly around the room. "You look like you've just seen a ghost," Sir Nicolas said.

"I have," Robert said. "My own."

"I saw a ghost once," the shipbroker recalled. "I was living in Mozambique living on Quinine and working for a Dutch shipowner who gave me the unseemly task of…"

"Stop!" Robert interrupted. "Don't get me wrong, Sir Nicholas, I love hearing all your old shipping stories, I really do, but I need your help before it is too late."

"I'm always happy to work for red Burgundy and 1% fee," Sir Nicholas said and flashed a macabre collection of wine-stained teeth.

"Here's the deal," Robert said as he leaned forward across the table so the Dippers were sure not to overhear the conversation. "What you said earlier about American Refining Corporation defaulting on the ten time charters to Viking Tankers is only half the story," Robert said.

"That's more truth than most broker gossip," he said.

"The other half is that ARC is threatening to default on us in order to induce Coco to do something else," Robert said.

"What's the ask?" Sir Nicholas inquired.

"There are fifteen LNG carriers currently under construction at a shipyard in Korea called Regal," Robert said.

"I am familiar with the units," Sir Nicholas said.

"Rocky DuBois at ARC has apparently told Coco that if we can gain control of those ships, he will keep paying the charter hire and we can finish our IPO."

"It sounds like you have a lot riding on those fifteen LNG carriers," Sir Nicholas said.

"More than you can imagine," Robert said.

"It's astonishing how popular those boring LNG carriers have become lately," Sir Nicholas said.

"You don't need to broker me, Sir Nicholas," Robert said. "I want the ships and I am willing to pay for them. I am a willing buyer and all I need now is a willing seller. I know your client just bought those ships from Great Dane a couple of months ago and now I want to make them an offer they simply can't refuse."

Sir Nicholas closed his eyes and said, "I'm afraid I can't help you."

"Why not? I thought everything was for sale in the shipping business," Robert said. "I thought shipowners weren't supposed to fall in love with the ships. I thought that's why they never name them after their wives and daughters."

"Yes, but LNG ships are a unique species," Sir Nicolas said.

"Why?"

"Because for anyone who actually needs to move gas, and I speaking now of nations and not just private shipowners, there is simply no substitute for an LNG ship; unlike most types of vessels, you can't just sell one unit and go into the market and charter-in another one. Nor is there a steady flow of 're-sales' available for purchase from shipyards."

"What? But I thought there were always too many ships," Robert said.

"Ah yes, but only when you don't need them," the shipbroker replied.

"So what the heck am I supposed to do now?" Robert asked.

"The best advice I can give you, Mr. Fairchild, is to just forget about this deal, forget about shipping and try to return to a life on land that is safe and predictable," he said.

"But you haven't heard my price," Robert shouted. "Nobody has *ever* heard my price! What is wrong with you people?" Robert exclaimed. He was ready to jump out of his chair. "Why doesn't anyone care about the price?"

"Because, to be honest," the old shipbroker said. "I have no idea who my client was on the transaction."

"Hold on," Robert said. "You just brokered a deal to sell $3 billion worth of ships and you don't even know who bought them? How is that possible?" Robert asked.

"It is possible because the general manager at Regal Shipbuilding, an old mate of mine from Cardiff University, approached me with the deal *on behalf* of the buyer; all I did was to make the phone call to my old friend Mr. Juhl to see if he would be willing to sell. My secretary filled in the blanks on the MOA and added a few riders," Sir Nicholas said. "I was actually at my house in Provence at the time."

"And you never thought to ask who the buyer was?" Robert asked.

"Don't ask, don't tell," Sir Nicholas said.

"What about all that stuff you said about shipping being a personal business that should be conducted face-to-face? What about *Our Word, Our Bond*?"

"I live by a different motto now, a more modern one: *If the Wire Clears, Have No Fears*," Sir Nicholas laughed.

"But what am I supposed to do now?" Robert whined. "I only have a few days to get those ships on subjects or I am in serious trouble!"

"Mr. Fairchild, if you really want to gain control of those vessels you must pay a visit to Him," he said.

"But you just said you don't know who the buyer was," Robert complained.

"That is precisely why you need to see Him," Sir Nicholas repeated. "He is your only hope."

"Who is?" Robert asked.

"Him is," the Englishman repeated.

"What are you *talking* about?" Robert shrieked as he pulled on his hair.

Sir Nicholas replied and a calm and clear voice. "I am talking about Mr. William Him, the general manager of Regal Shipbuilding in Busan, Korea. He is the one who represented the buyers when I brokered the LNG carriers and he is the only person who knows the identity of the new owner."

"In *Korea*?" Robert pleaded desperately, his eyes bulging. "You actually want me to go to *Korea*?" Robert repeated.

Sir Nicholas's suggestion was highly distressing to Robert Fairchild who had been hoping London would be the third and final stop on his odyssey to find the owner of the LNG carriers before it was too late. The only thing he really wanted to do was go home, take a hot shower, put on pajamas and curl up on the couch with Grace watching *Seinfeld* re-runs.

If he did continue on to Korea, it was highly unlikely that he would make it home for his own fortieth birthday. Robert Fairchild was just about ready to give up once and for all when he remembered what Aphrodite had said to him just before he left Jimmy the Fish – *This is shipping, Robert. Just when you are ready to give up, you need to hang on a little longer and you will be okay.*

"Okay," Robert sighed as he got up from the table. "Please inform Mr. Him that I will be paying him a visit."

Chapter 26

The Power of People

There are three tenets upon which Navios is built – good people, open communication and prudent business practices. It is the people whom we entrust with making multi-million dollar decisions. If we do not hire and retain the best people, we will not be the best company. In addition, we cultivate a free exchange of ideas within the company – between groups and team leaders. It is this free exchange that allows good people to make wise decisions. And long-term success can only be achieved with a conservative business practices. This means that the controlling factor in all our decisions is "have we protected the company?"

Angeliki Frangou, Chairman & CEO,
Navios Group of Companies

As Robert Fairchild waited for the elevator to carry him up to Regal Shipbuilding's executive offices on the top floor of the five-story building, Mr. William Him sat in his office proudly watching a two-hundred-ton crane nicknamed "Big Boy" insert a prefabricated bulbous bow into a partially constructed LNG carrier.

As Mr. Him's army of highly skilled workers flawlessly performed the complicated industrial procedure, the Korean couldn't help but feel philosophical; he had worked tirelessly for thirty-five years to become CEO of the largest and most technologically advanced shipbuilding complex in the world, and reinvested almost every dollar of profit back into the physical plant, yet he was lucky if he could make money one year in five on his $10 billion of annual revenue.

But despite the economic struggles, Mr. Him firmly believed in the nobility and importance of his contribution to global seaborne trade. He also knew that shipbuilding wasn't a purely capitalistic enterprise, but a socio-capitalistic one that stimulated employment in economies transitioning from agrarian to industrial.

That was why Japan had increased its shipbuilding capacity in the 1960s and 1970s and why Korea had done the same thing in the 1990s. Both expansions of shipbuilding had temporarily oversupplied the market with ships and both were dwarfed by the expansion of shipbuilding capacity in China during the shipping boom of 2004-2008. During that four-year period the Chinese had nearly *doubled* global shipbuilding capacity which left shipowners, lenders and investors to wonder whether the world could *ever* absorb the excess capacity.

Mr. Him also knew that shipbuilders like him bore all the costs of shipping's volatility but reaped few of its benefits. If the ships he was building dropped in value while under construction, his customers could renegotiate the contract price or abandon the vessels altogether. But if the ships *increased* in value during the construction period, those same customers could flip the half-built machines to another shipowner for a quick windfall – leaving Mr. Him with the original profit margin and a demanding new owner – which was precisely the case with the LNG carrier coming together before his eyes.

"Are you Mr. Him?" Robert Fairchild asked when he popped his head into the office.

"I am Him…and Him is me!" the Korean smiled warmly after using a well-worn ice breaker. He rose to his feet. "It is such a pleasure to see you!"

Mr. Him extended his right hand while ceremoniously brushing his left hand across his forearm, a Korean tradition which harkened back to the ancient kings who pushed back the sleeves of their robes as they greeted their visitors. Robert took a moment to study his affable host; thick head of dark hair, official shipyard jacket over a white shirt and tie, black work shoes with thick rubber soles.

"My name is…"

"Robert Fairchild," Mr. Him finished his sentence. "Nico told me to expect you."

Mr. Him continued to shake Robert's hand as he inspected the man. Like most of the intelligent and hardworking Americans who took day trips to Korea in search of cut-rate ships, the man before him looked exhausted. But although Mr. Him had received many HP calculator-toting, coffee-seeking, value-hungry visitors with unshaven faces and dark circles under their eyes, never before had he seen one who looked quite as haggard as Robert Fairchild. That the American had not changed his suit since walking into the swimming pool at the Delano Hotel in Miami with Luther Livingston one week earlier would not have surprised Him.

"So," Mr. Him said. "What can I do for you?"

"*What can you do for me?*" Robert asked with panic in his voice. He had fantasized that the London shipbroker and the Korean shipyard boss had cooked -up the deal during the entire day that Robert had just spent on the airplane. He hoped all he would have to do upon his arrival in Korea was to sign the MOA and race home for his fortieth birthday, but it wasn't going to be that easy – deals never were.

"Yes," Mr. Him said slowly as if to a young child. "Why are you here, Mr. Fairchild?"

"Didn't Sir Nicholas tell you?"

"Who is Sir Nicholas?" Mr. Him asked.

"Sir Nicholas Eaton-Hardy," Robert said.

"He didn't even tell me who you work for," he said.

Although Robert Fairchild had eagerly anticipated this moment during the long trip from London to Busan via Dubai and Seoul, he suddenly found himself without words. His strategy of being direct had gotten him nowhere in his meetings in Athens, Copenhagen and London, so he decided to try a different approach.

"Mr. Him, I am a private equity investor from New York City and I am here to buy some boats," Robert said, deliberately using the term "boats" as many novice investors did in order to appear like a rookie to Mr. Him.

"The ships we build *carry* boats," Mr. Him said.

"Then I want some ships," Robert said.

"Today is your lucky day, Mr. Fairchild, because today is a very good time to order new ships," Mr. Him said and switched into his salesman persona. He was eager to test-out his new pitches and Mr. Fairchild's visit provided an ideal opportunity for a dry run.

"Why is that?" Robert asked.

"Because of the eco-ships, of course," he said. "You see, shipping is usually a business of *evolution* in which small changes are made in vessel size, configuration and design, but today we find ourselves in a rare moment of *revolution*!" he oozed with excitement. "We believe that today's low prices and new technology could make the current fleet of ships economically and environmentally obsolete."

"That sure would be good for your business," Robert said with the sort of skepticism often associated with owners of fuel-inefficient vessels. "But let's face it, Mr. Him, reduced fuel consumption won't change time charter rates; only supply and demand can do that."

"That's shocking," Robert said, recalling that Mr. Him's characterization was exactly how he had first analyzed his purchase of the *Lady Grace* that fateful evening in Greece. He thought he'd purchased the old ship at one times EBITDA but ended up having to fight for his life and work seven days a week for a year just to get his money back.

"Please, come with me," Mr. Him said as he carefully placed an orange hardhat emblazoned with the shipyard's logo on Robert Fairchild's head. "Let's go have a look at the shipyard, shall we, so you can do some shopping for ships."

Ever since the collapse of the shipping market in 2009, Mr. Him had entertained dozens of investors in search of bargain-basement pricing on ships. In the spirit of ginning up some orders during those dark days, Mr. Him had given away windbreakers, baseball hats and fountain pens and spent countless hours educating investors about shipping – all of which amounted to not a single order.

He had learned the hard way that very few investors had the type of capital that was patient enough to wait the two years it took to build a ship before it generated any revenue – irrespective of how attractive the contract price or how high-quality the vessel. But no matter how much time he'd spent courting investors, Mr. Him had never grown tired of showing off his shipyard and his amazing workers.

Over the course of his career, he had given hundreds of tours – to Greeks, Norwegians, Turkish, Russians, South Americans and more – and his launchings and christenings had been attended by everyone from members of royalty to famous Hollywood actors to government dignitaries.

But never had he encountered an investor as intensely fascinated by the shipyard as Robert Fairchild. Even after the two men had been sitting in the back of the fiercely air-conditioned black Hyundai Equus station wagon for more than an hour, official flags flying on either side of its gleaming hood as hundreds of workers bowed toward the vehicle everywhere they went – Robert Fairchild wanted more.

So they zoomed through robotic machine shops the size of aircraft hangars, zipped along pipe-bending facilities and careened across a climate-controlled computer nerve center from which a battery of laser lathes cut, numbered and stacked the two inch-thick plates of gray steel. They watched a computer-controlled crane welding plates of steel onto the skeleton of a ship – all without any visible human intervention.

"I feel like we're inside the Matrix," Robert marveled.

"Welcome to the future, Mr. Fairchild," Mr. Him said with a slow laugh as he admired the orderly industrial activity being conducted in a spotless environment.

"It's truly amazing."

"This is one of the largest commercial shipyards in the world, Mr. Fairchild. We have nine graving docks spread across seventy-two billion square meters – equal to about seven hundred football fields in your country," he said. "We have spent close to $1 trillion developing this plant to ensure that it produces the highest quality vessels as efficiently as possible."

"Holy cow," Robert said as he struggled to process the numbers Mr. Him was reciting.

"Yes," Mr. Him agreed solemnly. "It is indeed a sacred place. Shipbuilding is the crown jewel of the Korean economy and Regal Shipbuilding is among the best shipyards there are," he said.

"It is very impressive," Robert agreed.

"And yet some people come here to tell me there are too many shipyards," Mr. Him said thoughtfully. "They tell me I should reduce my capacity. But I ask you this: did your Barack Obama, who I admire very much by the way, close General Motors when they were having some trouble?" he asked rhetorically.

"He bailed them out," Robert said.

"Correct. President Obama provided critical assistance to a critical industry at a time when they needed it. But what is the alternative – for me to tell my 13,000 workers who provide for more than 15,000 children that they are fired, just because the shipping markets do not happen to be strong at a particular moment in time?"

"Of course not," Robert said.

"Am I supposed to force my community to shut down the schools, hospitals and everything else that relies on the revenue of this shipyard just because the shipping markets are weak?"

"No."

"And the truth is, Mr. Fairchild, that while there are always too many shipyards and there always will be, there are still not enough shipyards that are capable of building very large, very complicated, very high quality vessels. We can. We deliver a beautiful, new, well-built ship every four days," Mr. Him said.

"Every four days?" Robert asked.

"When the shipping market is strong, yes," Mr. Him said.

"How about when it's weak?" he asked.

"When the shipping market is weak we still build the ships, but it is like an orphanage around here," Mr. Him said. "The new babies are lying around everywhere because nobody wants to take the new babies home to start losing money every day; they want to wait as long as they can; sometimes they never come."

"Oh, that's terrible," Robert said. The exhausted, dehydrated, hungry and emotionally-drained Robert Fairchild felt like he might actually weep from the metaphor of ships as abandoned children.

When he turned to hide his moist eyes from the Korean, he was paralyzed by what he saw in the 2,000-foot-long graving dock. He didn't need to be a shipping expert to know that the unusual raised deck could only belong to one type of vessel – an LNG carrier.

"Stop the car!" Robert shrieked.

"I agree," Mr. Him said. "We have had a nice tour, but let's return to the office and have a cup of tea."

"Stop the car *now!*" he yelled again.

The moment Robert Fairchild screamed for the second time, the startled driver slammed on the breaks causing the black Equus wagon to skid across the sand-covered asphalt. Before the vehicle had even come to a complete stop Robert bailed out and tumbled to the ground. He'd scrambled to his feet, pausing only momentarily to inspect the blood seeping through the new hole in the knee of his suit pants. He sprinted the twenty-five yards that separated him from the fence where the road gave way to a one-hundred-foot drop into the graving dock.

As Robert Fairchild stared down into the vast canyon, it took him a moment to see the fifty men scurrying around the vessel in matching grey uniforms and the dozen plumes of smoke rising from welding arcs. As he gazed at the mammoth, partially-constructed machine, Robert experienced the same rapture that King Arthur might have felt when he first laid eyes on another famous vessel – the Holy Grail. The semi-assembled ship below him might not have been as significant to humanity as the chalice that Jesus Christ shared during the Last Supper, but gaining control of the LNG ships held the key to Robert Fairchild's own salvation.

"I'll take that one!" Robert boomed when Mr. Him finally joined him at the edge of the canyon. "I want the LNG Carrier," Robert said.

"I am afraid this is not possible," Mr. Him said.

"Oh yes it is," Robert replied.

"Oh no its *not*," Mr. Him countered. "She is not available to you," Mr. Him said. "She is going home with someone else."

The sudden and intense interest that Mr. Him had received toward the fifteen LNG ships his yard was building was both flattering and troubling to the seasoned shipbuilding executive. He was flattered because the ships were his brainchild. After growing weary of building small, standard ships he had convinced his Board of Directors to license the proprietary technology required to build state-of-the-art LNG carriers.

LNG wasn't a big market at the time and he had selected it because he figured the ships' complexity would eliminate fierce competition from aggressive Chinese shipyards – which would provide him with more pricing power. He also assumed that a serious, long-term industrial business like LNG would attract the sort of serious, long-term shipping companies that were willing to invest a huge amount of capital for a long period of time – when most shipping speculators were after exactly the opposite.

Mr. Him had been wrong on both counts.

More than a dozen shipyards had followed him into the LNG market which meant that he now competed for every order. His yard still won most of the desirable contracts, but the competition had compressed his margins to dangerously low levels. The long-term owners he'd been expecting to serve hadn't behaved as expected either. Even the most serious shipping man of them all, Cornelius Juhl, proved incapable of resisting the temptation of selling the ships for a massive profit a few months earlier; shipping behavior, as it turned out, was the same as human behavior.

"But I want her," Robert said, "and her sisters, too."

"Those ladies are spoken for and that is the end of the discussion," Mr. Him said sternly as he dried the sweat from his forehead. "I do, however, have some very good news for you."

"What's that?" Robert asked.

"The good news is that I just so happen to have some very nice post-Panamax container vessels that a German bank has given me full authority to sell on behalf of a bankrupt KG fund," Mr. Him said. "Come on, let's jump back into the car and I'll show them to you."

"I don't want post-Panamax container vessels," Robert said. "I don't even know how wide the new Panama Canal will be."

"Good point," Mr. Him agreed. "Then perhaps I can interest you in a pair of very nice LR1 tankers? These ships will be very profitable just as soon as the Reliance refinery gets up and running in Jamnagar and the stem size and ton miles increase for refined products."

"I don't want those *either*," Robert repeated like a picky child refusing food.

"How about a self-trailing hopper dredger?" Mr. Him asked hopefully as he recalled the vessel that an Indian company had abandoned two years earlier.

"A *what*?"

"It is like a seagoing vacuum cleaner. It is a very useful machine now that climate change is affecting the coastline, especially in your part of the world."

"I don't want a seagoing vacuum cleaner."

"How about a shallow-water accommodation rig for four hundred men?" Mr. Him asked. "A group of Norwegians ordered the vessel with money from the bond market but now they don't have the cash to make the final payment. I can make you a very nice deal on that one if you tow her out of here by the end of the month. It would make for a smashing hotel in New York Harbor."

"I don't want an accommodation rig or anything else from your island of misfit ships," Robert said. "I want the LNG carriers!"

"But-they-are-not-for-sale," the Korean said slowly, his controlled, reserved demeanor offering no indication what-so-ever of the total frustration he felt regarding this situation.

As Robert perseverated over his demand, he watched the group of men who had been working on the bow of the LNG vessel begin dismantling a tower of blue scaffolding. When the orange nylon safety curtain drifted slowly to the ground, Robert squinted to read the partially obscured white letters.

"I want the..." Robert paused as he attempted to read the name, "*Hispanic*. I want the *Hispanic*!"

"She is called the *Hispaniola*, Mr. Fairchild, the workers haven't quite finished putting her name on. And she is not for sale. I don't know how else to explain this to you."

"Did you just say *Hispaniola?*" Robert asked incredulously as he realized he'd stumbled across another reference to *Treasure Island*.

Yet another wave of homesickness washed over Robert. He had only been away from home for a week but it felt like he'd been gone for a lifetime. While perpetual international travel was one of the great things about working in the shipping industry it was one of the sacrifices as well; he had seen a lot, but he had missed so much.

"Furthermore, we are the only shipyard in the world that can build an LNG vessel like this one," Mr. Him said. "We have the exclusive license on the necessary technology and because we have so many large graving docks we will deliver six of them to the owner in a few weeks."

"How much are they?" Robert asked.

"Based on what's happening in the charter market," Mr. Him said, "these ships are probably worth close to $200 million each."

"Fine, I'll give you $200 million each," Robert said, as though he were committing to the last of the cookies on a bakery tray and not $3 billion worth of high-specification gas tankers.

Mr. Him's eyes narrowed as he stared at Robert Fairchild. The acrid shipyard air was now momentarily silent but for the creak of a colossal crane loading steel plates in the distance and a sandblaster performing a "haircut and shave" on the hull of a ship in dry dock for her periodic hull cleaning.

"I admire your persistence, Mr. Fairchild, but the company that originally placed the order for those ships only recently sold them to a new owner who apparently has a very specific use for them," Mr. Him said. "Therefore, they are not for sale."

"Then I'll pay $250 million each," Robert interrupted and the words plunged into Mr. Him like a dagger; at that price the new owner would make a $750 million profit and he hadn't even fully paid for the vessels yet. This was how people really made easy money in shipping: flipping ships under construction.

"If you are really willing to offer that much money, I suggest that you approach the owner of the ships directly," Mr. Him said clinically "Because I want nothing to do with it."

"With pleasure," Robert said with the punch-drunk smile of an exhausted man who believes he is close to rest.

Robert Fairchild had spent the last six days circling the world, from New York to Athens to Copenhagen to London to Korea via Dubai, trying to find out who owned the LNG carriers. As he neared the end of his Homeric odyssey, he felt himself becoming philosophical.

During the course of the past week, he had witnessed some of the key drivers of global shipping markets; he'd experienced a small family owner in Greece, a large one in Denmark and a major charterer in America. He had seen a veteran shipbroker at work and pitched an investor hungry for risk. He had witnessed a cartel of leading lenders exhibit grace under pressure and gotten to know the manager of a world-class shipyard. He'd even had the pleasure of meeting Prasanth in the engine room of the *Viking Alexandra*. The truth was that to really understand the forces that affected international shipping, you had to understand what motivated everyone in the marketplace.

But all that was history now. Judging from the pensive look on Mr. Him's face, Robert estimated he was no more than sixty seconds away from finally discovering the truth – a truth he believed would finally set him free.

Chapter 27

The Channel Islands

Like most beautiful and strategically located islands, the Channel Islands have been the prize for many fights over the centuries. The last remnant of the medieval Duchy of Normandy, the tiny archipelago has been battled over by naval forces, Aragonese mercenaries, Vikings, Calvinists, Louis XIV, Reformers and Royalists whose Castle Cornet in St. Peter Port was the last stronghold to finally capitulate in 1651. Even Adolf Hitler had taken an interest in the place, fortifying the castle to secure it as a tactical lynchpin in the North Atlantic. The Channel Islands also have a rich history of piracy dating back to the seventeenth century. Their proximity to mainland Europe made the islands an ideal spot for privateering. Today, thanks to favorable tax regulations, the Channel Islands are a safe harbor for international hedge funds, trusts and shipping companies.

When Robert Fairchild regained consciousness in a pitch-black room twenty-four hours after leaving Korea he was lost in time and space.

As his perennially pampered body struggled to adjust to life in the shipping business – having entered his fifth time zone in as many days – he wondered if he had suffered a stroke or some other insidious neurological malady. He opened and closed his eyes as slowly as a butterfly at rest and stared into the infinite darkness unable to ascertain where in the world he was – or even remember that it was his fortieth birthday.

He took a deep breath and allowed his mind to drift, hoping it would bump into something and it quickly did – the memory of sitting next to Aphrodite in the Captain's Escalade. Using that as his reference point, Robert began to retrace the steps that had led to his present and still unknown location.

Memories came back slowly. He remembered sitting at the harbor-side restaurant called Jimmy the Fish in Mikrolimano and touring the maritime morgue packed with dying aquatic life. He remembered the Swiss Air flight through Zurich and wandering the idyllic streets of Copenhagen the following morning. He remembered the story of the Great Dane's rescue ship and visiting the Baltic Exchange and having lunch at Harry's Bar with Sir Nicholas Eaton-Hardy. He remembered being assaulted by Alistair Gooding.

Guilt-tainted details started coming at him fast as Robert stared into the inky darkness; he remembered Mr. Him giving him an endless tour of the shipyard and then claiming not to know the identity of the new owner of the LNG vessels. He remembered storming out of Mr. Him's office and pretending to leave the premises but in fact aggressively barging into the accounting department three floors down where he demanded to know the origin of the recent wire transfers associated with the LNG carrier named *Hispaniola*.

Even in his foggy and fragile frame of mind, Robert could clearly remember the expression of terror on Mrs. Park's face just before the trembling bookkeeper finally divulged the name, "Fjord Bank." And he would never forget the moment when she surrendered the name of the British banker who had signed the wire transfer – Mr. James Hawkins.

Robert remembered the long flight to Paris via Mumbai followed by a heart-pounding race through the sprawling Charles De Gaulle airport the previous night to catch his connection. He remembered being fortuitously offered the last seat on the last flight of the evening, an old Air France turbo prop, which hadn't touched down until well after midnight.

As Robert Fairchild lay in bed and massaged his temples he could visualize the old white Peugeot taxi rumbling under the light of a full moon, careening alongside paddocks and pastures, dairy farms and ancient stone walls before finally delivering him to his present location: a harbor-front suite at The Old Government House Hotel on the Channel Island of Guernsey.

He was momentarily relieved to know his location on the planet, but he was not particularly happy about the state of his life or the fruitlessness of his odyssey. At least the ordeal was almost over and he was closer to home and on the beautiful little island of Guernsey, a place he had always wanted to go.

Ten years earlier he and Grace had been snowbound for three days on Martha's Vineyard in a rented house with just one movie that someone left behind – a creepy *film noir* starring Nicole Kidman called *The Others* that was filmed in the Channel Islands. He remembered once telling Grace that the Channel Islands were one of the places he wanted to visit before he died, but she seemed not to have heard him.

Robert untangled himself from the starched white bed sheets, switched on an oversized lamp and walked over to the sliding glass doors on the opposite side of the enormous hotel room. Excited to experience his first impression of an island he'd always dreamed of visiting, Robert dramatically pulled apart the heavy floral drapes to take in the view from the terrace – but instead he saw *nothing*.

He didn't see the picturesque, Colonial clam-shell shaped harbor of St. Peter Port or the fleet of ferries shuttling people and cargo between France and England. He didn't see the ochre ramparts of famous Castle Cornet or the crystalline blue waters of the North Atlantic. What Robert Fairchild saw instead was a heavy blanket of fog that closely mirrored his own mental state.

For the first time in a week, checking his BlackBerry for a menacing text message with a fiery-faced emoticon from Coco

Jacobsen, counting down the days until Robert's demise, was not his first conscious act. Instead he was totally focused on getting in touch with Grace to make sure she and Oliver were okay. But when Robert dialed her mobile number it buzzed with an unusually heavy European-sounding ring before going into her perky, ten-year-old voicemail greeting.

Robert knew Grace was in New York because Oliver had school that week, but between the twelve-hour time difference in Korea and his spending most of the previous week living on airplanes, he hadn't been able to reach her by telephone since he left London four days earlier. He tried her number three more times with the same unsatisfying result before giving up.

Fighting his natural inclination to panic about the welfare of his wife and only child, Robert took a cold shower and pulled on the rumpled grey suit – a second skin he was ready to shed. He swilled a pair of $14 skim lattes served on a silver tray from room service and headed downstairs to finish his quest once and for all.

No matter what he learned from Mr. Hawkins at the Fjord Bank branch office in the town of St. Peter Port on the island of Guernsey, Robert decided that it was over. It was all over. He was going back to New York on the last British Air flight from London to JFK that evening. Whatever the consequences, Robert's quest to gain control of the fifteen LNG carriers from Regal Shipbuilding would be officially over – together with his much-loved career in the stylish and exciting international shipping industry.

As Robert exited the elevator and entered the hotel lobby, he experienced that haunting sense of anticlimax present in resort towns in the off-season. The place was mostly deserted but for a few older couples who were lingering over breakfast, flipping through newspapers, sipping tea and playing cards in front of the propane fireplaces.

Fully laden with a nineteenth century English breakfast, Robert walked down the hotel's majestic staircase and stepped onto

Trafalgar Street. When he walked outside, he was relieved to discover that the fog hanging over the harbor just thirty minutes earlier had been miraculously burned off by the warming sun. The island air was refreshingly cool, in the mid-60s, and the sky had been scrubbed to the deep blue of an American mailbox.

In front of the hotel, the sea breeze was ruffling the flags of Britain, France and the distinctive red "X" that dominated the flag of Guernsey. He didn't know what or why, but for the first time since he started his journey it felt like the kind of day when something was finally going to happen – one way or another.

Armed with unintelligible directions delivered by a concierge with a heavy Scottish brogue, Robert Fairchild turned right on Trafalgar Street and walked up a cobblestone street over-looking the harbor. As he strolled along the lanes of the Colonial Seaport, he realized why its low white-and-yellow buildings looked so familiar; they reminded him of Bermuda. And as he always did when he had the opportunity to visit a beautiful place, he vowed to bring Grace and Oliver back there before it was all over – though he feared he never would.

After making several quick turns, passing by an incalculable number of offshore trusts and banks from which an inconceivable volume of money was pushed through sub-oceanic cables like blood through arteries, Robert finally arrived at the address Mrs. Park had blurted out during her moment of terror.

Now all he had to do was find Mr. Hawkins. He pulled open the glass door and walked inside the bank. It was show time.

Chapter 28

The Barclay Brothers

Born ten minutes apart, the identical twin Barclay brothers have worked side-by-side their entire lives, amassing billions of dollars through successful, if controversial, investments ranging from the Ritz Hotel in London to the Sunday Telegraph. David and Frederick Barclay first entered into shipping in 1983 through the purchase of Ellerman Lines, a London based shipping company, which they sold in 1988. The Brothers returned to the shipping industry through their purchase of Gotaas-Larsen, an oil tanker and LNG tanker company, the same year. They sold the company for a profit in 1997, but retained a stake that they later sold over a "brief cell phone conversation" to Norwegian tanker tycoon John Fredriksen.

The moment Robert Fairchild entered the Fjord Bank branch office in St. Peter Port, he feared for the worst. A far cry from what he imagined an offshore bank would look like, the institution he'd just wandered into seemed no different than the retail branch of a local savings bank in suburban America.

The place had the standard-issue linoleum floor and a row of teller windows beneath a sign hanging from the ceiling that trumpeted very low interest rates on twelve-month CDs. The only elements missing were an offer for a free toaster, a velvet rope to corral customers and a jar filled with lollipops to reward children for their patience. Robert approached the cotton-haired teller who had just greeted him with an anemic wave.

"Good morning," he said, trying to remain composed. "My name is Robert Fairchild and I am here to see Mr. James Hawkins, please."

"*Who?*" she crowed.

"James Hawkins," Robert repeated. "I believe he works in the, um…" he paused momentarily as he considered what to say next, "I believe he works in the *offshore bank*." Robert had leaned forward and whispered the final words as if the act of merely uttering them was a punishable offense.

"I believe you must be mistaken, sir," she said.

"I believe *you* must be mistaken, miss," Robert replied aggressively.

"There is no one by that name who works here," she said.

"Listen to me," Robert's said, his heart was now pounding furiously in his chest from a toxic overdose of coffee and much stress. "Mrs. Parks in the accounting office at Regal Shipbuilding in Korea specifically told me that Mr. James Hawkins works in the Guernsey branch of Fjord Bank!"

"Korea?" she asked with her face twisted in a dumbstruck expression.

Robert sincerely believed he had come to peace with the fact that the IPO of Viking Tankers was a complete and utter failure – and that he had senselessly gambled his son's financial security on a foolish lark. Nevertheless, upon learning that Mr. Hawkins didn't even work at the bank he suddenly felt like he was in the throes of an anxiety attack. He'd been had yet again – and this time by a bookkeeper in Busan.

"I would appreciate it if you would at least check the directory," Robert demanded now suspecting that Mrs. Parks had given him a fake name in order to get him to leave.

"I can't," she said.

"Oh yeah, and why not?" Robert challenged.

"Because we don't have a directory," she laughed. "We are only ten people who work here and seven of us are ladies. In fact, there is only one private banker in this office and his name is…"

"Young James Hawkins at your service," called out a man of Robert's age after emerging from a doorway in the back corner. "But please call me Jim. And excuse my tardiness," he added. "I got stuck behind a lorry heading down to the ferry dock with a load of arugula en route to London."

The man quickly shuffled across the room and extended his hand. When Robert grabbed onto it he felt as though he was being pulled from peril. As he pumped the man's hand and looked him over from head to toe, the disheveled American was soothed by what he saw. He was reassured by the banker's dark blue woolen Savile Row suit, silver Rolex, recreational suntan, Hermes pocket square and freshly polished loafers. Robert was visibly relieved when he caught a glimpse of the man's cufflinks – silver ship propellers engraved with the tiny letters KS.

"I am Robert…"

"Fairchild, yes, yes, I know," Jim Hawkins said quickly as he discretely peeled Robert's desperate fingers off his own hand. "Mr. Him warned me that you might be dropping in," he said and then quickly retreated back from which he came. "He also said you got a little loony out in Korea. Now please, follow me."

Robert followed the natty banker down the long hallway and they emerged in a wood-paneled reception area located in a different building from the one he'd entered. The new environment had the milieu of mega-money management; the air was warmer and drier and the hardwood floor was covered with Persian rugs. On the navy blue and mahogany-paneled walls hung a dozen oil paintings of ships and the people who had owned and financed them over the centuries.

Robert felt a rush of adrenaline the moment he saw a scale model of an LNG tanker encased in glass against the wall in the far corner. The ship's name was *Katherine Juhl* and Robert figured that was the ship's original name before the mysterious new owner renamed her *Hispaniola*. It had been a long, hard journey, but judging from the ship model, Robert Fairchild knew he was finally in the right place.

"You must excuse me for what happened out there, Mr. Fairchild," James Hawkins said. "You see, the place that you stepped into is our registered address, but it is not the manner in which our private clients typically enter our offices."

"No apology necessary," Robert said, grateful to have been plucked from the branch office. "I'm just glad we found each other."

"I bet you are," he said. "May we offer you a cappuccino?"

"Can you make a macchiato?" Robert asked hopefully.

"Of course we can!" the banker boomed. "You've had a long trip so perhaps you would care for a *doppio*?"

"Ah, macchiato *doppio*," Robert said the words lovingly as he fell into one of the two leather chesterfield chairs stationed in front of the banker's desk. "*Che sono marveloso*," Robert added with a dramatic flurry of his hand and a bogus Italian accent. He was suddenly feeling euphoric from a combination of exhaustion and the exquisite anticipation for the conversation he was about to have.

"So," the banker asked in a solemn tone inconsistent with the amused look on his face, "just what brings you to our quiet little island? I suspect it's not to see the sights."

"I am here to buy *that*," Robert spat the final word and pointed to the ship model encased in glass.

"Don't be ridiculous!" the banker laughed.

"I am not joking," Robert said.

"But we don't sell our ship models," Jim Hawkins said. "They are gifts from our clients."

"It's not the model I'm after," Robert said, "it's the ship – the *actual* ship."

"That's even more absurd than you asking to buy the model," he said. "Are you working for a SPAC that needs to make a quick acquisition? Is that what's going on here?"

"No," Robert said and attempted to read the banker's eyes. "I am here to buy that ship and her fourteen sisters."

After a considerable period of silence during which the banker appeared as though he might either laugh or cry, he said, "I sincerely hope you didn't come all the way from Korea to tell me *that*."

"That's precisely why I came all the way from Korea," Robert said flatly and lowered his head to glare at Jim Hawkins "And I am not leaving until I have a signed MOA to buy those ships."

"I wish you had used the telephone, or even sent me an email, before making your journey," Jim Hawkins said and picked up his BlackBerry from his desk and held it up, "because it was a real fool's errand."

"And why's that?" Robert grumbled.

"Because those ships simply are not for sale," he said.

"But you haven't even asked the owner," Robert grumbled slowly through gritted teeth.

"That's because I don't wish to waste the owner's time on such an absurdity," the banker said. "I know how much those ships earn and I know how much my bank has lent against them, which means I know what sort of equity will be required, which means I know the return on that equity – and I know it will not clear the American market. But I do have some good news?"

"What's that?" Robert asked.

"The good news is that I am in the position to offer you a fleet of eighteen-year-old product tankers of which my organization has recently taken possession," he said. "Yes, they are out of class and due for special survey, but…"

"I don't want your lousy product tankers!" Robert cried. "And I am not rational!"

"Clearly," the banker said with huff. "But if you aren't rational then I wouldn't be able to conclude a transaction with you in any case because that would be immoral."

When Jim Hawkins said the word immoral, Robert couldn't help but envision Luther Livingston sleeping in his poolside cabana at the Delano Hotel on South Beach eating take-out from Nobu as he anxiously awaited his boatload of preferred share certificates in Viking Tankers.

"But you haven't even heard my price," Robert begged.

"Your price does not matter, Mr. Fairchild," he said. "My client did not purchase those ships on speculation. The new owner purchased them to perform a specific contract. This type of vessel is not bought and sold at cocktail parties like ancient bulk carriers," the financier said, suppressing a chuckle.

"What is that supposed to mean?" Robert challenged.

"It means that LNG is a serious industrial business that is not well-suited for dilettante punters or gentlemen shipowners."

"I'm afraid this is not that simple, Mr. Hawkins," Robert said.

"I'm afraid it is old chap," Jim Hawkins explained coolly. "And don't get all wonky on me the way you did on Mr. Him or I'll be forced to call security."

"But…"

"Look it, if LNG carriers are what you're after then turn right around and go back to Korea and order some," the banker said. "I am quite sure Mr. Him would be happy to start delivering them to you thirty-six months from now." He pushed back from his desk and stood up.

"I can't wait thirty-six hours," Robert said, "never mind thirty-six months. I am out of time."

"And you are out of luck. Julia dear," the financier called into the intercom on his black telephone, "please pour Mr. Fairchild's macchiato into a paper cup. He will be leaving us now."

"I don't think so," the American said as he walked around the desk until he was no more than six inches away from the nervous banker. Robert was so close that Jim Hawkins could smell the stale kimchee on the crazy American's breath.

"You are going to tell me who owns those ships so that I can at least have my offer heard, or else I will…"

"Or else you will *what?*" the lender peppered him as he waited for a reply.

"I will…"

"What?" The banker taunted him again.

Robert's mind raced and his eyes shot furtively around the chestnut-paneled room as he thought of what to do next. Despite its short-term temptation he had learned earlier in life that physical violence was the ultimate form of failure. Instead he narrowed his eyes and struggled to come up with another alternative.

"What can you possibly do to me, Mr. Fairchild?" the banker ribbed him again. "Nothing; you can do nothing. You are powerless."

In one fluid and spontaneous maneuver, Robert Fairchild snatched the banker's BlackBerry off the leather blotter on his antique French desk and quickly stepped away – gripping the device over his head.

"Oh, don't be ridiculous," the banker laughed. "I have all the files on that machine backed up on my laptop," he said. "In fact, I am due for an upgraded device this week anyway so you are probably doing me a favor."

"Then I guess you won't mind when I send this thing to all the shipping newspapers," Robert said and he watched the banker's smile melt away. "Or perhaps to the Exchequer's Office, or to the taxing authorities in the U.K or Greece or Norway or America," he added. "I am sure there is plenty of incriminating correspondence on this filthy little device as it relates to foreign corporations in which you clients have an undisclosed beneficial interest."

Robert had been expecting James Hawkins to erupt in yet another fit of humiliating laughter at the sheer absurdity of his amateur threat, but he didn't. After a full minute, during which the lender was apparently running his own personal cost and benefit analysis, James Hawkins pulled down on the lapels of his Savile Row suit, cleared his throat and spoke in a very small voice.

"As it just so happens, the new owner of those fifteen LNG vessels you are so fond of was with me yesterday," Jim Hawkins said. "He was here reviewing the details of the acquisition financing that we are providing upon the delivery of each vessel."

"Where is he now?" Robert said slowly as he held the machine above his head.

"He is taking a few days of holiday on the island of Herm," Jim Hawkins said.

"Oh great," Robert sighed. "Where's Herm – in the middle of the South Pacific Ocean? Next to Vanuatu or Majuro or Monrovia or wherever else these globetrotting shipowners register their ships?"

"As a matter of fact, Mr. Fairchild, Herm is just a short ferry ride from here," Jim Hawkins said. "It is a Channel Island, you see, one of our smallest and loveliest."

"Are you serious?" Robert asked with disbelief. "He's near here?" His pulse was racing with excitement at the prospect of ending the torturous process of finding the ships at such a nearby location. He didn't know whether or not he would be successful in buying the fifteen LNG vessels but at least he would preserve some shred of self-respect if he was able to present an offer to the new owner.

"I am always serious," the banker confirmed with a solemn nod. "That is my job."

"Where is this shipowner staying on the island of Herm?" Robert demanded as he rose to his feet.

"There's just one hotel out there," he said. "It's a small place and quite old-fashioned. It goes by the name..." the banker lowered his head beneath his desk when he answered so that Robert could not see his face. "It is called the Admiral Benbow Inn."

"What is the shipowner's name?" Robert asked.

"That I cannot tell you," Jim Hawkins said. "It would be a breach of my fiduciary duty. But if you want to meet him, I suggest you go quickly," Jim Hawkins said.

"Why?" Robert said.

"Because the Coast Guard has cancelled the rest of the ferries to Herm due to the high winds," he said. "The *Trident* will be the last one to depart from St. Peter Port today and she leaves in just ten minutes."

Robert tossed the banker's BlackBerry onto his desk and ran out of the office.

Chapter 29

Shipowners & Philanthropy

Shipping tycoons are famous for their philanthropy. In 1975, Aristotle Onassis directed in his will that his fortune be divided 55% to his daughter Christina and 45% to a foundation bearing the name of his deceased son, Alexander S. Onassis. The Alexander S. Onassis Foundation was designed by Mr. Onassis as a shipping company, Olympic Shipping and Management, which continues to exist for the sole purpose of funding public benefit efforts in the name of the Foundation. 40% of the year-end profits are distributed for public benefit projects and the remainder is reinvested back into Olympic Shipping and Management. Thanks to excellent management, Mr. Onassis's structure has proven successful and has inspired the creation of similar structures.

Robert Fairchild burst aggressively through the heavy wooden door of the private bank and slid across the freshly washed sidewalk on the leather soles of his battle-worn Gucci loafers.

After narrowly avoiding a small white pick-up truck with a payload of freshly-cut tulips, he bolted back down Trelawney Street and past the Old Government House where he barely dodged a gaggle of elderly tourists boarding a tour bus. By the time Robert reached the harbor, the lone ferry boat called *Trident* was preparing to depart.

"Sorry sir," the ship's mate said to Robert over the sound of the gurgling diesel engines and the rising wind. "I'm afraid I cannot allow you to board unless you have a confirmed room reservation for the night."

"Why?" Robert snarled like an angry animal as he handed the man his ticket and stepped down onto the deck.

"Because the only hotel on the island is quite small and it's fully committed tonight for a private party and this is the last ferry of the day. The *Trident* will tie up on Herm for the evening and won't return to St. Peter Port until tomorrow morning."

"I'm a guest at that party," Robert lied as he moved toward the deserted bow of the ship, "the guest of honor." Surprisingly, the crewman did not give chase.

Thirty gut-wrenching minutes after leaving St. Peter Port, the *Trident* made a hard landing on the stone quay of the island of Herm, a primitive mile-and-a-half-long swath of land comprised of rugged brown cliffs, verdant green pastures and stunning white sand beaches surrounded by an unbroken expanse of cobalt blue; it was like Eden in the Atlantic.

"Where's the Admiral Benbow Inn?" Robert barked at an old ferryman draped in yellow foul weather gear as he disembarked.

"Top of the hill, sir," said the man without looking up from the thick braided line he was carefully coiling.

Robert Fairchild trudged up the steep slope from the harbor toward the highest and driest location on the island where Herm's modest amount of commercial activity had been established. When he reached the top of the hill, the only hotel Robert could see was called The White House Hotel and Ship Restaurant.

Robert entered the hotel lobby to ask for directions to the Admiral Benbow Inn but he couldn't find anyone to ask. It was a sensation that reminded him of his arrival at the Delano Hotel one very long week ago. Robert stood motionless at the reception desk for close to ten minutes before he heard a muffled melody coming from the other side of the hotel.

As Robert focused on the sound, he recognized the tune of "Happy Birthday" and it was only then that he remembered that it was his *own* fortieth birthday; too bad he would be spending it alone and sleeping on a street on a tiny island off the French coast. He just hoped that kicking off his forties as a homeless man in a torn and bloody suit wasn't a harbinger of what was to come during the next decade.

Robert walked toward the sound of music that was coming from the other end of the dark hallway. When he tentatively moved beneath the arched doorway and into the taproom, he was assaulted by an explosion of light and sound.

Chapter 30

Crowley Maritime

Crowley Maritime, one of the largest maritime companies in America, was founded in 1892 when Thomas Crowley purchased an eighteen-foot Whitehall rowboat to provide transportation of personnel and supplies to ships anchored in San Francisco Bay. Today, the company is run by Thomas B. Crowley, Jr., grandson of the founder, and has 5,300 employees and around $2 billion in revenue.

"*Happy Birthday!*" a chorus of voices erupted along with a flood of light.

At that moment Robert Fairchild believed he had reached the end of his life. He had heard theories about what happens to the human spirit in its final seconds, including precisely the sort of hallucination he was experiencing right then; this must have been his mind's way of saying goodbye – by briefly revisiting the many people and places that had formed the final chapter of his life. Rather than attempt to deny the dream he decided to soak in every last detail.

As his blank stare finally began to move around the room absorbing the tableau of characters grinning at him, he immediately realized that he knew almost all of them. Alistair Gooding and Sir Nicholas were presiding over pints of bitter at the polished wooden bar. Next to them was Aphrodite Bouboulinas who was sitting on a high stool with her bare legs crossed and a tanned arm draped affectionately around Mr. Him from Regal Shipbuilding. Mr. Him seemed to be so focused on the beautiful Aphrodite that he appeared not to have even noticed Robert's arrival.

Reclined on the leather couch directly in front of Robert were the two elder statesmen Robert had encountered on his odyssey around the world in search of the elusive gas carriers. Captain Spyros was calmly rolling a string of worry beads between his fingers as he spoke with Mr. Cornelius Juhl who was wearing nothing on his feet but pale pink cashmere socks. Sitting in a club chair next to the two octogenarian shipping tycoons was his friend Spyrolaki who was smiling brightly and motioning for Robert to look to his right, which he did.

Robert Harrison Fairchild had been blessed with many wonderful moments during his forty years of existence. He had felt the agony and the ecstasy, the success and failure, the satisfaction and the frustration that came from being a child, a father, a husband, a brother, a friend, a teacher, a student, a coach, a caregiver and a patient. But when he slowly turned around in that dimly lit English tavern on that remote island in the North Atlantic Ocean, all of those things came together. It was a scene so sweet he would remember it forever – even as he slipped into the darkness of his own final moments.

Standing in that Channel Islands pub and looking at the people looking at him, Robert Fairchild was finally present. He wasn't thinking about what he had to do next or where he had to go or the things he should have done or worrying about some boneheaded mistake he'd made or the stuff he wanted to buy or the places he hadn't gone or the well-being of the people he loved. He wasn't even thinking about his BlackBerry, even though he hadn't checked it for at least five minutes. For that one moment everything Robert Fairchild cared about in life was together in that historic room – and it all seemed okay.

"Happy fortieth honey!" Grace Fairchild shouted with joy as she jumped up and ran to her husband. "We made it to the Channel Islands!"

"Heel, Black Dog!" Oliver shouted. "Daddy doesn't want your hair on his suit."

"I don't think daddy needs to worry about that suit," Grace told her son as she observed the blood stained hole in the knee that had grown so large that much of Robert's leg was now exposed.

"Did you say *Black Dog*?" Robert asked. These were the first words he'd spoken since entering the tavern.

Before the boy had responded to his father's inquiry about the name of his new puppy, Robert Fairchild began to make a series of connections, like traffic lights turning from red to green. First there was the Treasure Island Navigation placard in the Piraeus office Blue Sea Shipping & Trading, then the Long John Silver Holdings deal binder in Copenhagen, the LNG carrier at Regal Shipbuilding was called *Hispaniola* and the banker in Guernsey named Jim Hawkins had directed him to a hotel called the Admiral Benbow Inn where he met a dog named Black Dog. There were six references to *Treasure Island*, the novel that had inspired Oliver Fairchild to become a pirate, and Robert realized he'd been played.

"Happy Birthday, Daddy!" Oliver smiled as he quickly scrambled to his feet. He ran toward his father with open arms but immediately recoiled. "Argh, ye smell scurvy, matey."

"*Garcon*, bring this man a bottle of Aquavit!" Coco boomed to the lone barman.

"And some deodorant," Oliver said.

"So, Fairchild, did you have a good trip?" Coco asked with a hearty laugh.

"*Did I have a good trip?*" Robert finally repeated the words as he glared at the Norwegian through squinted eyes. "Did I have a good trip?"

"Yes, sweetie, Coco and I knew it wasn't exactly a vacation, but was it fun?" Grace chirped energetically. "We tried really hard to make sure it was fun for you."

"Fun?" Robert repeated, stunned.

"I am so jealous that you got to go to Copenhagen," she said. "The hotel that Mr. Juhl booked for you looked absolutely fabulous when I saw the photos online," she said and turned to smile at the Great Dane. "Thanks, Corny."

"What is going on here?" Robert asked as his exhausted mind struggled to process so much new information.

"Ja," Coco said, "but Robert do you remember when we were at that little hotel in London and you tricked me into putting ten of my VLCCs on charter to Kraken DuBois?"

"I didn't exactly trick you, Coco," Robert said. "I simply articulated the value proposition of exchanging income security for…"

"And do you remember what I told you that night?" Coco interrupted.

"You told me that I wasn't really a shipping man," he said. "That's what you said."

"Ja, I'm sorry I lost my temper," Coco said, "but do you remember what else I said?"

"You told Alistair that you were going to have a surprise party for my fortieth birthday," Robert said.

"How did I do, Allie?" Coco asked his banker.

"You've taken this tradition to another level, Coco," Alistair said.

"But Robert, I also told you that if you weren't so old and busy I would enroll you in Cass Business School for an advanced degree in ship financing with Professor Grammenos, because you have so much to learn. Do you remember that?"

"Yes," Robert said.

"And I said something else, too," Coco said in a serious tone of voice. "I told you that I would be your mentor, in the same way Hilmar was a mentor to me, because everyone deserves a mentor in life."

"Yes, but you also said you had decided to give up on me because I was too much work."

"Ja, but this was before you came up with the MLP idea," Coco smiled. "Anyway, because you are too old for graduate school and since Viking Tankers doesn't have an around-the-world training programs like the shipping banks do, Alistair and I decided to put together our own little mini-course for you," Coco explained.

"You did *what*?" Robert recoiled.

"I needed to stall Rocky DuBois for a couple weeks while Captain Bouboulinas and I put together a deal directly with Mr. Xing," Coco smiled. "I also needed to get you out of the picture, which provided the perfect opportunity to have this all-star faculty teach you a thing or two about how the shipping business works," Coco said and cast his arm around the room.

"Let's not forget the work of the Dean," Alistair added and gestured toward the man standing behind the Captain; he was only person in the room that Robert didn't recognize. "He is the real star of the show."

"The Dean!" Robert shrieked and tugged on his thinning, graying hair with both hands.

"Robert, I would like to introduce you to Professor Costas Grammenos from Cass Business School in London, England,"

Alistair said. "Your friend Spyrolaki is a proud graduate of his program as well."

"Hello, Robert," Professor Grammenos said with a strong Greek accent as he stepped out of the shadows. "I am very pleased to finally meet you," he said, meticulously pronouncing each word. "You have done nicely so far and you have shown that you do not give up which is very important in the shipping business."

"Thanks," Robert said and shook the professor's hand. He shot a look of appreciation at Aphrodite for her words of encouragement whispered into his ear at Jimmy the Fish.

"I know you have learned much from the small curriculum we put together last week," Professor Grammenos said solemnly, "but I must remind you that we still have more work to do."

"We do?"

"Oh yes. In fact, we will begin to talk about the topic of your thesis over dinner this evening," the professor said.

"My *thesis*!" Robert wailed. "Is this some kind of joke?"

"Shipping might be fun, but it's no joke," Alistair offered. "That was one of the key points on the syllabus."

"Ja, and by the way, your little Oliver is the one who came up with the *Treasure Island*-naming theme that we used on this project," Coco said. "We will name each ship for a character in the book."

"We do not like pirates," Captain Bouboulinas said, "but we are so happy that the boy likes reading. I can only hope that my little Spyros will learn from your little Oliver."

"Hey, I read more than Aphrodite does," Spyrolaki retorted as he sat up from his reclined position. "The only thing she reads is *Marine Engineering Monthly*," Spyrolaki added, and a smile bloomed on Mr. Him's face.

"Me, too!" Mr. Him said. "I never miss an issue!"

"I hate to break the news to you, Laki, but shopping for Ferraris on your iPad doesn't count as reading," Aphrodite smiled at Mr. Him.

"I have absolutely no idea what you lunatics are talking about," Robert said with frustration. Try as he might, he just couldn't piece all the information together.

"It's all good, honey," Grace said.

"How can it all be good?" Robert said. "The reality is that I tried to find out who owns those gas vessels and I failed. That means the ten time charters will be cancelled, the IPO is dead and I have lost all of Oliver's money, not to mention my job and the house on Martha's Vineyard!"

"*Minn Venn*," Coco said as he winked at Grace and Alex.

"That means 'don't worry', honey," Grace chimed in. "It's Norwegian."

"*Don't worry*? Why shouldn't I worry?" Robert demanded.

"Ja, because we already control those fifteen LNG carriers," he said casually and studied his silver Knut Shipping propeller cufflinks; they were the same ones James Hawkins had been wearing. "We've controlled them for months."

"*You what?*" Robert asked and tossed back the first of many glasses of aquavit. "You own those ships!"

"Captain B. and I teamed-up to buy them from our old friend Mr. Juhl a few months ago – long before you even dreamed up that crazy idea to charter our ships to the Kraken and do the IPO in America," Coco said.

"So that's why you were spending so much time on the island of Chios," Robert said. "You were with the Captain."

"Uncle Coco has spent a lot more time in Kardamyla than I have," Aphrodite said. "He and Baba lived in that little taverna for more than a month."

"Uncle Coco?"

"Actually," Spyrolaki said, "he's our Godfather."

"Are you telling me this entire thing was a coincidence?" Robert asked. "You're telling me you bought those ships *before* Rocky DuBois even knew he needed them?" Robert asked.

"There are no coincidences in this business," Coco said. "There is only timing and patience. Oddleif and I have been studying the gas market for five years and when U.S. export demand looked like it was going to triple, we decided to invest in Mr. Juhl's ships. I felt it was important for Viking Tankers to be diversified."

"Diversified! You told me diversification was just a crutch used by shipowners who lack confidence!" Robert cried.

"I never said that," Coco said.

"Oh yes you did."

"Ja, okay, but the gas carriers will really help strengthen our balance sheet by allowing us to have long-term relationships with our clients."

"Strengthen our balance sheet!" Robert cried. "You told me a strong balance sheet is the sign of a weak management! And you also told me you didn't believe in the long-term relationships!"

"Do you really think that, honey?" Alexandra asked Coco.

"Absolutely not," Coco said.

"You told me you are a hunter, not a farmer!" Robert reminded his boss.

"Okay, fine," Coco caved under Robert's crushing glare, "but even if I did say those things that was the old me talking."

"The *old* you?"

"Do you remember when my friends in Egypt closed the Suez Canal just to get me out of trouble last year and you and Alistair told me to learn from my mistakes and diversify my fleet," Coco said.

"I remember saying it, but I don't remember you listening," Robert said.

"He's always listening," Alistair interjected. "He has the ears of a bat."

"And I'm now in charge of training him to listen," Alexandra said. "And he's doing better – not great, but better." Coco smiled.

"Besides Fairchild it's not just me I am responsible for anymore," Coco said softly and put his hand on the knee of Alexandra who was slowly rubbing her pregnant bump. "I need to be a little more conservative now in order to protect my family," he said.

Robert turned to look at Captain Bouboulinas. "But why are you involved with this deal?" Robert asked. "I thought Blue Sea Shipping & Trading was a traditional family shipping company with dry bulk carriers?"

"Mr. Fairchild, Greek shipowners take advantage of opportunities whenever they arise," the old Greek said. "For many years the opportunity came in the form of carefully operating older bulk carriers, then it come from ordering newbuildings and now modern tankers for gas appear to look the most attractive based on the fundamentals. I made this investment for my children and their children," the Captain said and added softly, "if they ever give me grandchildren, that is."

"Give it a rest, Baba," Aphrodite said without taking her eyes off Mr. Him.

"Ever since the children returned to Greece after studying aboard they've wanted to bring Blue Sea Shipping & Trading into the twenty-first century by teaming up with investors in America and buying the kinds of ships that will carry the next generation of cleaner energy," the Captain said. "Spyrolaki and Aphrodite said they believe this is the next logical step for the shipping industry."

"And you listened to them?" Robert asked.

"He was happy to," Aphrodite said and put her arm around her brother. "I think it's the only thing my brother and I have ever agreed upon."

"But how do you people even know each other?" Robert asked.

"That is a story for another time," Coco said as he thought momentarily of the steamy night in Haiphong Harbor in 1970 when the two men met while smuggling cargo on behalf of their mutual client – the United States Government.

"But Robert my friend," Spyrolaki interjected, "didn't you ever wonder why the *Viking Aphrodite* deviated from her course and saved the *Lady Grace* from those nasty pirates?" Spyrolaki asked.

"I thought it was the sort of selfless act of kindness and generosity that still existed among people at sea," Robert said. "I thought the closest ship was obligated to do that."

"Yes," the Captain said softly, "but Coco's ship wasn't the closest ship. He came to the rescue of the Blue Sea officers and crew who were still sailing on the *Delos Express* after Spyrolaki sold her to you. My nephew from Chios was the chief engineer on that ship, you know."

"But you've put me through hell for the last ten days, Coco," Robert wailed as he returned to the situation at hand.

"That was exactly the point," the Norwegian said.

"What was exactly the point, to torture me?" Robert asked.

"Yes! The point is that shipping really *is* torture a lot of the time; and it can be hell. I needed you to learn that there's more to this business than doing multi-million dollar deals in five star hotels with my money, Fairchild. Don't you remember when I told you the only way to really understand shipping is to lose money?"

"They all told me that," Robert sighed and glanced at each of the Greeks, the old British shipbroker and the Great Dane just as Coco offered each of them an earnest smile.

"That was excellent reinforcement, boys!" Coco winked and offered a double "thumbs-up" toward his faculty. "Alistair and I really wanted that to be the central theme of our curriculum; we wanted you to feel like you had something at stake," Coco said, "because without having something at stake..."

"You can't properly price risk," Robert finished one of Coco's favorite maxims. "It's called moral hazard."

"By the way, Moral Hazard in ship finance would make an excellent thesis topic for you, Mr. Fairchild," Professor Grammenos said.

"Animal spirits in ship finance would be better," Robert replied. "Which reminds me, Coco; how could you possibly have bought $3 billion worth of ships when you don't have any money?" Robert said plainly.

"A lack of money never stops a good shipowner," Coco said.

"But where, exactly, do you plan on finding your $500 million if the IPO is dead?" Robert asked.

"Tell him, Alex," Coco said and turned toward Alexandra.

"Robert, when I went to Davos to see Coco last week to apologize for the incident on St. Bart's and tell him he's going to be a daddy, Coco showed me the prospectus for the Viking Tankers IPO that you drafted."

"And what do you think?" Robert asked and braced for her critical reply.

As he waited for Alex to speak, Robert realized there was something very different about her. It wasn't just her swollen tummy or her shorter hair or the absence of the tiny blonde dreadlock she had always tried unsuccessfully to conceal. It was something else. Then it hit him. What looked different about Alexandra Meriwether was that she was actually looking him…and not glancing at her BlackBerry every fifteen seconds.

"I think you totally nailed it, Fairchild," she said.

"Really?"

"Absolutely," Alex replied. "The idea of using the Master Limited Partnership structure as a mean of financing shipping assets was pure genius."

"It was?"

"Your concept was absolutely right; the long-term cash flow generated by long-lived assets like ships really should be given a lower cost of capital and therefore a higher valuation," Alex said.

"I know, right," Robert said with surging confidence. "It makes no sense for all shipping risk to be priced the same way."

Hearing Alexandra Meriwether, one of the most talented transportation bankers on Wall Street, praise him profusely in front of Grace, Oliver and Coco was one of Robert's proudest moments.

"The only problem is that you missed something really obvious," she said.

"What?" Robert asked slowly as he prepared to hear the glaring fault in his logic.

"What you missed is that Coco's VLCCs are too old, the five-year time charters are too short and the capital structure is too highly leveraged to have the risk characteristics of an MLP," she said.

"I'd like to remind you that Luther Livingston committed to take $250 million of the deal," Robert said in his own defense.

"I'd like to remind you," Alex said, "that the preferred shares Luther was demanding were more expensive than the unpaid balance on a Visa card."

"Hey, I did the best I could with what I had to work with just like every CFO does. Besides," Robert said, "I actually think Luther's pricing was appropriate based on the risk."

"In retrospect, you're right," she said. "But the important thing is that you built a beautiful piano; all we need to do now is tune it."

"Okay," Robert said as began to feel better about his prospects. "Now I get it what's going on here; we're going to sell the LNG carriers to China and make enough money to pay off our loans with Allie so we can do the IPO of the crude oil tankers," Robert said.

"Come on!" Coco exploded with laughter. "Do you actually think I'm would let Rocky DuBois out of the boxing ring by helping him sell his company to the Government of China?"

"China? What are you talking about?" Robert asked. He was lost once again.

"That's the reason why Rocky needed the gas ships in the first place," Coco said. "Because the Peoples' Republic of China agreed to buy ARC but only if ARC came along with control of those fifteen LNG carriers which they need to export shale gas from America to China," Alex said.

"I finally found a way to get even with that wily old wrangler for putting me on the naughty boy list!" Coco said and clenched his fist triumphantly. "Oh yeah, baby!"

"Now I'm confused again," Robert said. "If we don't sell the LNG carriers to China then we won't have any charters to ARC. If we don't have any charters to ARC then we won't have an IPO and if we don't have an IPO then we won't have any money to complete the purchase of the LNG carriers," Robert said as he attempted to connect all of the new information.

"Tell him, Alex," Coco said.

The Norwegian leaned back and admired the woman to whom he would soon be married in an unusual ceremony aboard the *Kon Tiki*. The mega yacht would be anchored three miles outside Ambrose Channel, the entrance to New York Harbor, and guests would be shuttled back and forth by helicopter. As long as Coco stayed out of America's territorial waters, Wade Waters had advised him, Coco would not be subject to search and seizure by the United States Government.

"Tell me what?" Robert asked and turned to look at the pregnant investment banker.

"The thing is, Robert," Alex explained, "Mr. Xing and China never really needed to buy ARC or the LNG ships in the first place," Alex said.

"You just said they are keen to buy clean energy," Robert stressed.

"They are, but that doesn't mean they needed to buy ARC," she said. "They just needed to buy ARC's gas. And they didn't need to *own* the gas ships – they just needed to control them."

"I see," Robert said even though he didn't. "So what happened?"

"So Coco, Mr. Xing and I put together a simple deal that works for everyone: China agrees to buy enough gas from ARC to fill the fifteen gas carriers for twenty years and Coco agrees to time charter the gas carriers to China for the same period," Alex smiled as she began to maneuver her pregnant body in preparation for getting off the couch.

"So now we have twenty-year charters with China, but Viking Tankers still doesn't have the $500 million we need to *pay* for our share of the equity in the ships," Robert insisted.

"That's where you and my investment banker come in," Coco sang and looked at Alexandra.

"She's your investment banker?" Robert said. "But you told me you'd never do another deal with Allied Bank of England as long as you live," Robert reminded his boss.

"I never said that," Coco said and swatted his hand. "Anyway, Magnus and Alex have teamed up to underwrite the IPO of our MLP in Norway *and* America," Coco said. "That how everyone does it these days."

"The IPO of what?" Robert asked. "What are you *talking* about?"

"The IPO of *Viking Gas*," Alex smiled. "Wade Waters re-filed the IPO prospectus with the S.E.C. while you were on your little road trip last week. As it turns out, the fifteen gas carriers provide exactly the type of high credit quality, long-term cash flow visibility we need to make Viking Tankers into a *real* MLP and maybe even achieve that 200% valuation you promised to Coco."

"And Coco even said that if you get the deal done as you promised, he will buy us the house on Martha's Vineyard as your bonus," Grace said.

"Wait a minute," Robert said. "Does that mean…"

"Yup," Coco said by way of a sharp inhalation of breath. "The Viking Raid is about to begin!"

"You and your co-CEO have your first investor presentation in Boston on Monday morning," Alex added.

"And who, exactly, is my *co*-CEO?" Robert asked.

Just then, Spyrolaki Bouboulinas stepped out of the shadows, draped his arm around Robert's shoulders and pulled him close.

"It is me, my friend," the Greek said in the same smoky voice that had first drawn Robert Fairchild into the shipping business. "I always told you we would find a way to be together again."

As Robert considered how to reply to Spyrolaki, Coco Jacobsen slowly rose to his feet and climbed up onto the couch.

"What are you doing?" Robert asked, staring up at his boss.

"Come up here with me," the Norwegian said with a smile. "I think it's time I taught you how to sing Helan Går."

The End.

Post Fixture

You've reached the end. Thank you very much for reading *Viking Raid*. I hope you enjoyed the book. I would be grateful for your feedback. My email address is: mmccleery@marinemoney.com.

Finally, I just couldn't resist including the image below which was created by my friends at Northern Shipping Funds. Although the external factors that influence each individual shipping cycle are unique, the process of having too many and too few ships (relative to demand) are generally the same in each boom and bust. The picture below provides a simplified but effective summary of how the shipping cycle works.

Source: Northern Shipping Funds

MARINE MONEY, INC.

Lightning Source UK Ltd.
Milton Keynes UK
UKOW04f1939100817
307099UK00001B/9/P